How do you evaluate books when you haven ι ѕɛɛ̃ ρ...
here is a selection of reader's reviews for my last three books from US ana
UK Amazon. Nobody pays readers to post reviews—so thank you, readers!

MISS TERRY

Julie Greeman	Loved this book!
Pam Caswell	Well told story
Kathleen O'toole	Brilliant
C. Fairweather	Wow! Miss Terry is one of the best books I have read in a long time… Wow!
K. Maxwell	Different, thought-provoking mystery
iChas "Biologist"	An unusual—and very topical—book that I strongly recommend.
Lovetoread	A great read

BALLAD OF A DEAD NOBODY

Kathleen O'toole	Fascinating
Kathryn Bennett	So glad to see Liza Cody is still writing
Hilde	Another great Liza Cody
iChas	A gripping story very well told…
A. B. King	What a writer!
Esskayee	Good outing by Cody
Ian S. Maccarthy	Half of a good novel

GIMME MORE

Merle K. Gatewood	Fresh and Different
Likesmysterystories	Liza Cody's the best!
Jacques Coulardeau	A masterpiece, of sorts
A Customer	I loved this book/Leading the field again (*bought 2 copies—yay!*)
Mrs L C Harvey	The Truth About Rock and Roll
Ed "ramblingsyd"	The music biz, the seventies, born again rock chicks…

Other books by Liza Cody

LADY BAG

Liza Cody

iUniverse LLC
Bloomington

Lady Bag

iUniverse books may be ordered through booksellers or by contacting:

iUniverse LLC
1663 Liberty Drive
Bloomington, IN 47403
www.iuniverse.com
1-800-Authors (1-800-288-4677)

ISBN: 978-1-4917-0746-3 (sc)
ISBN: 978-1-4917-0747-0 (e)

Printed in the United States of America

iUniverse rev. date: 11/18/2013

Cover drawing and design by Elsie and Emzel

For Mike

And with love to Sue, Brigid, Ben and Nell—in memory of Brian Garvey who, in a very real way, made all this happen.

With a big thankyou to Julie Lewin for her sharp eyes and generosity.

Contents

LADY BAG

Chapter 1

In Which I Bump Into The Devil

//

The silvery man looked plump and prosperous in his fine wool coat. Through the glass door he'd seemed good natured as well. My mistake. Never judge a man through glass. Always wait till you can smell him. This one smelled of tomato soup and single malt—a smug smell.

He said, 'We've all got to work—except, apparently, you. Why should I give you money? No one gives me any.'

He pinned me back against a no-parking sign with contemptuous eyes, and in front of all the city workers rushing to go home he said, 'I'm not going to feed your habit or encourage your laziness.' He had a rich brassy voice, loud enough to be heard a mile off.

Then he walked away. I hate it when they do that. It's like saying, 'I don't even want to *look* at you.'

What does he mean—no one gives him any money? What about all the tax breaks, business expenses and bonuses? People are giving him money all the time.

You think I don't know about playing the system? I haven't always looked like this, you know. I wasn't born out here. If you make your mind up about me too quickly you'll be as guilty of bigotry as that snotty guy.

Electra pushed her wet snout into my hand and I stroked her sleek narrow skull. 'Never mind,' I said.

Public rejection is hard to recover from. Bastards like him in their clean wool coats never imagine you might need a pick-me-up to help swallow their self-righteous words.

A woman in a black city suit said, 'I heard that.' She held out a pound coin. 'I'm not saying I disagree, but what about the dog?' She smelled far more womanly than she looked—of breath mints and rose-water.

I held my hand out for the coin. At the last moment she snatched it away and said, 'This is for the greyhound; not you. You've got to promise you'll spend it on him.' Like she was offering me a fortune instead of one measly pound coin that would hardly feed Electra her supper.

'Her,' I said. 'She's called Electra. She's a rescue dog. If I don't look after her the animal shelter people can take her away.'

'I should hope so,' the woman said. 'Why did you name her after a girl who killed her own mother?' Maybe the breath mints covered the acid scent of cheap white wine.

I said, 'Her racing name was RPA Radiovista's Electra of South Slough. Nobody murdered a mother.'

'Electra did.' She released the coin into my hand and started to walk away.

'Why?' I followed. I love stories.

'Sorry, I've a train to catch. Look her up. Google her.'

Of course I will, on my thousand quid laptop which I can plug into any fucking lamp-post in London. Know what? The shelter where I sometimes sleep makes you buy a key before they let you charge your mobile phone for an hour. If you've got a mobile phone and haven't been robbed when you were sleeping rough because your stupid dog was too much of a pussy-cat even to bark and wake you up. Murder her mother? Hah! You got that one wrong, office lady—this Electra couldn't kill a crippled bunny. Unless of course she just stared at it with her big tragic eyes and the bunny committed suicide out of sympathy.

Those eyes are why I got her in the first place. Electra can screw coin out of the coldest of hard hearts. Me? They don't care if I live or die, but then I'm not Ms Pitiful like she is. Sometimes when I really need extra cash I bandage her paws. It isn't dishonest: she actually does have arthritis in her legs and feet. A lot of ex racing dogs do, and trudging around on stone-cold pavements doesn't help. Bandages just make her pain visible. And they make me look like the caring owner I am when normally nobody sees me at all.

People like dogs more than they like people. And they're right. You can actually help a dog but you can never really help people.

Look at me and Electra—she's old and arthritic. The bastards who raced her would've put her down. When I first got her all she knew how to do was run, but not fast enough anymore to escape a lethal injection. She didn't know how to sit on a sofa and be sociable or sleep snuggled up. She'd never seen a sofa in her life and greyhound trainers don't snuggle worth a damn.

I took her and fed her and kept her warm. I'll feed her and keep her till the day one of us dies. I wouldn't do that for a broken down old human athlete with social problems, would I? And nor would you, unless you were maybe a saint or related by blood or way better at solving human problems than I am.

Then again, if you look at it from her point of view, I'm not the disappointment you'd expect me to be. She was brought up in a cold concrete kennel block without human kindness. I'm not letting her down in that department, am I? She isn't lonely because she's got me twenty-four seven. If she didn't like me she could just walk away—she isn't tied up.

When I first got her she used to stand with her tail between her legs, shivering and not making eye contact. She used to flinch when anyone tried to touch her. Now she lets strangers give her a pat and she sticks her nose into my hand when she wants to be noticed and petted. We didn't go for

3

couples therapy or any of the shit you'd have to go through with a human being. No. Electra just got into the habit of trusting me and trust made her happier. You could never do anything that simple for a human being. I think people are too complicated to be content with simple happiness. That's why I'd rather talk to Electra than anyone else on earth.

We collected about seven quid and when rush-hour was over we walked west to get ready for the evening entertainment crowd. When people get too drunk and abusive, we go to the hostel if we managed to keep enough coin to pay for it or we find somewhere safe-ish to put our heads down. Or we do the rounds of the charity shops to see if there's anything in the bags outside that'll fit me.

First though I had a little taste of the Algerian red—just enough to recover from the insults and to make the evening warmer. Then I wandered down St Martins Lane towards Trafalgar Square. If you can't get a seat on a bench there, you can always sit on the steps. I like Trafalgar Square. There are masses of tourists to listen to and someone always makes you laugh by jumping in the fountains or falling off one of the bronze lions.

That's when I bumped into the Devil, also known as Gram Attwood, coming out of the National Portrait Gallery. Him with his cool blue eyes and his vicious little smile. I didn't think it was vicious in the old days—I thought it was cute. I thought *he* was cute. And he was—for a thief and a killer.

Chapter 2

I Follow The Devil And His Doxy

//

I saw him but he didn't see me. He was with a woman, of course. She was a few years older, of course. Not beautiful but well constructed and carefully dressed. Of course. And of course he was charming and attentive. Of course, of course, of course.

I could smell his soap, his shampoo and moisturiser, his laundered shirt. So clean, so fresh and so inhuman. However close I came to him I could never smell his body. The Devil leaves no scent. Maybe that should've tipped me off.

I stood for a second, stunned, and wondering if Electra could catch a whiff of Gram Attwood. Maybe that is a dog's superpower—distinguishing between the merely evil and the Devil by smell alone. But she stood patiently, waiting for me to move on. Dogs are sweet creatures who know nothing about evil so maybe they won't recognise the Devil when they see him.

Gram Attwood walked across Trafalgar Square towards Haymarket without a flicker of recognition. His right hand lightly grasped his companion's elbow. His touch was intimate, the touch of ownership. Maybe he paid for something. He'd certainly gone up in the world since I knew him. When I knew him I paid for everything—including the price of his freedom.

'Come on,' I said to Electra, and we followed the Devil.

The woman parted from him outside a theatre. She kissed him on the mouth, laughing and lingering a little. His smile was a work of art. I'm so interested, his smile said. Fascinated. Treat me right and I might just love you.

I was in the dock the last time I saw that smile and I did treat him right. I did exactly what he asked of me. Or rather it was what I didn't do that was important. And you could write a hundred books about what I didn't say. When I finally realised that he was never going to visit me, that he'd left me inside to rot, I understood what hatred actually is. Hatred is love with maggots gnawing at its living flesh. It's love turned inside out, its guts and soft places exposed to the maggots and the acid rain.

That's what I learned in prison. Pretty, eh?

They gave me tablets—three a day—to stop the hatred. They buried it under layers and layers of gauze which muffled sound and hung between my eyes and the world.

I fitted in better after that. Time slid by day by day without leaving footprints on my memory. It was just time and I did it the way you have to. But my personality was eaten away just like my memory.

Then it was over. I left prison and there were no more tablets. I was free. Free to hate again. Free to hurt again. I woke up one morning and the gauze that hung between me and sights and sounds had blown away. Everything hurt my eyes, ears and skin. Sights and sounds became slights and wounds. If I'd had any money I would've turned into a junky because they say that junkies feel no pain at all for hours at a time. But I had no money, my mother was dead and my house had been sold.

At first I did what you do to get back to normal. I tried to find a job so I could rent somewhere decent. But then I discovered that I'd been left at the bottom of a deep chasm called Debt. I'd given Gram Satan Attwood power of attorney to sell my house to cover legal fees—which is much the same as giving the Prince of Thieves the key to your treasure chest and saying, 'Go ahead, my dearest one, help yourself.'

There I was, with less than nothing. Even so I tried to get back into the system and become a proper person again. I really did. The trouble was that I wasn't a proper person anymore, and everyone could see it. Or maybe they could smell it; like I can every day of my life.

It's well known how hard it is to get a job when you have a prison record and a hostel address. But did you know that you can't get a doctor or a dentist either? If things become bad enough you can go to A & E and they're forced to treat you. But you can't do that when all that's happened is that you've run out of Prozac or Largactil.

They give you emergency housing in a bed-and-breakfast miles away from your benefit office. You've got no money for the bus so you spend hours walking there, only to find it closed or they've invented some other reason for you not to qualify for assistance. So you trudge all the way back. It's a filthy house, and there's no lock on the bathroom door. The other residents are drunk, barmy, druggy, or have a cocktail of problems you wouldn't want to meet in a dark corridor outside a dirty bathroom. Or inside.

When you can't stand it for another second you leave and make yourself 'voluntarily homeless'. And, know what? It's a relief. You're at the bottom. There's no further to fall. You can stop trying to haul yourself back into society and concentrate on survival.

You can stop hoping that one of your job interviews will succeed. You can stop hoping you'll qualify for better housing. You can stop hoping, period.

Hope is the great deceiver. It whispers in your ear and keeps you on the treadmill thinking that if you do everything you're told—fill in all the forms, go to all the interviews—one day you'll be able to climb out of the pit and live an ordinary life.

Once you've dumped hope you're free. You don't have to keep clean and respectable. You don't need a roof over your head or food on the table. Things are a lot simpler without a roof or a table. Nobody cares if you're crazy. It's the struggle to stay sane which drives you mad. Stop struggling, I say, stop hoping and learn to survive. Give up hope and adopt a dog. It's the only self-help tip I can give you.

But when you're left in pieces by the sight of your lost demon lover with another woman you'll need a little help from a reliable source. Mine came in a bottle. It was running dangerously low and I had to make a decision. Should I find more wine or should I follow Gram Attwood?

'Well?' I asked Electra. She turned her head and seemed to be watching Gram Attwood as he walked away towards Piccadilly. Maybe she *can* smell the Devil after all.

'Your call,' I said and we followed him.

He walked close to the kerb and I realised he was looking for a taxi. He saw one, stepped off the kerb and hailed it. The driver ignored all the other outstretched hands and stopped for him. The Devil always was a lucky bugger. I hurried closer and heard him say, 'Harrison Mews.' I was so close to him now that he was forced to notice me. He turned, frowning.

I said 'Spare a little change, please?'

'Piss off,' he said.

'My dog's hungry.'

He just laughed and opened the cab door.

As the cab pulled away he glanced indifferently in my direction. There was absolutely no recognition on his handsome face. Not one jot. Either I had changed completely or he had erased me from his screen—total deletion.

'I've ceased to exist,' I told Electra as his cab disappeared. 'I'm not even a ghost that haunts him.' She looked at me with the beautiful gold-flecked eyes which told me I was at the centre of her universe.

'Thank you,' I said and crouched down to kiss her forehead and stroke her ears.

'Get a room,' Joss said, 'get a man and get a life.' Joss and Georgie were on their way down to St Martins-in-the-Fields for food and beds.

'Get rid of the mutt,' Georgie said, 'and it'll be way easier to find somewhere to sleep. No one wants to share a room with a farty old flea-bag like that.'

'He's talking about *you*.' Joss thinks he's funny.

We backed across the pavement into a doorway. The boys had to empty their bottles before going to the shelter so we all had a quick shlurp and a smoke. Joss kept an eye out for the cops.

I said, 'Either of you know where Harrison Mews is?'

'Kensal Rise,' Georgie said, because he was born without the skill to say, 'I don't know.' He's an expert on every damn thing in the world.

'Tony at the shelter has an A–Z,' Joss said. 'Come with us.'

But I didn't want to. I wanted to wait outside the theatre for Gram Attwood's new woman. Maybe I could warn her. Maybe I could kick her bony arse. Maybe I could steal her nice shoes and exchange them for a ham sandwich and a bottle of wine.

'What's at Harrison Mews?' Joss asked suspiciously. 'Evangelicals?' He's always joining new cults because to begin with they feed him and give him money. Then they get wise to him and give him the cold shoulder like everyone else with any sense.

'It's personal,' I said.

'People who sleep in public don't got nothing personal,' Joss said.

'I got my pride,' Georgie said, and we all burst out laughing. I wished we could stay together always.

Except of course Georgie's a pain in the arse and Joss is paranoid and both of them stink and neither one of them likes Electra. Also if there are three of you together no one will give you any money but the cops will move you on

LIZA CODY

much more quickly. We're pathetic singly, but in a bunch we're intimidating.

I wandered up past Piccadilly Circus and bought a couple of litres of red. Then I came back and sat down outside the theatre to feed Electra some of her biscuits and a little water. A bride and her hen party came by shrieking, trailing pink net and wings. The bride stopped and gave me a five pound note. 'For luck,' she said, shuddering.

I said, 'Your kindness will save you from a fate like mine.' They love that karma stuff when they're tiddly. So the bridesmaids coughed up too and suddenly I had more than enough for a bed *and* a meal.

As usual, when I didn't need it anymore, people started to be lavish with their spare change. Electra was at her best—soft eyed and dignified—acknowledging gifts with a gentle dip of her head.

'You're much better at me than this,' I said. 'I mean, you're much better than me at this. You're my lucky charm, my doovoo, my voodoo doll, mo myjo, my mojo.' And I had a little drink to celebrate.

Then without me noticing, time had passed and people started piling out of the theatre. They came too fast, trampling on me and Electra, talking, talking, talking. There was no room to move, no air to breathe. Electra started shivering.

I said, 'Hey, watch out. Give a dog a break.' And a man said, 'She's drunk.'

'My dog is not drunk,' I said, because it was true and he had no right to insult her—him with his hair all slick with pomade and his fingernails buffed and clean. What does he understand about a dog who's been walking all over London since six in the morning?

'She's mo myjo,' I said. 'She's worth you of ten.'

'Don't shout at us,' his wife said. 'We don't understand you.' They walked away. I was going to follow and explain but then I saw her, Gram Attwood's new woman, and I remembered why I was outside the theatre in the first place.

'You,' I said, 'hey, you. I'm talking to you.'

She was with a girlfriend and they were a matching set in their silk suits and gold, talking, talking, talking, and not paying any attention. I said, 'This is my winal fawning—stay away from Am Grattwood. He's dangerous.'

'Excuse me,' she said politely and she and her friend tried to walk round me.

'You seem like a nice lady,' I said. 'Listen to me. Gram's dangerous. He'll take you for everything.'

'What's she shouting about? Did she say 'Graham'? What would she know about him?'

'What wouldn't I know?' I said, trying to stop her walking away by running backwards in front of her. 'Look at me. He did this to me. Beware.' It came out like 'wee bear' so I repeated it till I got it right, 'Beware, beware, beware!'

'You're upsetting the people,' a man said. He worked at the theatre. I could tell because he had a badge which read 'Deputy Sub-manager. Front of House.'

'She *should* be upset,' I said, 'but not by me. Beware of Gram Attwood.'

Maybe I shouldn't drink so much before delivering an important message. How could she take me seriously if what she heard was 'Wee bear o'Fam Greatwood'? Which is what it sounded like, even to me. Why would she listen to me when she smells of *Rive Gauche* and truffle oil while I smell of dirty feet and London gutters?

Chapter 3

I Am Advised By A Dog

///

E lectra and I were all alone in Jermyn Street. We were sitting in a bookshop doorway and she was looking miserable. I tried to stand up on boneless legs but fell back down.

'I'm sorry,' I said.

'You always say that,' she said.

'You're a dog; you can't talk.'

'You always say that too.'

'If you're going to talk, say something nice.'

'How can I?' she said. 'I'm cold, hungry and tired, and it's all your fault.'

'Guilt trip.'

'I don't understand,' a human voice said. 'You're mumbling to yourself. Are you hurt? Ill? I'm Melanie Jones, Floating Outreach, Ecumenical Aid.'

'Floating what?' The ground was heaving slightly, but quite dry. 'I was talking to my dog.' I dragged my coats around my shoulders and made a half-hearted stab in the direction of dignity.

'He's a lovely dog.'

'She.'

Electra said, 'Why do they all think I'm a boy?'

'Well *I* think you're very feminine,' I said, stroking her cheek.

'Thanks,' said Jelly Moans, or whatever her name was, 'but not entirely appropriate. I'm here because a member of the public reported that you need help.'

'Uh-oh, now you're for it,' Electra said, and I had to agree with her. Members of the public only report you as needing help if you've seriously upset them. The help they mean usually involves a short stay in the monkey house. Without your dog.

I sat up straight and said, 'I do need help, actually. I was trying to find someone to direct me to Harrison Mews. Maybe they misunderstood and thought I was begging. People don't always understand me since I had my little cerebral mishap.'

'Stroke, eh? I was told you were roaring rat-arsed.' Smelly Jones was not as mimsey as she looked.

'I only had the one.' Bottle, that is—but it's unwise to mention amounts to Floating Outreach. It's also unwise to claim absolute sobriety when you stink of Algerian red and you've been found in a heap in a bookshop doorway. 'I was cold,' I went on. 'But maybe I shouldn't drink at all these days. It only seems to take a tiny amount to affect my balance and speech.'

'If those are the same centres affected by your stroke you probably shouldn't.'

'And yet doctors recommend moderate consumption of red wine to protect against strokes.'

'Oh per-lease,' said Electra.

'Well,' Moany said, 'I'll give you a leaflet about alcohol abuse. Meanwhile do you have a place for tonight, and enough money to pay for it? Or should I arrange hospital accommodation and assessment?'

'There's a three-bed women's room at St Christopher's, Euston,' I said, pronouncing every word with great clarity. 'And I have my latch money. I'm alright, thanks so much for asking.'

'They don't like me at St Christopher's,' Electra said.

'Yes they do,' I said, checking all my pockets. The wonder of it was that I *did* have money. I hadn't thrown it away and no one had robbed me.

'They have a no-dogs policy at St Christopher's,' Electra said. She can be such a stubborn bitch at times.

'That's where we're going so, lump it.'

'I beg your pardon?' Lemony said. 'Did you just call me a bitch?'

'Certainly not.' I climbed cautiously to my feet. If you move slowly enough you won't fall over and give the game away. 'My leg's all stiff, and that's a bitch. You might've heard me mumble about that.' I stooped and took Electra's face between my hands. 'Hush,' I said, and I kissed her on the nose.

'You really love that dog,' Wallaby Jo said.

'I couldn't live without Electra.' I took hold of her collar and we moved carefully off.

'Wait!'

'What?'

'I thought you wanted to find Harrison Mews.'

'Where is it?'

'South Kensington, near the Science Museum.'

'Have you got a car?' I said. 'You could give us a ride.'

'Don't push your luck,' said Electra. 'One whiff of you in a confined space and she'll have you sectioned.'

'Shouldn't you get to St Christopher's before they lock their doors? Find Harrison Mews in the morning.'

'Absolutely tootly right,' I said. 'Goodnight, and thanks for stopping by. Your concern is appreciated.' I walked slowly and in a dead straight line. My head felt wonky but no one could possibly see that. Electra knew, of course, because she was sent to me by fairies and she knows all things and sees all things. But for once she kept her mouth shut. Although usually she's the perfect companion, sometimes she becomes critical. I wish she wouldn't. I'm only unwise when I've been under unbearable stress, and in those circumstances criticism from your best friend is the last thing you need. If meeting the

Devil outside the National Portrait Gallery doesn't count as unbearable stress I don't know what does.

Algerian red is good for whatever ails me, except when what ails me is Algerian red.

We walked north towards Euston until I was sure I was out of reach of Floating Outreach; then I turned left. Electra wasn't talking to me anymore but she was limping. I stopped and sat down. She lay with her head on my thigh and went straight to sleep. She's a dog—she sleeps when she's exhausted. She closes her eyes and she's gone. I wish I were a dog.

Chapter 4

Plagued By Joss, Beer And Jealousy

///

B ut sometimes I too sleep like a dog. And sometimes I sleep better outdoors than in. Instead of putting the legs of your bed inside your shoes and lying on top of your money so that no one can steal anything, you just curl up in a doorway. You think you'll take the weight off your feet for twenty minutes and the next thing you know it's daylight and someone's tapping you on the shoulder offering you a paper cup full of hot sweet coffee. An ordinary guy on his way to work gave me his coffee and walked off before I could say thank you. Sometimes people are so lovely I could cry.

We walked west to Hyde Park where I could use the public facilities and Electra could feel the grass under her toes. She likes that. She drank from the lake and wandered between the trees reading the messages left by other dogs. A walk in the park for her is like a fresh newspaper for me.

I found a packet of nearly unopened cheese sandwiches in a bin and shared them with Electra. It was a brilliant morning—free coffee, free sarnies and hardly any headache. I'd expected worse. I deserved worse.

I had twenty-six pounds and forty-seven pence in various pockets about my person. Alone in the park I was able to count it and conceal most of it next to my skin, keeping only enough to get by for the next few hours. I promised myself and Electra that I wouldn't buy any Algerian red till after lunch.

I was going to South Kensington and South Kensington is not in my territory. My patch is the West End where all the tourists go. It's messy and there are loads of all-night burger bars—it's a land of opportunity. To get to South Kensington you have to bypass Belgravia and Knightsbridge because that's where all the toffs live, and toffs don't want to see me and Electra outside their billion pound pads. And they don't go in for the amenities that make life liveable like twenty-four-hour convenience stores and public lavs.

It was a good grey day for those of us who live outdoors—no sun, no wind, no rain. People who look forward to a hot sunny day should remember that it's nearly as stressful to us as snow—we can't escape either.

Now, the problem was Harrison Mews. I couldn't loiter there. It was a tiny dead-end cobbled stage-set of twee little cottages covered with wisteria and clematis.

'We're buggerised,' I told Electra. 'They don't even have dustbins to hide behind. These people are so precious—I bet you it won't be five minutes before someone sends the maid to find out what we're doing.'

Electra stared in amazement at a little stone lion that Mr and Mrs Precious of Harrison Mews had placed on the edge of a horse trough outside a house with a yellow door. There's nothing so rustic as a mews in central London.

Gram Attwood came here last night, I thought. He might be asleep in one of these houses right now. He might be lying flat on his back hogging the bed the way he used to when he lay under my duvet in Acton. He lay with his throat, his chest, his stomach, his groin, unprotected. Obviously he never feared attack from me. The Devil doesn't fear attack.

I never sleep on my back anymore and I don't know anyone who does. Everyone I know curls like armadillos around their soft parts and possessions.

The song says, 'When you got nothin' you got nothin' to lose.' But that was written by a guy who didn't understand the concept. There's always something to defend even if it's only your soft parts or your right to feel no pain.

But Gram Attwood can sleep without fear. Think about *that* when you talk to me of justice. He stole from rich and poor alike and then persuaded me to take the blame. Why? Because, he assured me, as I had no prior convictions, I would not be sent to prison. I was a respectable forty-year-old woman, previously of good character, with a house and an ailing mother to look after. Yes, I was a home-owner and I worked in a building society. I was in a position of trust, and that was what finally did for me—I betrayed so many expectations: I was worse than a thief—I was a bad woman. You can't be more wicked than that. So of *course* I was sent to prison—as he must've known I would be.

But Gram Attwood can sleep on his back without protecting his soft parts.

Even his story about a previous conviction turned out to be a lie. He wept real tears when he told me about the youthful indiscretion that'd put him in the dock. When he threw himself on my mercy.

The Devil cries salty tears and can sleep on his back without fear.

In the last four years he has not acquired a single wrinkle or a grey hair. He has been cosseted. I wonder how many women have bought him clothes and shoes, provided freshly laundered sheets and towels. Did they pour his coffee and champagne like I did? Do they know that he doesn't like mushrooms?

Electra whimpered softly. My hand was cramped around her collar—a clenched fist. I released her and my fingers ached.

'I need a drink,' I said.

Electra licked my thumb—so discreetly that I almost missed her message. I looked into the huge topaz eyes that said, 'You promised.'

'I know, I know,' I said, 'but what do I do about the rage?'

'What're you mithering about now?' Joss said. 'You're always mithering. People think you're barmy.'

'What're you doing here?'

'You told us about it. I want to check it out. You shouldn't keep the good stuff to yourself. We're muckers, ain't we?'

'Where's Georgie?'

'Kensal Rise. That's where he thinks you'll be. We had a bet. Well screw him.' Joss shifted uneasily from one foot to another. Obviously they had a fight last night. Georgie drives him insane but he's lost without him.

'Rich pickings?' Joss looked down the little mews with its cute cottages and immaculate paintwork. Then he looked at the grand Victorian facades of Harrison Road. 'What's the story then?' he asked. 'What we doing here?'

'I know why *I'm* here,' I said, 'but I didn't invite you.'

'That's right, you didn't.' His face darkened with suspicion and he moved a few steps into the mews staring at the cobbles through his long lank hair.

You'd never guess he was only twenty-four—his hair and beard make him look fifty.

'It's not a new mission, you said? Yeah, this'd be a weird place for a mission. So what is it? Someone chucking out stuff you can sell?' He whipped round and stuck his face into mine. I could smell cornflakes and his first beer of the day. 'Why're you holding out on us?' he hissed. 'Mates don't hold out on mates.'

Electra whimpered. I took a step back. 'It's nothing like that. Last night I saw an old... I saw someone I used to know.'

'Someone rich? From before? See, I always said you was never one of us. You come from higher places, you. I told Georgie, I said, one day she'll go back to where she came from. She'll be with her rich friends and forget all about us.'

'Stop shouting,' I said. 'Someone will call the cops.'

'Mates stick together,' he snarled. And I remembered a story someone told me about when he was part of a 'recycling' team and another rough sleeper got badly beaten up when Joss thought his territory was under threat. That was before he met Georgie and settled down. But he was still paranoid—I could see that.

'Fancy a coffee?' I said. 'I'm buying.' I'd have to come back later—Joss was making me conspicuous.

'What about your old friend?'

'I don't think anyone at this address is going to want a reunion with me. I shouldn't have come.'

'I don't want coffee,' he said, 'but I could murder a can of Special Brew.'

I looked at Electra. 'I'm sorry,' I said, 'it's not my fault.'

He led the way with unerring instinct towards the nearest off-licence. He moved quickly. I was carrying my back-pack and bedroll and followed more slowly, so, turning for a last look at the mews, I saw the woman from last night come out of the house with the yellow door. She checked her bag for keys—a Louis Whatsisname handbag—and hurried out of the mews to Harrison Road where she was picked up and driven away by someone I couldn't see in a sexy red German car.

It's her house, I thought, of course it's her house. I used to check my bag for keys in exactly the same way when I left for work. When I had a handbag, a house and a job. And I too used to sneak a last look at the bedroom window when I'd left Gram sleeping on his back in the middle of my bed.

I could soak a newspaper in alcohol, set light to it and stuff it through the letterbox in the yellow front door. When Gram came stumbling out, coughing and retching from the smoke, I would be waiting and I'd clock him over the head with a manhole cover.

'Do you want a fucking drink or what?' Joss said, striding ahead. Electra hung back looking miserable. She knows what I'm thinking.

'I'm jangling,' I told her. 'Because my mother would be alive today if it wasn't for what that Devil did to me.' Electra stared at me with sorrowful eyes and I knew I had her sympathy.

'Got any money?' Joss stopped so abruptly that I almost ran into him.

'Not much,' I said. You don't want to tell him how much you've got unless you're prepared to put up with his company till it's all gone. In that, he has a lot in common with Gram Attwood.

We clubbed together to buy a six-pack of Special Brew. It isn't Algerian Red, I thought; I'm not breaking my promise. Beer is more thirst-quenching than wine but it causes painful bloat. Then there's the question of where to pee, which is another problem with beer. Joss can do it in the underpass but I can't. Knowing what to drink and where to pee are just two of the skills I've learned the hard way. That is why I stick to my own territory. I'm lost in South Kensington.

By the time I found somewhere near Gloucester Road tube station I was nearly bursting. I hate the smell of wee, but I stayed in there for ages. I wanted Joss to get fed up waiting for me and bugger off. I had the place to myself because any woman who came in took one look at me and walked straight out again. The dirty spotted mirror told me why: multiple layers of clothes, bedroll and backpack bent me out of shape. I stoop and hulk. My face is bluey-pink from broken veins and the weather. The grizzled hair that escapes from under my woolly beanie is an uncontrollable frizz. Four years ago I went to the hairdresser every five or six weeks. I had it layered and streaked with hi and lo lights for my court appearance—as if looking my best would save me. But women get into the most trouble when they're looking their best. I met Gram Attwood when I was looking my best. That sort of trouble would never ever happen to me today.

I couldn't help myself. I cried like a baby. I often do when I'm stupid enough to take a peek in a mirror.

'Dogs don't get ugly with age,' I wept to Electra, 'so why should I? Is it cos I look after you better than I look after myself?'

'Don't bring me into this,' she said. Her amber eyes are more beautiful than any you'll see on a super-model. She stood on her hind legs with her front paws on the wash-basin and I gave her a drink from the running tap. Why don't greyhounds get bags under their eyes?

'It's the pure thoughts,' she said. 'I feel no hate or rage: only love.'

'Oh do shut up,' I said, and we went out into the stone-coloured afternoon.

Joss was there with a man who was circling him like a vulture, saying, 'I should fucking kick your ugly teeth in. This ain't your pitch, you nonce.'

'Bring it on!' Joss yelled. 'Who you calling nonce, arsehole?'

Both of them were working their insane technique. It's what certain guys learn in prison, and it's like they're saying, 'I can take more pain and dish out more hurt than you cos I'm crazier than you.'

The sight of two homeless guys trying to frighten each other over a small square of pavement was so depressing that I left Gloucester Road and tried to find my way back to Harrison Mews. But could I? You'd think I was lost in the space-time continuum. I couldn't find Harrison Road let alone the sodding mews.

'It's not like I'm... '

'What? Totally fucked up?' Electra said. 'Don't kid yourself.'

'Well you find it then. You can't, can you? I should've chosen a bloodhound over a greyhound.'

She gave me a look full of patience and accusation before turning right through a hidden entrance, up some stone steps and out into a tiny secret churchyard. The sign over the church door said, 'Apple Pip Montessori Pre-school.' Dotted among the ancient headstones were wire cages holding lop-eared rabbits and ginger guinea pigs happily munching on the grass and bits of carrot. Electra and I stared at them, astonished. She sniffed at a couple of the cages but the occupants showed no interest or alarm. They knew her sweet nature without even bothering to ask.

I unrolled a blanket and sat behind a grave. It was quiet and private, an island in a fast moving stream. I settled down, and when no one came rushing out to send me away I opened a tin of dog food for Electra, plopping it onto her red plastic bowl. When she'd finished I gave her some of the guinea pigs' water to drink. We were safe and comfortable in South Kensington and we celebrated by going to sleep.

Chapter 5

I Find Myself At The Wrong End Of A Boot

///

I was dreaming about walking up to a house with a yellow door. My lovely high heel shoes clicked and wobbled on the cobble stones and I was afraid I'd fall over and mess up my party dress. It was important I look my best. Love and success were waiting behind the yellow door if I could only get there in time.

I opened my eyes. Two very small children in Oshkosh dungarees were petting Electra who had rolled on her back to let them tickle her tummy. A young woman with shiny fair hair was shaking my foot and saying, 'You'll have to go now. Wake up—you can't sleep here.' Behind her several children stared at me curiously.

'Is she dead?' one of them asked cheerfully. 'Why's she making that funny noise?'

'Is she Big Foot?'

'She's snoring,' the teacher said. 'Go inside for your milk and biscuits.'

'Can Big Foot have milk and bikkies?'

'She isn't Big Foot,' the teacher said, 'and she's going home now.'

'Can the doggie have some milk and bikkies?'

'Go inside,' the teacher said, a note of desperation creeping into her voice as I sat up smiling eagerly.

'*Chocolate* bikkies?' I asked.

So Electra and I were given milk and chocolate biscuits because the people at Apple Pip Montessori were too nice to send us away empty-handed. They even gave us directions to Harrison Mews. And waved us goodbye, their faces wreathed with smiles of complete relief.

I am a bad person. I have received gifts today—coffee, sandwiches, milk and chocolate. Strangers have been kind. I should be more loving because of it. But I cannot free my mind from its pit full of boiling rage. In this pit I am hungry and thirsty, yes, but not for food and red wine. Nothing will fill the jagged hole but revenge. I would like to see some blood. My hunger would feed on the sound of a cracking bone or two. I want to witness Gram Attwood's pain and fear. He couldn't be bothered with mine but his will be the medicine that makes me whole again.

When I'm free of this unliftable weight of rage and sorrow I'll be able to walk free, to work for wages, to buy moisturiser for my purple face and cream-rinse for my splintering hair.

'And you shall have a sofa to sleep on,' I told Electra, but I couldn't meet her eyes. She doesn't understand the need for revenge. I don't think she would even consider laying a tooth on the human beings, so-called, who treated her cruelly when her winning days came to an end, who rejected her and left her to rot. Like me.

'Did you actually forgive?' I asked her as we walked. 'Acceptance is in your nature so it isn't a virtue. But if you forgave... well, that makes you a better bitch than me.'

She didn't answer, and at last we arrived at the house with the yellow door. I hunkered down opposite with my back against a wall and a trail of leggy buddleia tickling my ears. Electra sat beside me.

Two minutes later Joss hissed in my ear. 'You stupid fucking cow—you can't sleep here. Get the fuck out before someone sees you.' He grabbed my arm with one hand and Electra's collar with the other and started dragging us across the cobbles.

He was hurting me. I was going to start yelling when, to my complete astonishment, the yellow door opened and Georgie came skittering out like a ferret from a drainpipe. He sprinted past us to Harrison Road, turned left and disappeared. He was carrying three plastic bags that clanked as he ran.

'What've you done?' I cried.

Joss dropped my arm and bent over me. 'You ain't seen us,' he snarled. To drive his meaning home he drove his boot into my side with such force I felt ribs crack—even under all my layers of clothes. He hauled back to deliver the same message to Electra but I snatched at his foot and he fell over. Electra ran for her life.

He scrambled to his feet. 'You mad syphilitic old cow,' he said and aimed his boot at my mouth.

I can't remember the next couple of minutes, but when my eyes opened again my head felt like a smashed melon, all my teeth wobbled and my mouth was full of blood. Joss was gone. Electra was gone.

I badly needed a drink.

The yellow door was ajar and I crawled towards it. They always keep wine in nice little mews houses with yellow front doors.

I crawled on all fours across a blond maple floor to a tiny kitchen. There was a wine rack on the counter. I grabbed a bottle at random. The lady of the house didn't go in for easy-open bottles so I had to find a corkscrew. It was the only thing worth trying to stand up for. Even so I threw up messily in the cute round kitchen sink. Throwing up, I discovered, was not a kindness to the broken ribs. It was only the thirst for red wine that kept me from passing out. I found the corkscrew in a drawer, and a box of dissolvable aspirins in the one just below it. I dissolved three aspirins in a tumbler full of wine and nearly sicked up in the sink again.

26

The floor slid up to meet me and I sat gratefully with bottle and glass until the room stopped heaving and the bottle was empty. It was the first time in years that I'd drunk wine from a glass.

'This could've been mine,' I said to Electra. 'I should've been an area manager by now.' But Electra didn't answer. I looked round. An empty space had opened up at my side—a silent pocket that used to hold the warm doggy smell of her. Then I remembered. She ran away when Joss tried to kick her. I protected her but she didn't protect me.

'Fuck her,' I thought. No sofas for her. I opened the fridge: white wine, milk and fizzy water in the door. Oh yes! And packets of ham, cheese and smoked salmon, plus six little jars of chocolate pudding—all the stuff I buy specially for Gram because I know what he likes.

I opened another bottle of classy French red. I took a chocolate pud from the fridge and a spoon from the drawer and slowly, oh very slowly, made my way upstairs. When you come home after a hard day the first thing you want to do is have a little drink and then take a bath; or maybe have a little drink *in* the bath. Sometimes when Gram is at home, waiting for me, we have a bath together, drinking wine and talking by candlelight. Today I think I'll have a bath with lots of bubbles, the jasmine bubbles that Gram likes. Hot water, bubbles and good wine are what you need when your ribs ache and your teeth no longer fit in your mouth. I always leave the boiler on so that there's hot water whenever Gram and I want it. And I always have candles. Candlelight is kind and forgives the years. It makes Gram forget I am older than he is.

I lie wallowing in hot jasmine water, healing from the day's hurts, and wait for my one true lover. The only one. The one and only. The love and lonely.

I woke up when I heard the screaming.

The water wasn't hot. The bubbles had burst. The bottle was empty but the stub of a candle still flickered on the edge of the bath. I struggled to sit up but my back and ribs went into spasm. So I screamed too. I grabbed for a towel, slipped and fell back, whacking my head. The candle went out. A door slammed. Darkness and silence.

Chapter 6

Hospitalised

///

A man said, 'Ma'am, can you hear me? Can you stand? Ma'am?'

Strong arms lifted me and swathed me in warm fluffy towelling.

'Gram?' I said.

'Concussion,' the voice said. 'Watch out, her head's bleeding. What about the other one?'

A woman said, 'Resuscitation failed. I called it in.'

'Cops?'

'On their way. What a bleeding mess, eh?'

'And such a posh little neighbourhood—just goes to show—no one's safe.'

My eyelids weighed a ton. My fingers felt like walnuts. I smelled of jasmine. The man smelled of cigarettes and disinfectant. The towelling...

The woman said, 'Can you hear us, love? What's your name?'

The towelling smelled of aftershave and cologne.

'Gram,' I said. 'The Devil.'

'What did she say?'

'You won't get much sense out of a mouth like that till the swelling goes down.'

'Icepack?'

LIZA CODY

'I know the cops said wait, but I really think we should load this one up and go.'

'Think of the traffic on the Brompton Road. It could be half an hour before we get there. She needs to be in Emergency.'

'We're taking you to hospital, dear,' the woman said loudly. 'You'll be more comfortable there.'

'Ow,' I said, 'ow, ow, ow.'

'Take it easy,' she said. 'It's all very well—these bijoux mews houses, but you try getting a sodding full-length gurney down the narrow stairs without getting stuck or doing yourself an injury.'

I felt cold air on my aching face and smelled London's pollution. 'My bags,' I cried. 'Electra!'

'What's she saying?'

'I think she wants her handbag,' the woman said.

The man stroked my hand and said, 'Don't worry; the police'll make sure your house is secure. No need to worry about the electricity.'

Gently, the woman put a bag on my chest. It was a Louis Whatsisname handbag.

'Not that one,' I said.

'Don't thank me,' she said. 'I'm just doing my job.'

———

I woke up from a dream about a trespassing woman who poured a foul perfume all around my house, on my clothes and on me. The perfume was sanitary and carbolic—the stuff you put down drains. The woman was unstoppable and treated my house as if it belonged to her; like she treated my man, my Gram, as if he was hers.

I woke in a rage of frustration and fright. I could smell blood as well as Draino—it was clogging my mouth and my nose. Worst of all, ringing in my ears, was the memory of someone saying the cops were coming.

30

The cops don't like me. They wake me up to push me off benches and doorsteps. They accuse me of begging. They call me a vagrant. They try to persuade doctors to put me in the Nut Factory.

I wanted to get up but I was in bed and someone had tied me down.

A nurse came along and said, 'What's all the fuss about, Mrs Munrow, or can I call you Natalie?'

I tried to tell her, but my mouth was sewn up like a big fat purse. I struggled to sit up.

'Wait,' she said, and loosened the sheet. 'Maybe they were afraid you'd fall out. I imagine you're a bit disoriented. People often are when they've been admitted unconscious. Do you want the loo? A drink?'

I nodded eagerly. But my head fell off and rolled under the bed. The nurse didn't notice. She said. 'I'm afraid you'll have to drink through a straw for a few days.'

'I don't care,' I said. 'Just get me a drink.' But it sounded like, 'Inerf ferf frink.'

She put a straw between my blobby lips and I drank Draino, blood and… water. 'A proper drink,' I cried. 'Affroffer frink.'

'There, there,' she said. 'I know it hurts, but you'll soon get used to it. When the swelling goes down and the stitches come out you'll be as good new.' She disappeared for a few seconds and I realised I could only see out of one eye.

'Fneuf?'

'Your bag's in the bedside cabinet and your robe's on the chair. Try not to talk, Natalie. You'll need your energy. The police wanted to interview you last night but Dr Dat said they'd have to wait till this afternoon at least. I'm going off shift now. Bye-bye.'

I was completely wankered—I'd lost all my stuff and the buggerizing cops were coming. I didn't understand. Who the fuck was Natalie Munrow? Sure as sugar she wasn't in my bed.

And then, as I lay there getting used to all my new aches and pains, it came to me: Natalie Munrow wasn't in *my* bed, but maybe I was in hers.

A tiny old lady appeared at my side. She wore a frilly pink dressing-gown and said, 'That Suzette's so bleedin' lazy—of course you'll want the bleedin' toilet—you've been asleep for nine hours. Come on, I'll show you.'

It was agony. Knives stabbed my head, my back, my sides. I was walking on pins and needles. I said, 'Ow-ow-ow.' It was the only thing I could say that came out the way I meant it.

'I know, I know,' the tiny lady said. 'Gawd's tooth, some bugger really played knickety-knack-paddy-whack with you, dint they? I heard them nurses saying your whole house was covered in blood, and where you wasn't covered in blood you was covered in bruises. There you are now. I'd have a wash too, while I was at it. They dint clean you up too good. I'm lucky me daughter comes in every day. I'd be dead ten times over if I left it to them lazy cows.'

The bathroom was all white but it smelled of blood and Draino like everything else. Then I looked in the mirror and at first I didn't recognise what I saw. My hair was all stuck together with dried blood. The stitches on my lips were like black pits filled with it. My nostrils were stuffed with it too. I couldn't open my mouth but I could taste blood on my tongue and down my throat. My jaw and one eye were so lumpy I looked like the Elephant Man.

I wanted to stand under the shower but I was wearing one of those hospital gowns that fasten at the back and I couldn't reach because my shoulders and arms tore off when I tried. I did what I could in the basin but I couldn't touch my own face. It hurt too much.

The little old bird was hovering outside the bathroom door when I got out. 'Tweet tweet,' she said. 'Locking up's too good for the likes of them. They should be strung up from the nearest lamp-post where you can watch 'em choke. And what they done to your poor friend... all for a few trinkets. I blame the drugs.'

'*Pherf?*'

'Oh my Gawd's wrinkly billibow, dint they tell you? Battered to death—face like mashed beetroot. You was ever so lucky.'

I crawled into my white bed that smelled of blood and ironing and closed the only eye that opened. I was ever so lucky.

'Fag?' the little old bird sang. 'If you can get a straw in your gob you can manage a smoke.'

A man said, 'Back to bed, Mrs Barnes. You should be ashamed—leading new patients astray. I'll tell your daughter.'

I cranked my eye open again just in time to see the old bird flutter away.

'Dr Dat.' The man in the white coat sat down next to the bed. There was marmalade on his tie and butter on his breath. Soft fingers closed over my wrist. 'You won't be able to say much, so nod or shake your head. Okay?'

I nodded and my skull crushed my brain.

'First of all, don't worry about brain damage or bleeding. We gave you a CT scan last night. You have a hairline fracture and some nasty gashes but nothing serious. I'm afraid we had to cut off some of your hair to suture your scalp. That couldn't be avoided. You have three broken ribs on the left side. Several broken teeth too, but nothing a good cosmetic dentist can't cope with. Obviously there are multiple contusions and abrasions and I bet you think we've been stingy with the painkillers.'

I nodded more cautiously.

'We have to be careful what we give someone who's slipping in and out of consciousness but we'll try to improve on that.'

'*Phow?*'

'Yes, very soon. And we've phoned your brother in York. His number was in your mobile phone in your handbag, OK? He should be here after lunch.'

'Pho phit!'

'I thought you'd be pleased. I'm hoping he'll be present when the police return. Now I must be off. I'll send a nurse along with the analgesic. Get some rest.'

'Oh phugger,' I moaned to his retreating back.

The crap I was swimming in was getting deeper and skankier by the minute. Someone was dead. Everyone seemed to think I was Natalie Munrow who was maybe Gram's girlfriend and the owner of the house with the yellow door. Her brother was coming and he'd dob me in as soon as he saw me. My head hurt like a bursting boil. I'd lost Electra. I'd lost my bedroll, all my gear and at least twenty pounds I'd had hidden in my clothes. The cops were on their way.

My good eye stung with tears and my bad one ached like a broken leg.

Tiny Mrs Barnes perched on the end of my bed. 'Cheep-cheep,' she said. 'Lend us some gelt for the phone? My Margi'll pay you back when she comes.'

And I had a roommate on the cadge.

'You got a handbag stuffed full of goodies. I heard that lazy cow Suzette saying.'

'Phugh foff.'

'You're a pal,' she trilled and bobbed out of sight, reappearing seconds later with the Louis Whatsisname handbag with all the buckles and pockets. It looked heavy. I held out my hands. 'Orright if I help myself?' she said, ignoring me.

'Pho!' I shouted, stretching and tearing my shoulders out of their sockets. 'Ow-ow-ow.'

'Mrs Barnes!' Big arms appeared and wrestled my handbag out of the old bird's claws. 'Why you tormenting this fine lady? Ain't she got enough torment already? You go back to your own bed now.'

The mountainous nurse drew curtains round my bed. 'I'll be hiding this nice bag under your pillow.' She pulled me this way and that as if I was a baby who weighed no more than an armful, and when she settled me back down I could feel the pillows fluffed up on top of the handbag.

She handed me a plastic beaker full of green Draino and told me to rinse and spit. So I rinsed with green and spat out mucky brown. 'Ow–ow–ow.'

'They sure messed you up good,' she muttered and advanced on me with a syringe.

Just one tiny scratch and I dived deep down into soft black pillows and arms where there was no pain, no loss and no fear.

Chapter 7

I Become Natalie

///

'**K**nock, knock.'
I struggled through layers of loft insulation just in time to see a fair curly head poke through the curtains.

'Natalie?' she said. 'I know I'm supposed to wait for your brother, but I just got a call and I have to attend.' A skinny woman in uniform came through the curtains.

Uniform. Dark blue uniform. A cop.

'Pho phug!'

'I'm supposed to return your house keys to you and have a chat.'

'Phan fout?'

'You know, about what happened... and your friend— so sorry about that—but I can see you're not up to much conversation. So I'll leave your keys and come back in a couple of hours.'

A handful of jingly-jangly metal dropped close to my fingers. I tried to thank her but my blubberous lips got in the way.

'I'm PC Cole, by the way, Sally Cole, victim support officer. Here whether you need me or not, and all that malarkey.' She pressed a square of cardboard into my hand and turned away.

Tall, fair-haired and no arse whatsoever. I was never more pleased to see anyone leave in my life. Cops hate me when they know it's me. Good job they don't hate Natalie Thingy… Muldrow… Bloodrow. I closed my eye. Cops don't hate you if you've got house keys.

My eye jerked open again. My brother was coming. He would hate me and make the cops take my keys away.

There was a white towelling robe on the chair next to the bed. I put it on. I put my keys in my pocket and wrapped my arms tightly round my Louis Whatsit handbag as I staggered to the bathroom.

It didn't hurt quite so much this time. I was still walking on glass, but I wasn't treading as heavily. In fact, I was sort of floating.

Out of habit I put the spare toilet roll in my pocket before leaving.

Birdie Barnes was lying on her back on top of her bed, snoring. She was going to steal all my coin. So I stole her slippers. They were too small by nearly six inches so my heels dragged on the floor. Which is exactly what you'd expect from an enemy like her—something small and inconsiderate.

But I had to have slippers. People notice bare feet. They can see vagrancy, poverty, madness and martyrdom when they look at ten naked toes. Bare feet carry tortured refugees across scalding deserts, and no one wants to be reminded.

My mother used to say, 'If your hair and shoes are clean, no one cares what's in between.' Like a lot of things my mother said it turned out to be bollocks, but even so she didn't deserve to die of shame knowing her daughter was in chokey.

I drifted down a corridor or two, floated down some stairs and followed a tragic flock of slow bathrobes to a canteen. I was going home.

All the smokers huddled outside the main entrance coughing their lungs up. What a way to treat sick smokers! It's a police plot. And when all the smokers are dead they'll turn on the eaters and drinkers. Then hospital entrances will be surrounded by fat drunks.

My brother smelled of blood and Draino but not of tobacco. He got out of a cab, pushed his way through the smokers and went into the hospital to look for me. He didn't recognise me.

'Tee-hee, ow-ow,' I said.

I stole his cab.

'Harrison Mews,' I said. But the driver said, 'Huh?' So I searched in my bag till I found an ivory case with my business cards in it. After that he called me ma'am and started to drive. Cradled, rocked and on the move at last, I went to sleep.

'Harrison Mews. Wake up, ma'am. Oy, shake a leg, we're here.'

'It's the one with the yellow door. Phwon fiff phellowfor.' I pointed. 'Ow.'

'I'll have to reverse out.'

'Phellowfor.'

'I can't turn round,' he grumbled.

Rain was pouring down. Pools of water glistened between the cobbles. Heavy-headed wisteria drooped. Electra's coat would be sodden. She hates getting wet. She shivers.

Tutting and sighing, the man drove his cab to the yellow door. 'Uh-oh,' he said, 'police tape. I don't think you're supposed to go in there.'

I gave him a twenty pound note because I suddenly had lots of them, and he shut up. He even got out to help me with the keys after he'd watched me drop them twice. It's amazing how much people want to help you when you've got lots of twenty pound notes and a house with a yellow door. But he wasn't my friend. His eyes tore little strips of skin off my face so I didn't invite him in for a drink.

Draino and blood waited behind the front door. I don't know why I hadn't seen it before. Maybe it wasn't there before. Maybe the cops smeared the maple floor with blood and smashed the telly. Don't ask me why—they hate me.

But they forgot to steal the wine. That's because they're stupid. There was wine, a corkscrew and a glass in the kitchen. I opened the bottle and ignored the glass. But I couldn't get my lips round the neck of the bottle and I couldn't find a straw. When I poured the wine into what was left of my mouth it stung like a swarm of bees, so I staggered upstairs for a lie-down. I wasn't feeling too clever.

I lay down on a big soft bed and covered myself with a crimson duvet. I closed my eyes. Just for a moment… just for a…

Light squirmed in through the curtains. The clock on the table said eleven-thirty. I stared at it. Eleven-thirty a.m. I did the arithmetic—I must've slept for over twenty hours. Or maybe it was for twenty days. I got up and went to the bathroom.

I'd been standing in the shower for five minutes before I realised that half my hair was shaved off, that I had fifteen stitches in my scalp and they were all screaming at me for putting shampoo on them. I wrapped myself gently in a towel and looked in the mirror. There were four stitches in my upper lip, seven on my cheekbone and five over my right eye. I was black, blue, angry red and sick yellow all over. I looked like one of Dr Frankenstein's failed experiments—before he finally got it right and created a monster.

I went back to the bedroom and sat on the bed. Memories, like coloured beads, began to hit me in no particular order. A bottle of red wine. A boot hurtling into my face. A voice saying, 'Sorry about your friend.' An old lady trying to steal my handbag. Electra running away. An ambulance. A cop-lady. Cops. Oh shit—my brother.

A massive headache smashed my skull like a train. I had to find my stuff and move on. I knew it wasn't *my* brother I needed to avoid, but the brother of whoever lived in the house with the yellow door. Because he would know I wasn't her. But he would be *like* my real brother—full to the brim with blame and contempt.

I had to collect my stuff and find Electra. But the cops had stolen my things. My backpack, all my spare clothes, spare change, my bedroll and dog food were gone.

I couldn't go out on the streets in a towelling dressing gown and slippers six sizes too small. If I couldn't go out on the streets I'd be chucked in chokey and I'd never find Electra.

I began to shake so I went back down to the kitchen and opened a bottle of wine. I thought my mouth was less swollen but I still couldn't get it to fit round the neck of a bottle without tearing stitches. The shakes turned into rattles. The rattles are to the shakes what earthquakes are to vibrations. The shakes are amateurs.

But I am a survivor, a woman who can solve nearly as many problems as she creates. I was in a kitchen, after all, and most problems surrender to kitchen utensils.

I found a turkey baster. Turkey baster, my old friend, I thought, and sucked up red wine which I then squirted into my mouth.

When I had enough of the red inside me to control the shakes I went upstairs to the bathroom. I wasn't expecting to find anything better than aspirin in the cabinet so I was surprised to find a stash of moggies, zopiclone, fluoxetine and co-codamol. It was all stuff I could use, and if I couldn't use it I could sell it.

Sometimes I have this feeling right in the dead centre of my chest. It's like a tumour growing inside and I think that if I could puncture my chest, cut a hole exactly the right size, all the darkness and evil would come rushing out leaving me light and airy and free. I know to the last millimetre where I'd make the hole. I can put my finger right on the spot. Sometimes it seems almost ready to explode. Sometimes I think it will implode and suck me in like a black hole.

Moggies and zops are good for that sort of hurt because they're sleepers, but co-codamol can't touch it. Unfortunately now was a bad time to have a sleep. But fluoxetine is an anti-depressant—a cheaper form of Prozac. It wouldn't act immediately and in the short term it might make me a little crazy. But I was willing to take the risk. I took one two-tone capsule and squirted it down with red wine. Then I took a tab or three of co-codamol to give the aspirin a helping hand.

One day, when there's no wine or pills left, I'll have to take a skewer to that spot in the dead centre of my chest. But not today—there's too much evil on the maple floor already.

Chapter 8

Leaving Harrison Mews

//

I was looking for a backpack but I found a wheelie case
in the bottom of a fitted wardrobe. I packed the crimson
duvet, a pillow, three toilet rolls, the three remaining
bottles of red, a corkscrew, the turkey baster, the Louis
Whatsisname bag and all the pills.

I found a drawer full of exercise clothes—sweat pants,
fleecy tops, t-shirts, socks and sports bras. Natalie and I weren't
the same size but it doesn't show so much with sports clothes.
I put on as much as I could. Layers are important. I took
four large silk scarves and wound them, African style, around
my head to hide the stitches and the bad haircut. I found a
big loose Aquascutum raincoat in a downstairs cupboard.
That only left the shoes, which are always a problem when
you have feet the size of cocker spaniels. In the end I took
her tennis shoes to the kitchen and cut the toecaps out with
a carving knife. They wouldn't be much good in the rain but
they were better than nothing.

You think I'm stealing. So what? I have absolutely fuck-all
and this woman had ten of everything. Besides, she was dead.
I *need* a bedroll for sleeping outdoors. She barely needs a thin
blanket, given all the central heating she's got in her bedroom.
Also, when my nose clears and I can smell something other
than blood and Draino, I may be able to catch the scent of
Gram Attwood on the pillow. Not his real scent, of course,

because he's the Devil and doesn't have one. But that citrus aftershave and the almond-like shampoo that costs fifty quid a bottle. I used to buy it for him. Convincing Gram to love me wasn't cheap.

I parked the wheelie case by the front door and noticed that in spite of the police tape the postman had delivered some letters. They were addressed to Miss N Munrow.

I noticed too that some of the bloody smears on the floor ended at the front door. I imagined Natalie dragging herself, bleeding and dying, out of the house, into the rain.

Then I remembered. I had dragged myself, bleeding, *into* the house. The blood didn't end there—it began there. Maybe I had dragged myself past a dead body without noticing. I'd badly needed a drink, but all the same it was quite an omission.

I started remembering fragments of yesterday—or was it the day before? Or even the day before that? I was in a lovely hot jasmine-smelling bath to soothe my ribs and then somebody screamed. Someone had a key to my yellow door. Gram had a key. But Gram is a devil and a killer so he doesn't scream at the sight of death. He smiles that vicious little smile that I once found so cute and turns his head away.

A simpler explanation might be that I didn't close the yellow door after I dragged myself through it. A neighbour saw the open door and came in.

When pain begins to ebb away it leaves behind it a clean stretch of sand without footprints. In a sudden rush of clarity I picked up one of the letters from the doormat, the one from the National Bank. I opened it and saw that the woman whose handbag I'd been toting around had a healthy wedge of coin. If I was in charge of her handbag I was probably also in charge of her credit cards.

I used to know about that stuff. After all, I was a branch manager with access to customer accounts. I would have been an area manager if I hadn't given someone who smells of citrus aftershave access to my access.

I sat for a moment at the bottom of the staircase and looked around. It was a small living room with an even smaller kitchen and dining area leading off it. There were original oil paintings in curly gold frames on the walls, and blood-stained damask on the sofa and armchairs. From the look of her bank statement and her expensive but bloody Persian rug, Natalie Munrow was loaded.

Now that I was looking properly I could see that her CD player and some other electrical goods were missing because there were three plugs in wall sockets from which the wires had been cut. Her CDs were in a mess, as if someone had grabbed a handful without looking. The same was true of her DVDs. CDs and DVDs represent quick cash and they are portable. It looked to me as if everything that had been stolen would fit in carrier bags. The big flat-screen TV and state-of-the-art DVD player were smashed but unstolen.

'Phorgey 'n' Foss,' I said out loud, remembering the clanking plastic bags Georgie had been carrying. Georgie was inside ripping stuff off while Joss was outside keeping watch. Georgie wasn't the violent one. That was Joss. He'd nearly killed me. *Everyone* said he was one mean, mad dude. We got along because I'm a woman and women don't count in his testosterone-fuelled world. Until they cross him or get in the way. What could be more in the way than knowing about theft and murder? If he realised I was still alive I'd be a threat to him. I moaned.

Wouldn't I be safer staying here in the mews behind the double locked, double bolted yellow door? Surely this was the last place Joss would come back to.

But it was the first place my, sorry, her brother would come to. He might be on his way right now, with the cops. I had to go. Quickly.

Where? There are no limitless possibilities for the homeless. And the places we can go are well known to all of us. Joss would track me down easily unless I left town. But

London's the only town I know. And I couldn't leave without Electra.

Then I realised I could use one of the credit cards to get a hotel room. Joss would never look for me in a hotel. It'd been a long time since I'd had a credit card but I still knew I'd need a Personal Identity Number. When I was a real person I used to keep mine disguised as the last four digits of false telephone numbers under the entry 'Pine Furniture' in my phone book. Pine, PIN, gettit? Well, so did Gram Attwood, damn his lovely blue eyes.

I unpacked the Louis Whosit hand bag and found a mobile phone with more gadgets, buttons and symbols than the flight deck of a jet fighter. I couldn't deal with it. Instead I looked round the room and saw that a cupboard close to the fireplace was in fact a cubby-hole containing a whiz-bang, space age computer and, oh thank the lord for little favours, an old fashioned Rolodex.

I stared at the tiny desk packed with computer, scanner, printer and something scary that was probably a hands-free phone set. And it made me cry. Life on the street had turned me into prehistoric woman. I couldn't imagine my swollen, bruised hands with their torn yellow fingernails playing arpeggios on the clean cream keyboard.

'Phawful,' I whispered and went straight upstairs to the bedroom where Natalie kept a little woven basket full of luscious, subtle nail varnishes. I sat on the antique chair in front of her make-up mirror and began to paint my nails the colour of unripe blackberries. They looked alien, like a frog's hands. I stopped. A frog's hand trailed, clammy, down Gram's hairless, scentless chest towards his lean, clean belly.

I squirted myself with her Issy Miyake perfume but it made me gag so I went down again to the Rolodex. I looked up P for PIN and pine. Nothing made sense. I was losing focus. I crammed the whole damn thing into my suitcase. I hadn't achieved anything but a waste of time. Every second brought my brother's taxi closer.

Even so, my good eye stung with tears when I closed my yellow door and hauled the wheelie case onto the cobbles. I wore the Aquascutum raincoat and a large pair of Ava Gardner sun-glasses I'd found in the pocket. Expensive eyewear, I reasoned, would distract attention from the mutilated tennis shoes and buggerised face.

I struggled down the mews with my case hip-hopping, tip-toppling behind me.

I wanted a taxi to take me to Battersea, to the dog's home where Electra came from in the first place and where lost dogs go. It's where I'd find her, looking sad and anxious. I could imagine her expression when she saw me: she'd grin with relief and if I'd had a drink or two she'd say, 'You took your time.' She wouldn't turn her back and walk away.

But astonishingly, I could see her in the distance, *walking away*. Her brindle flanks just a little lop-sided as she favoured her right hind leg because of the arthritis.

That's what too much co-codamol does, I thought. It makes your dog appear in front of you, walking away, wearing a lemon-yellow chiffon scarf.

She looked so very real... but a chiffon scarf?

'Phlectra?' I called.

Electra stopped and turned her head towards me. Lemon-yellow was *not* her colour. And the nun who held the other end of the scarf was not her owner. A nun or a non-nun?

I took off the sun-glasses to get a better look at my analgesic dream. Electra *was* there, waiting for me. The lemon chiffon scarf was there. The nun looked annoyed. She tugged at the yellow scarf.

'Phlectra!' I shouted and started across the road, the wheelie case lurching dangerously behind me. Electra obligingly sat down and waited.

Chapter 9

A Dodgy Nun And Electra

//

'Fuck off, freak,' growled the nun through gritted teeth. She smelled of tobacco. I was elated— something had bypassed the blood and Draino in my nose. It was a breakthrough. I *would* survive and recover.

I squatted painfully and threw my arms round Electra's neck. I was too choked up with tears to speak, but Electra said, 'I might've known—you go missing for three whole days and then you turn up wrecked.'

'Foo phays.'

'Three. I should know. You abandoned me.'

'Bugger off, tit head,' the nun said. 'What the fuck d'you think you're doing, slobbering all over my dog?'

'Fmy fog,' I said, standing up and grabbing for the chiffon scarf.

The nun gave up so suddenly that I tipped over onto my arse. 'Okay, okay. But shut the fuck up shouting.'

'You're making a *scene*,' whispered Electra, her warm breath tickling my ear.

Over her shoulder I saw a police car draw up to the entrance to the mews. A fair-haired cop with no arse at all got out. I couldn't remember her name but I had her card in the pocket of my bathrobe. I buried my face in Electra's neck. The nun saw the police car too and crouched down beside us.

A man got out of the passenger side. He was balding, bespectacled and paunchy. He was my, no, Natalie's brother.

A cold sharp point poked me under my chin. The nun said, 'Shout and I'll stick this screwdriver in your throat.'

The cop glanced in our direction and said something to my brother. He was standing there with blame flames bursting out of his bald head and rage glinting off his bifocals.

The nun waved her hand at the lady cop. The lady cop was too far away to see the nicotine stains. She raised her hand too and set off down the mews. She and my furious brother disappeared.

I knocked the screwdriver away from my neck. 'Phgerroffme,' I muttered. Suddenly I felt quite comfortable on the ground with Electra in my arms. I could sleep now, I thought, I'm used to sleeping on the ground. It doesn't smell of blood and Draino in the gutter.

'You're stoned,' the nun said, 'you're abso-fucking-lutely arseholed. What you on, you battered old tart? Eh? C'mon now—share.'

'Need a hand, sister?' A passer-by with two Airedale terriers stopped a few feet away.

'How kind,' the nun murmured in tones that were suddenly light and refined with a trace of an Irish accent. 'But we're quite alright—just a stumble. We're on our way to the doctor's right now.'

'Phelp!' I cried, but I could only watch the retreating backsides of one passer-by and two Airedales.

'Oh give your hole a holiday,' the nun said. 'You're coming with me.' She grabbed my arm and pulled me to my feet.

'Ow-ow-ow,' I shrieked. My fine Aquascutum raincoat and trendy dark glasses weren't saving me. The nun could see my tattered vagabond soul. There was no hiding place. She'd pull my arms off like butterfly wings if I didn't go with her.

'Don't make such a fuss,' Electra said. 'Where were you going anyway?'

'Phoo fie phoo.'

'Well *I* found *you*, so come along. It isn't that bad.'

'It is.' And to prove it the clouds burst open with a crack and a screech, and rain came tumbling down, slapping my bruises with tiny wet fists. Electra started to shiver.

'Oh crap,' said the nun. She grabbed my wheelie case and started off down Harrison Road. But I caught up and grabbed the handle too. I had Electra's chiffon scarf in one hand and the handle in the other—all my worldly goods and chattels. I wasn't going to let go of either one. You'd have to kill me first. Which is exactly what the nun looked as if she wanted to do. But now we were on the Cromwell Road and there were hundreds of people hurrying past with umbrellas or in tourist busses watching the Natural History Museum get wet. The nun knew she'd attract attention if she was violent, so we trundled through the rain, an undignified trio, heading west.

We came to rest nearly an hour later in a tiny room in a boarded up, fire-damaged house. I was too tired and hurt to stand so I sank down to my knees, huddled over to protect the wheelie case. Oddly enough I felt nearly safe. The cops wouldn't find me here; or my brother; or Joss and Georgie. All I had to worry about was the nun. All the nun seemed to be worrying about was drugs.

'C'mon butt-brain,' she said. 'Whachoo got? You screwed up my evening so you bleeding owe me.' She tore off her wimple and revealed bleached blonde hair with sky blue and violet streaks in it.

I had to turn away. I was experiencing one of those crumples in the material of reality—I didn't know if the nun was a boy or a girl. Hanging from the fire-scarred picture rails were nine or ten pretty dresses. But unless my undamaged eye was telling mighty white lies the nun had an Adam's apple and a shaving rash.

I wanted to tell Electra that I couldn't cope, but she said, 'Oh for goodness sake, just share. Then we can all get some sleep.'

So I rummaged in the case until my hand hit my purloined pharmacy. I snatched up zopiclone and co-codamol.

'Goody, goody, goodies,' the nun said. He brought over a bottle of water.

I took two of each. I didn't see what the nun took because I was too busy unpacking the scarlet duvet and making a nest for Electra inside the case. She could curl up on the towelling bathrobe and be protected from draughts.

I struggled out of the soaking raincoat and wrapped myself in the duvet. I lay down with my head on the handbag. I was hurting so much I couldn't have cared less about being ripped off. All I wanted was a way out of the pain. I wanted blankness, nothingness, and to pass many hours without having to feel anything.

Chapter 10

I Am Persuaded To Move South Of The River

///

I lay on the hard floor and listened to Electra scuffling and whimpering. I was warm and I didn't want to move. But my bladder was bursting. We both relieved ourselves in the tiny overgrown back garden. It wasn't raining now but the bushes and shrubs were dripping. The light was as grey as dirty curtains. I don't own a watch so I couldn't tell if it was dawn or dusk. I was just glad to have a roof over my head.

The nun was lying flat on his back with his arms outstretched like Jesus on the cross. He didn't stir when I bent over to examine his face. He wasn't a natural blond. His lashes were lush and his eyebrows, plucked to a perfect arch, were dark.

Electra sniffed at his long bony fingers before settling back in the wheelie case. She seemed quite friendly towards him but I didn't like him, because in spite of the absurd coloured streaks in his hair, the severe black habit and the shaving rash, he was prettier and more feminine than I had ever been— even in my teens and twenties.

He smelled of young sweet sweat and chocolate. This told me that he was not the Devil. I lay down, wrapped myself in the duvet, took another few painkillers and tipped off the edge of the world.

The next time I woke up the nun was washing shaved armpits with bottled drinking water and Electra was eating a can of tuna. I was so stiff I could barely move.

'What do I call you?' I mumbled through sliced and diced lips. They still hurt but the blubber had shrunk enough to make my speech understandable.

'Hello Ms Momster.' He turned, his pale supple body flickering in the candlelight. 'That's the best sleep I've had since someone gave me eight Vicodin and I slept right through the Reading Festival. I didn't even wake up when someone stole my tent.'

'Yes but what do I call you?' Notice that I didn't ask his name. If people trust you they might tell you. But what most people go by are tags. Some of us have several.

'You can call me Sister.' He batted his thick eyelashes shyly. Or was it slyly? I couldn't tell by candlelight.

'What time is it?'

'Dunno. Two days later? It's night-time; I know that. And we got to move.'

'Two days later than what?' My sense of time lurched wildly. 'Why do we got to move?'

'How do you fancy sharing a river view apartment? No rent. No landlord. No leaks, no drafts and no pellet-shitting rats.'

I reached out and stroked Electra's sleek snout for comfort.

'What's the matter, Momster?'

What's the matter is that the guy who's calling me Mom and Monster is a Sister. It's two days later and I badly need a drink.

He said, 'We could share your dog. With a face like yours you don't need a dog to help hustle. You can do the battered wife act without her, but she's a real asset to the weak-bladdered nun.'

My hand scrambled like a rodent through the wheelie case until it found the neck of a bottle. I seized it and hung on for stability. 'Rent-free?' I said.

'A team thing?' Sister suggested with a winsome smile. 'You lend me your dog and I'll let you stay rent-free until I've made enough dosh for a ticket.'

'Yesterday you called me a tit head.'

'I say stuff, okay? How come you remember? You were boiled, fried and scrambled.'

'I remember stuff, okay? Especially insults. And you can't have Electra till I see the river view.'

'Well get your arse in gear. We're going now. And do something about your head. You look totally random.'

Electra shook her head and gave me a look which said, 'That about sums you up... Momster.'

Mister Sister held out a mirror while I righted my silk turban. My face looked worse but it felt better. I thought about the little mews house with the yellow front door. While I was there I wanted it to be mine. I even painted my nails the colour of unripe blackberries so that I'd deserve it more. But it could only be mine if I was Natalie Munrow, and then I would also have to pay her bills, pay council tax, learn how to use her terrifying technology, learn how to be a 21ˢᵗ century woman again, instead of being the creature that lives under a stone who expects nothing and from whom nothing is expected.

But Mister Sister offered me a rent-free flat and a dry bed. He is the worm that corrupts the hopeless apple. He said, 'We could take a cab if you pay.'

So that was it: he'd been using his eyes, nose and ferrety little fingers and he thought I was Natalie Munrow. He didn't know that if I was Natalie I'd be dead. Probably. Almost certainly. I should find out. I should have a drink and buy a newspaper.

'Don't start gargling yet, butt-bonce,' he said with a charming scowl. 'I need you walking on your own two kipper boxes and making sense.' He adjusted his wimple, gave himself a flirtatious wink in the mirror and swept all his pretty dresses into a backpack along with his toiletries. 'Remember,' he said, 'if anyone asks, we're looking for sheltered housing for you and your dog. And we *are* taking a poxy taxi, okay? If I really was a fucking thief I'd have nicked your wallet as well as your phone.'

Not a thief? Self-assessment on the street isn't *close* to realistic. Even I would never say that about myself.

'But we buy proper food for Electra,' I said. 'Tuna makes her shit soup and you won't want that in your river view flat. Also she needs a waterproof coat. This rain plays hell with her arthritis and she hates the cold. You can't use her unless you treat her right.'

'Who d'you think she is—the Princess Royal's pampered Pekinese?'

'Not much good at psychology, are you? People are generous if it looks like I care more for her than I do for myself. If she looks neglected they give me bugger-all and get straight on the blower to the cops or the RSPCA—listen, cos I'm telling you what you need to know.'

Electra was limping. Of the three of us she was the one who needed a taxi the most. Even so I would never have agreed if I'd known how far we were going. If I hadn't been so woozy from all my hurts and all the pills I'd taken I'd have stayed where I was; or gone back to the West End where I know who I am. But I was woozy and she was limping. It was as much her fault as it was mine.

Crabbily, I decided that if Mister Sister kept on calling me Momster I would call him Smister. See how he likes that, I thought, as we rocked and lurched across London. Electra was breathing tuna breath in my face.

I warned him, didn't I? But my life is splattered with the memory of guys who didn't listen. And now so is the lift at South Dock High Rise. Poor Electra—not only was she suffering from painful joints but she'd also been given the wrong food and had a jolting taxi ride. On top of that she'd never been in a lift before. So first she freaked, then she got the shits and then she got the shakes.

There wasn't much I could do about it because by that time I had the shakes pretty bad myself. I didn't know where I was, and I hate tower blocks. Instead of a little house with a yellow door there was dripping rainwater, runny dog-do, a nun dry-heaving in the corner because of the smell. The lift slid to a queasy stop and the doors glided open. A man in a high-visibility jacket looked in.

'Genius,' he said to Smister. 'You *do* know how to pick 'em.'

His yellow jacket was hurting my eyes. Cops wear jackets like that when they... I don't know when they wear them. Oh yes, at night. It was night. I was going to the lock-up, no doubt about it. They'd take away my dog, my bottles, my pills. I'd have nothing between me and the rattling terrors except a thin plastic mattress.

I couldn't persuade Electra to walk past the yellow man. We were trapped. In the shit.

My legs melted and I smashed my cracked ribs on the wheelie case as I went down.

They dragged me away down a burning brown carpet. I might've yelled. I can't remember.

Chapter 11

Abiding In Babylon

//

Smister took away my pills and my shoes.

Cops and nuns work together, you know. They say they're into salvation but they steal your shoes so that you can't run away from eternal damnation. Even if they don't steal your shoes they steal your shoelaces. They don't want you to hang yourself, you see; they want to do it for you. They try to throw your dog out.

The nun said, 'She's crazy about the dog.'

The cop said, 'She's crazy. She should be behind bars.'

Electra spoke up for me: 'It isn't craziness, it's love. I'm the only thing left she can love since the Devil murdered her heart. He killed her mum and then she lost her baby.'

Now why would Electra accuse me of losing my baby? Why did she even tell the cop and the nun about it? She swore she'd never tell a soul.

There's a little pink shell that sighs like the ocean and smells like oysters. If you make yourself small enough you can slide into it as if it's a helter-skelter. Right at the end of the slide, at the very centre of the shell, nestling in a bed of shiny soft mother of pearl, is a tiny baby.

The baby said, 'You didn't lose me. I dumped you. Do you really think I wanted to be born in prison? What on earth made you chose Satan for my dad? Surely you could've done better than that.'

'No,' I cried. 'No, no, no, I couldn't. It was my last chance.'

An ogre in a white nighty appeared at a doorway and thundered, 'Shut the fuck up—there's people trying to sleep in here.' He was obviously shouting at me. It's what ogres do.

I didn't hear what the nun or the cop said to the ogre because they shoved me into a small blue room and slammed the door.

———

In the morning I found the nun and the cop in bed together. No I didn't. It was just Smister and a big guy with a buzz-cut. On the floor next to the bed was a yellow high-visibility jacket. The word 'Security' was written in white on the back. He wasn't a cop at all.

My pills were there on a table plus an empty bottle of fine French wine. I'd been sleeping with thieves and fornicators. No I hadn't—I don't know where all that religious shite comes from. I just wish it wouldn't. It doesn't make me happy.

I collected as much of my stuff as I could find and took it to the living room.

Smister had told the truth about one thing: there was a fabulous view of rain on the river. The picture window in the living room was curtained by the downpour and the narrow balcony drummed with the sound of bouncing water. Electra wouldn't go onto it and I couldn't blame her. I let her out into the corridor to pee instead. I couldn't leave the flat because I had no keys to get back in and I wasn't well enough to leave for good.

Georgie, Joss and the cops couldn't find me if *I* didn't know where I was myself. I never go south of the river. Also I was just one aching bagful of hurt wrapped up in a bruised and sewn-together skin. I wasn't fit for street life.

There was a grim little kitchen with milk in the fridge and cornflakes in the cupboard. There was no wine or dog food. I gave Electra a bowl of milky cornflakes and made a cup of tea for myself. The clock on the stove said it was six-fifteen. I took one co-codamol because I wanted a clearish head. Smister hadn't left me many. It wouldn't matter so much if he hadn't drunk all the wine, but he was the greediest nun ever. He snuffled up intoxicants like a giant anteater. He said he wasn't a thief but I know for sure there were more twenty pound notes in the Louis Whos'is bag before he got his sticky fingers on it.

Back in the big bedroom I stood and listened to the two bodies breathe. They smelled of sex, wine and weed.

'Hey,' I said, in an ordinary voice. No one stirred.

'Hey, *fire!*' I yelled loud enough to make Electra jump. Neither Smister nor buzz-cut guy even twitched a muscle. So I ran my hand under their pillows and found more of Natalie's money and pills. A great jangling clump of keys was still attached to Buzz-cut's trousers by a dog chain. I took them and spent twenty minutes trying to find the key that opened the door of the flat.

We didn't take the lift—Electra absolutely refused for one thing, and for another no one had cleaned up the dog poo from last night. Not that the stairs were much better, they too were decorated with pee, poo and gang tags; which didn't say much for the residents of this tower block, my new neighbours.

The rain skipped and jumped off Buzz-cut's high-viz plastic coat and after a couple of minutes Electra was soaked to the bone. Even so she seemed glad to be outdoors. Me too. It's amazing, if I'd been sleeping out in the night's rain I would've been moaning my head off for a dry place to live. But stick me in a flat, eight floors up in a tower block, and I feel like I'm in chokey. I wouldn't say living rough's a lifestyle choice because I only chose it when I'd run out of other choices, but it does become normal quite quickly.

About half a mile away from the tower block a mangy line of shops cowered sadly in the rain. This is why I hate London south of the river: it looks derelict even when it isn't. But there was a mini-mart that sold wine and dog food.

As I stood in front of a shelf stacked with cheap wine I couldn't remember when I'd last had a drink. I tried to think but my brain kept slamming doors. When did Joss kick me in the head? How long was I in hospital? I held my head in my hands. It was still wrapped in Natalie's silk scarves which seemed to be stuck to my scalp with dried blood. Maybe while I still had the pills I wouldn't need the wine. But wine is predictable. It tiptoes up behind you, wraps you in a soft woolly cardigan and cuddles you. It doesn't just stick its fist out and wallop you on the head like the pills do.

I grabbed three two-litre bottles of red and stuck them in my basket along with dog food for Electra and went to the till.

There were three hard girls in hoodies lolling at the counter. One of them sniggered at me and said, 'Security? My arse!'

Taller and broader than her by far was the woman who checked out my purchases. She said, 'They found you then.' She had stark white hair floating like lambs wool round her head, but her eyes, brows and lashes were coal black. A pair of gold-rimmed half glasses gave her a teacherly look. 'You don't look like you should be out of bed yet,' she added sternly.

'I'm alright,' I said. I couldn't remember if I knew her—if I'd seen her on the street or in hospital.

'You don't look alright.' She sounded so certain that I tried to find a reflection of myself in the cigarette cabinet behind her. 'You don't hardly look no different from them photos they printed in the Standard.'

'What photos?' I couldn't help myself—my fingers, holding out the money, started shaking. Two of my fingernails were painted the colour of unripe blackberries. They were flaking and looked ridiculous.

'Them photos they took in hospital. "Death shock, brutal beating." Didn't no one show you?'

LIZA CODY

Another hard girl seemed to wake up out of her iPod coma. 'What she gwan do? Stick it in album, innit?'

'Nobody told me,' I said, trying to keep my voice level.

'Din't want to upset you I s'pect,' the older woman said. 'But you went missing, right?'

'No,' I said. 'I went to my... my daughter's convent. She's a nun, see. They looked after me there. That hospital was filthy.'

'They breed their own sickness, for true.' She gave me the concrete stare. 'So now you work for fat King Belshazzar, take the gold of corruption, huh?'

'Huh?'

'And that wine, it's for communion table? At £1.25 a litre—I don't *think* so.' The hoodie girl reached out and flicked my highly visible yellow sleeve with a fingernail that looked like an opal dagger. 'There ain't no security thuggies at no convent, you axe me, and there ain't no convent neither, you lying old cow, you.'

'I-I-I...' Their aggression and powers of observation nailed me to the sticky floor. 'I borrowed the jacket,' I stammered, 'from my, my brother-in-law. I'm staying with my sister now. It was raining. What photos? No one said I was in the papers. Have you still got one?'

'Not while you abides in Babylon with the servants of the fat Corruptor.'

I still didn't understand what she was raving about.

'We ain't giving no handouts, innit.'

'I can pay.'

'Go look in the back, Shawshawna.'

'Recycling, Nan, innit?'

'But you did forget, Shawshawna. Go look in the back.'

I waited, wondering what it would be like to have the personal power to make even hard girls in hoodies obey me. And while I waited I shook. Apart from one co-codamol I was sourly, bitterly sober. Teaspoonsful of milky cornflakes erupted from my belly and hit the back of my throat making me swallow nervously and too often. I was crushed by Nan's slab-like stare. Electra scratched at the door with her long middle toenail. She looked soaked and almost as nervous as me.

I said, 'I need some first aid stuff—clean dressings and antiseptic. Is there a chemist anywhere near?' My voice trembled. I was pitiful and I hated myself but I carried on, trying to make Nan believe I was a real person. 'And a pet shop? My dog lost her waterproof coat.'

'Oh, you got a dog then? I was wondering why you buy cheap wine and dog food. Hungry and thirsty, I thought.'

I looked down at my Louis Whos'is handbag. Why wasn't it saving me from insults? I had money. I wasn't begging. 'Are you always this rude to customers?'

'Only ones who work for Babylon,' she said, 'and lie to me and don't clean their teeth.'

'Pardon me?'

'I sell toothpaste, you know. And toothbrush. But no, you guzzle up alcohol by preference.'

That was too much. 'They split my lips and gums and broke my teeth,' I said. 'You can scrub your gnashers with a rusty fork and it'll hurt you less than it hurts me.'

'I sell mouthwash too,' she said, implacable. 'You ain't got no excuse to forget your dental hygiene.' To demonstrate she flashed me her white picket fence of enamel. I gave up and followed her pointing finger to a few bottles of green mouthwash.

Shawshawna came back with a damp, creased copy of the Standard. It was open at page four. 'Glamour shot or what,' she said and the other two hard girls joined her staring alternately at the picture and at me. Nan shooed them away. She folded the damp paper neatly and held it out to me.

'Ten pounds,' she said with no shame in her eyes whatsoever. 'You soldier in the forces of corruption at South Dock High Rise. You profit from greed and coercion. I ain't giving you nothing for free. Someone got to pay for what they doing over there.'

'I haven't done anything over there. I don't know what you're talking about.'

'Then why I going out of business? Where all my old customers gone?' She glared at me over the top of her half-glasses.

'I don't know,' I said faintly.

'Then you ignorant, but you ain't innocent.' She waved the Standard in front of my nose. 'Ten pounds or bugger off.'

'You tell it, Nan,' Shawshawna said, and the other hard girls growled in agreement.

'You come in here wearing the uniform of the Corruptor and ask for my charity.' Nan was almost singing in her rich contralto.

I was defeated and I knew it. I'd known it since I first set eyes on her with all her certainty and respectability. The street has taught me how to wheedle when I want something from the strong; not to do battle with the righteous. I should never have stolen Buzz-cut's highly visible waterproof. I crept away, ten pounds poorer, with a wet newspaper in my plastic bag full of mouthwash, wine and dog food. Electra crept away behind me. We both had our tails between our legs.

Chapter 12

In Which I Try To Review The Situation

///

E lectra ate proper dog food at last and I dried her off with a tea towel and the hairdryer I found in Smister's bag. She lay down and went to sleep in my wheelie case, snuggled up in Natalie's towelling bathrobe. She'd had a traumatic outing, poor thing.

I sat on the bunk bed with a bottle and the turkey baster and wondered how I'd let myself be bullied by Nan and her feral granddaughter. It was the handbag, I decided. Far from protecting me, the sight of it had set me up as a mark. It was a badge of prosperity and I was foolish to cling to it. But it was a lovely bag even banged about and soaked with rain water.

The other clue nestled on page four of the Standard: a picture of me, unconscious, bandaged, bruised, swollen, lumpy and drooling because of a tube in my mouth—a portrait of the archetypal victim. They said I was Natalie Munrow who worked for a firm of corporate investment sharks called Goodall and Jett. I was thirty-eight years old, divorced, and living in a trendy area of South Kensington. The other victim had not yet been identified. The neighbours were shocked out of their socks. An Australian au-pair claimed to have seen three or four suspicious characters in the mews earlier in the afternoon.

You'd think that someone would've noticed the difference between high-flying Natalie and bottom-crawling me. But as I say, it was the portrait of an archetypal victim. A woman beaten beyond all recognition is, after all, beyond recognition. The paper didn't say so but I had to assume that the other victim had been beaten too. She, Natalie, must have been unrecognisable too. The only reason anyone mistook me for her was because of the bag. I asked the ambulance lady for my bags and bedroll, but my mouth was too broken and she brought me Natalie's bag instead.

I squirted more red wine into my smashed mouth and tried to think.

It was Joss and Georgie. Natalie caught them burgling her house so they beat and kicked her to death. They were going to do the same to me because I was a witness but Georgie panicked and ran off.

I sucked more red out of the turkey baster and tried to get my head around the idea that my friends were killers. Joss always went mental when he thought he was being ripped off. He had, reputedly, kicked a guy half to death and then stuffed him headfirst down a manhole. The guy would've drowned in sewage except his beer belly stuck in the hole and three firemen had to rescue him.

Georgie had better people skills but once you got to know him you discovered that he was sly and annoying.

They sometimes shared booze and smokes and that counts as friendship in some levels of society. Not for me though. Giving me a few ciggies and a swallow or two of beer did *not* make up for my teeth, my concussion or my ribs. Plus I was still a witness. They were a real danger to me because I was a danger to them. I could send them down for murder if I ratted on them.

They'd be locked up for life or at least ten years. Then I'd be safe.

Except I wouldn't be. People who rat are never safe on the street. But you know what? Street law's as mad as a bag of weasels if it's okay for Joss and Georgie to kick the living shite out of me and Natalie but it's not okay for me to rat them out for it. I *should* call the cops. But I'd have to do it anonymously. The Dogs of Law would take me away if I ever told them my real name.

'Not you,' I whispered to Electra and laid my hand on her tabby-striped haunch. 'You aren't a Dog of Law. You're my one true friend.'

She opened a twenty-four carat gold eye and said, 'I'll be your untrue fiend if you don't let me sleep. Put that stupid bottle away—you're not making any sense. Again.' She sighed a tragically disappointed sigh and settled down with her back to me.

'If I don't drink I'll feel hungry,' I said. 'And if I don't talk I'll feel lonely.' But she ignored me.

If we were in the West End now, I thought, someone would give us some money and we'd amble off and share a burger. We'd have a little drink and wander around waiting for the next interesting thing to happen. If it was raining like it is now we'd stop in a doorway, I'd pull out a sheet of polythene and we'd shelter under it, steaming it up with our warm breath. No one would mistake us for soldiers in Belshazzar's army.

I wasn't always alone. Once I had a lover, a mother and a brother. But the lover was Lucifer, the mother died of shame and the brother blamed me. Now Natalie's brother will blame me for Natalie death. And who knows, maybe I *am* to blame. It was me who brought Joss and Georgie to her house. I didn't mean to, but it happened.

It was all Gram Lucifer Attwood's fault. I followed him. I couldn't help myself. I crave the pain of love and loss.

I watched them walk across the square in front of the National Gallery. I saw the palm of his scentless hand on her back. I saw her flirt, nuzzle and kiss him goodbye. And maybe my scaly-skinned, green-eyed jealousy wanted Natalie dead so that I could have her house, her handbag and her lover. She dripped jasmine oil into his hot bath and lay with her thighs and his thighs woven like silk. She let her breasts caress his knees when she leaned forward to kiss his sculptured mouth. Stealthily, like a sniper. I know she did. She broke my crumbling heart so she had to die.

If I am Natalie, *if* I am her, will he love me again? Once upon a time he told me that he would always love me. No matter what. He said this right before the first police interview. And he repeated it just as the trial started.

I used to be loved. I used to be intelligent. I lay down on the bunk bed.

With my eyes screwed shut, I fought with my memory which told me I was never loved—I was used; I was never intelligent—I was fooled. I showed him how to steal and he persuaded me to take the fall. I let him do it because I thought that if I gave him no trouble he'd find me more loveable; he'd need me so much it'd be impossible to leave me. I would be his heart and lungs and he wouldn't be able to live without me.

I was love's creature. But it turned out that he was the Devil, a slave to the cruelty and deceit just as I was a slave to him.

He used to tie me up with a biting clothesline and say, 'Do you trust me?' At first I thought he wouldn't hurt me. Then later I realised that he was teaching me to enjoy pain. A valuable life-lesson as it happened.

Sometimes I get cross. Not with him because when all's said and done he was only being true to his devil nature. No, I get cross with myself—not for being stupid—that too is nature; nor for being fooled—that can't be helped when you meet someone smarter and more ruthless than you. When I get cross it's because I was such a wimp, an abject servant of blind, buggering love.

I took a co-codamol for my ribs, and then another for my head. The last squirt of red laid my temper down to rest. I closed my eyes.

———

I woke suddenly and sat up, cracking my head on the upper bunk. That's how I caught Smister red-handed with his mitts in my handbag. He didn't even blush. He said, 'Where's your effing credit cards, Momster? I'm running out of readies and I got to take a cab back to civilisation.' He was wearing an off-the-shoulder apricot coloured sateen negligee and his hair was wet and tousled from the shower. Without make-up he looked unbearably young and clean.

I snatched the bag back.

'Kev!' he yelled.

Buzz-cut barged in growling, 'Where'd I put my fucking keys?' He saw his high visibility jacket on the floor and stopped dead. 'She nicked me coat,' he said plaintively.

'She won't lend us her credit card.' Smister sounded just as plaintive.

'Boot her out. She's more trouble than she's worth.' Buzz-cut bent to pick up his jacket. 'Keep the poxy pooch if you think you can use it. But she fucking goes.'

'I've got brain damage,' I said. 'I can't remember any of my PIN numbers. You can't use my cards without PIN numbers.'

'Good thing you kept them stored in your phone, then, isn't it?' Smister smiled, sweet, white and deceiving.

'You stole my phone! I remember now. You steal everything.'

'You stole my coat, and I bet you got my fucking keys.' Buzz-cut Kev glared at me.

'Did not!'

'I've given you a place to doss,' Smister said, offended. 'So what if I tap you for a bit of rent? You're loaded.'

'Doesn't mean you're getting any of it.'

'No?' Smister looked to Kev for support.

Kev said, 'What're you doing here anyway, Natalie Munrow? What you got to hide? That's what we want to know. Who you hiding from? You ain't kosher, that's for sure.'

I hugged Electra for support. She sniffed my head and wrinkled her nose. 'Yes,' I said, 'Brain damage. What *am* I doing? Why did you bring me here? Who the hell is Belshazzar?'

Kev loomed over me. 'Give me my fucking keys and shut the fuck up or I'll give you the boot myself. Right in the arse.'

'Kev, sweetie,' Smister said. 'You told me there'd be no violence.'

'That was before I met *her*. She made me change my fucking mind.'

'You said you wanted... '

'Don't fucking remind me what I wanted, you disgusting... ' Kev was looking at Smister as if he'd found him on his shoe.

'Disgusting what?' Smister smiled tauntingly. 'Poofter?'

'Freak, I said fucking freak.'

'And I say pot, kettle and black.'

Kev had a fist the size of a cabbage and he walloped Smister on the ear with it. It must've hurt like buggry but Smister didn't yell or fall over. He just looked patient, as if that was what he'd been expecting all along.

There was a moment's silence after that because Kev didn't seem to know what to do next. I was afraid he'd turn on me or Electra so I said, 'You left your keys by the front door.'

'Why would I do that?' he snarled. 'They're always attached to my belt.'

I looked at his belt and I looked at his cabbage-sized fist. I didn't feel like saying anything else. Electra whimpered and went over to nuzzle Smister's hand.

'Fuck you all,' Kev said at last. 'Don't get comfortable. I know you're fucking up to something.' He slammed the door behind him. Only then did Smister sit down on the bed. He rubbed his ear and moaned, 'Why do I always go for straight men?'

'I do too,' I said. 'I've had better luck with dogs.'

'Got anymore pain-killers?'

'You're going to get slaughtered again?'

'Why not? You already did.'

'I had an early start and I used my own money. Plus I've got a good excuse.'

'Yeah,' Smister said, 'brain damage. You said. Well, now I got an excuse too.' He drew his blond and lavender hair away from the side of his face and showed me his swollen ear. Then he pulled the negligee aside and displayed cabbage-sized bruises all over his back and torso.

He said, 'If he isn't big enough and mean enough he can't protect me, can he?'

'But *he's* who you need protection from.'

'If it doesn't hurt, it isn't love.'

I know that sounds perverted, but the moment he said it, in spite of the fact that he was a boy, he felt like my sister. So I rummaged in my bag and found him some co-codamol.

'You love him then?' I passed him the nearly finished bottle of wine to wash the pills down. His bruises reminded mine to come knocking so I took some pills too.

'He's a pig,' Smister said, 'but he's sort of what a man *should* be. I know I'm sick, but look—he's given me a home. I'm safe from every one else. That's what real men do.'

'I'll make us a cup of tea,' I said, because I couldn't bear to listen to him anymore. He could've been my son, or daughter, if I'd met someone when I was young.

I filled the kettle and Electra came in behind me. She said, 'You should be nicer to the kid. It's not his fault.'

'I'm making him tea, aren't I? How nice do you want me to be? Do you really want to go to work for him in Kensington?'

'My leg hurts. I want to rest. I want you to protect me. You can't help me when you're smashed.'

'I need a little drink to help me cope… '

'Then have a *little* drink but don't get absolutely stonkers. You're useless when you… '

Smister said, 'Who you talking to?'

'My dog. Her leg's hurting and it's pouring with rain. She shouldn't go out again today. You shouldn't either.'

'It's alright for you. You've got credit cards. You can go out and buy a bottle of this and that. You've got fancy doctor's prescriptions. What about me? How'm I going to get by?'

'Same way you always did before you met me,' I said, because that's what I was going to do once he'd blown out of my life—an occurrence I was looking forward to if he didn't stop whinging about Natalie's credit cards.

'I need an operation,' he said, staring at me with naked want in his eyes.

'I thought you said you needed a ticket.' I turned away from him and his eyes.

'I do—to Brazil. It's where they do the operation. Or Casablanca. I haven't decided yet. How come you remember the ticket but you're blank about your PIN numbers? Don't say "Brain damage," I'm so fed up of you saying that.'

He could be my little boy... with a serious need to self-mutilate. My eye ached and I poured boiling water into brown stained mugs. Electra moved closer so I made her some milky tea too. Dog experts say you shouldn't, but they don't know her.

I met Gram at a swanky hotel where my bank was having its annual awards dinner. He was working with the hotel hospitality team. He was wearing a snow white shirt with a black bow tie and looked unbearably young among the bankers, bank managers, wives and husbands. It's an important bank and we'd snagged a minor royal as guest of honour. Everyone was dressed to the nines and over-excited.

I don't know what Gram had done wrong but he was receiving a bollocking from a banker. He was blushing and utterly humiliated. I took the banker a fresh glass of champagne and pointed out that the guest of honour had arrived, thus saving Gram's pride from more pummelling. He said I was the only decent human being he'd met since starting work at the hotel. He told me he'd been in his third year at the London School of Economics when his parents died in an air accident. He'd had to give up his degree to find paid work until the insurance claim was sorted out. He was brave and uncomplaining.

I wanted to help. I did help. Look what happens when young men want my help. Just look. And learn.

I gave Smister his mug of tea. He said, 'Why are you crying?'

'My eye hurts.'

He looked carefully at the stitches round my eye and touched the swelling with his thumb. His touch was like a hovering butterfly. My eye abruptly stopped hurting but the tears continued to pour out. I had not been touched unprofessionally by man, woman or child for nearly four years. Unless of course you count a kicking.

'Maybe you should get your dog to lick your eye. They say a dog's tongue heals.'

Electra was slurping tea from a cereal bowl. She looked up, surprised. I could feel exactly the same expression on my own face. Smister started to laugh.

Chapter 13

Money, Violence And A New Flatmate

//

We all slept till evening. Buzz-cut Kev did not come back. At eleven we went out to find a cash point. Smister wore a cerise waterproof poncho with a matching umbrella. He wound a fresh checked scarf around my bedraggled silk turban. Electra wore a polythene bag with holes cut out for her head and legs. It was still dumping buckets out of the sky.

All this reminded me of the surveillance cameras that protect cash machines. I didn't want to say anything in case it tipped Smister off about my lack of identity. I had the credit cards which I wouldn't let him touch and he wouldn't tell me my personal security numbers. It was a matter of trust.

Usually when someone like me is at a cash point, it's when I'm sitting on the pavement, begging. Or it was before a young banker-wanker said, 'Are you out of your tiny mind? These machines only dispense tens and twenties. Do you really think I'm going to give you one of those?'

I said, 'But while you've got your wallet open you might spare a little... '

'Change? The reason I'm here is because I'm *out* of money. Are you mentally challenged as well as socially deficient? This is the *worst* place to beg. How much have people given you in the last hour?'

I had to admit no one had given me anything.

'Except me.' He looked smug enough to slap. 'I'm giving you advice: take your mangy dog and fuck off elsewhere.'

I associate cash points with humiliation.

This time I had a card but no confidence. I didn't know what would happen. But I stuck the card in and covered the slot with my hand in case Smister tried to pinch it when—or if—the machine gave it back.

Smister hipped me out of his way and covered the keypad so I couldn't read the numbers. I noticed that he tilted the cerise umbrella to shield us, not from the rain, but from CCTV.

'You've done this before,' I said.

'So have you.'

I was about to contradict him hotly when I remembered I was supposed to be Natalie. So I said, 'Of course,' in what I hoped was a lofty manner. 'It is my card, after all.'

'Uh-huh,' he said, 'and it's your PIN number you can't remember, stored in your fancy phone which you don't know how to use. So you won't mind if I give this camera a good look at your beautiful face, will you?'

'I don't think you understand head injuries,' I said, trying to disguise my quaking voice.

'I've been a rent boy,' he said simply. 'Now I'm a trannie. Of *course* I understand head injuries.'

I felt queasy, but, unbelievably, the machine gave me back the card and a few seconds later it whirred and spat five hundred quid at us. I was really glad I hadn't broken down and confessed everything. I'd been tempted after what he said about being a rent boy. But having a tragic life does not necessarily make you a trustworthy person. I know about that all too well.

When the money came out and he had it in his hand he gave me a very queer look indeed. Well, it was a queer situation—he didn't believe me, but the machine did.

I said, 'If you ever want to do that again you'll give me my half; right now.'

'Wait.' He turned us round without showing our faces to the camera and we tottered off like two skunked old women. In the back streets where there were no shops, cash points, or anything else that needed the protection of Mammon's eye, we divvied up the cash and Smister mumbled, 'Thanks.'

I said nothing because I was still trembly. I would never have thought of the umbrella so I'd probably have funked it at the last moment if I'd been on my own. I needed a drink. Electra looked up at me and I ran my thumb over her wet forehead. 'It's alright,' I whispered, 'Don't be scared.'

Smister said, 'What's to be scared of? You're legit, aren't you?'

'I was talking to Electra—she's gone all trembly.'

'If you say so,' he said, with the indifference of youth. 'You don't happen to have one of those big white tabs on you?' I rummaged in the bag and gave him one. I was tempted to take one myself but there was a pleading look in Electra's eyes that said, 'Please take me home and dry me off or I'll be paralysed by arthritis before morning.'

So Smister swanned off to club-land and Electra and I trudged back to South Dock High Rise while I could still remember the way. I was shaken and banjaxxed about how the cash point had coughed out money. Did it mean that no one had identified the mews house body as Natalie's and they thought she'd gone missing and was wandering around with amnesia? Or was it possible that someone had simply forgotten to stop a dead woman's cards and account? Or was it all a clever trick to catch me out?

As we emerged, breathless, from the eighth floor stairwell we almost walked into a violent confabulation. Buzz-cut Kev had his back to the door of our flat and he was surrounded by angry people. In front was the bearded man I'd mistaken for an ogre in a white nighty. He was saying, 'Don't you read your own fucking jacket, you moron? It says "Security". You've supposed to be protecting us from trash like them, not giving them free board and lodging. Security, my arse!'

'I've lived here for twenty-three years,' an old bird piped up. 'I've never seen the like. Pooh in the lift—syringes every-bloody-where. It's disgusting.'

'It just ain't good enough,' yelled a man with a shaved head, pushing forward belligerently. 'Do your bleedin' job!'

Kev retreated into the flat. Baldy banged on the door with his fist. Kev reappeared almost immediately with a billystick in one hand and a tyre-iron in the other.

I crouched down beside Electra and made myself as small and still as possible.

Kev advanced on the residents' committee. Baldy was the first one to scuttle away. The ogre vanished behind his own door. The old bird stood her ground for about ten seconds, saying, 'You can't intimidate me—I survived the Blitz,' before limping away as fast as she could, leading the rest of the residents in an untidy rout. I couldn't blame them— Kev followed them down the corridor like a bull chasing picnickers out of his field.

I remembered the fist-sized bruises on Smister's body. 'Quick,' I whispered to Electra, and we scurried into the flat while his back was turned. He'd left his keys in the lock. I grabbed them as I went past. I shut the door behind us, bolted it, slipped on the chain and wedged a chair under the knob.

I was shaking like a jelly on a plate. Electra's tail was between her legs. We looked at each other, horrified. I took her into the kitchen and, moving like an automaton, I stripped the polythene off her, dried her with a tea towel and opened a can of dog food. I'd promised her that I'd see to her first and that I would stay sober. But a woman can only take so much stress in one night. I opened a bottle of red wine and drank deep.

'I kept half a promise,' I said. 'It's better than none.'

She stared at me with sorrowful eyes.

The kitchen stank of wet fur, dog food and blocked drains.

'One day,' she said, 'you'll keep a whole promise.'

The doorknob rattled.

'What have you done?' she whimpered. 'He'll be rageous. He'll kill us.'

'Maybe he'll think the door blew shut. He didn't see us, did he?'

'But he'll hear us if you keep on blabbing.'

So I shut up and listened while Kev hit the door three mighty blows. It sounded as if he was running at it head first.

'Can I have a cuddle?' Electra whispered. We sat under the kitchen table, my arms tight around her. We were both trembling wildly. Her ears were pinned flat against her head.

'Jody?' Kev bellowed. 'Stop acting like a disgusting little fag and let me in.'

'Is that Smister's real name—Jody?'

'Could be it's one of those boy-girl names he picked for himself.' Electra's so wise.

Kev yelled, 'Let me in. I'll give you such a leathering.'

'Not much with the psychology, is he?' she murmured. I was glad I'd brought the bottle under the table with me.

'Fuck, fuck, fuck, *fuck!*' he screamed. 'I'll get a circular saw and cut the door open. Then I'll cut you open.'

He kept it up for twenty-five minutes and only stopped when the voice of the ogre threatened to call the cops. The door held and we stayed quiet. He couldn't be sure that Smister was inside. He couldn't be sure anyone was. And with any luck we'd stolen the key to the tool room along with all the other keys on the ring, so he wouldn't be able to make good his threat about the saw.

After a few minutes of silence we began to feel safe again. I finished off the bottle and then we tiptoed to the blue room and went to bed.

'Good old ogre,' I said, but Electra was already curled up in the wheelie case, snoring gently.

————⦿————

I dreamed I was locked in the little mews house with the yellow door. There was a huge lizard-like creature thrashing around outside trying to get in. Electra was crying. I thought she was afraid of the lizard, but it turned out she was trying to warn me about the nest of giant snakes that were waiting for me in the bedroom. There were monsters inside as well as out.

I woke up slowly and painfully. Electra was whining and pawing at me. Someone was knocking at the front door. For a moment I was petrified; but she showed no fear at all. Then Smister's voice said, 'Kev, Kev, let me in. I didn't mean to stop out all night, but I found you another one. I was only thinking of you.'

I pulled the chair away from the knob, unbolted, unlocked and opened up. He stood there, mascara halfway down his cheeks. His Wedgewood blue eyes were heavy and bloodshot.

'Momster,' he said uncertainly. 'What you doing up already? You stink. Don't you ever shower? Where's Kev?'

Electra pushed past us both and went out into the corridor for her morning wee. 'About Kev,' I said.

'Meet Too-Tall Tina,' he said. 'Too-Tall, this is Momster.'

'I don't like bag-ladies,' said Too-Tall Tina.

'And I don't like bean poles,' I said, stretching my neck to look up into eyes the colour of army camouflage.

'Girls, girls,' Smister said. 'Don't worry; I'm sure Kev will sort you out with places of your own. There are plenty to choose from.'

'About Kev,' I said.

'Later.' Smister began to weave towards the big bedroom. 'If I don't lie down I'll fall down.'

Too-Tall was the size of a giant skinny basketball player. She drooped like a cut flower in a dry vase and she held a black plastic handbag at breast height. She was Smister's friend so I couldn't be sure that she really was a she. But what bloke would want to look like a woman who looked like her?

I went to the door to find Electra. I needed to lock us in safe again.

Too-Tall said, 'Where's Kev?'

'Lucky for you—he isn't at home. You don't want to meet him, and you don't want to stay here either.'

'Josepha said Kev'd look after me. Josepha says he's the best boyfriend in the world. He may be a bit rough but he knows how to look after a girl.'

'With his fists,' I said, thinking, Hallelujah, I've met someone stupider and less observant than me.

'Josepha said you'd say that. She said you're jealous.'

I turned and gave her a full frontal of my stitches, bruises and broken teeth. 'Would you be jealous of this?'

Too-Tall leaned forward and stared at me through narrowed eyes. Maybe she wasn't unobservant; maybe she was just very short-sighted.

I said, 'Why do you think I've locked us in and barricaded the door? He's an animal.'

She looked away, and sat down on the broken backed sofa with her handbag on her lap as though she was having tea with a vicar. 'I get picked on too,' she said blinking her weak khaki eyes rapidly and twisting a coat button. Her coat was sopping wet. She smelled of cough linctus.

Electra came back in. She ignored Too-Tall completely and went to the kitchen. I shut the door, bolted it in two places and shoved the chair under the knob. 'Take off your coat,' I said, 'you can sleep on the sofa.'

The clock on the cooker said it was six-fifteen in the morning. I went back to bed.

Chapter 14

We All Wear The Mark Of Kev

///

I didn't wake up till Kev knocked the bunk bed over and tipped me out onto the floor.

'I might of known it was you!' He blew great gusts of whisky breath in my face, but the hands that grabbed for me smelled of baby powder. I should've been thinking of ways to save my life, but instead I thought, He's got a baby. I forced him to go home last night.

I rolled across the wreckage of the bed and scrambled under the fallen mattress from the top bunk.

He kicked it out of the way and hauled me to my feet by one arm.

My ribs shrieked. I shrieked. Electra started barking. She never barks.

Kev punched me in the guts.

I threw up on his boots.

'You dirty drunken old slag,' he bellowed.

I was bent double so I couldn't see his face; but when his pukey boots advanced on me I howled and pretended to fall over backwards.

I was shrieking, he was bellowing and Electra was barking. The noise filled my head, but even so I heard someone wailing like a gibbon: 'Stop it. Stop him.'

Then the voice of the ogre thundered, 'Shut the fuck up, all of you. I've called the cops. Can you hear me? THE COPS ARE ON THEIR WAY!'

I stopped shrieking, Kev stopped bellowing and Electra's bark turned into a whimper. Too-Tall went on wailing. I could see her through the bedroom door. She stood in the middle of the sitting room, making zoo noises. I scurried under the other mattress.

'Where are my fucking keys?' Kev yelled quietly.

There was a sudden silence. Then Too-Tall squeaked, 'I've got your keys. Don't hurt me. I let you in. Josepha said you'd find me somewhere to stay.'

The sound of jangling keys was quickly followed by the sound of fist on face. A body fell onto the worn out carpet. I made myself tiny and flat under the mattress.

Kev said, 'Stay with the freaks then. You'll fucking fit in great.' The door slammed.

I waited a minute and then crept out of the blue room into the living room. Too-Tall was lying flat on her back. Her chin was scarlet and already swelling to the size of a potato.

'Full house,' I said, 'now all three of us have the mark of Kev on us. And now he's got the key so we won't be safe here. Great.'

She sniffed a snail-trail of mucus into her long, sad nose and held up one skinny hand. In it was a key.

'My mate Charlene tried to teach me shoplifting,' she said, 'but I was too tall. Sales people kept picking on me. I really wanted to join the army, you see, but they said I had three too many backbones and I was too weak for my height. I'm too tall. Did I say that already?'

'You might have,' I said, taking the key. I relocked and bolted the door. I put a sofa cushion under her head and went to the kitchen to make some tea. There was too much of her to move and I needed more painkillers.

I made tea for Electra and Smister too, although I thought he must be dead or gone. No one could've slept through that ruckus. But he was lying stretched out on his stomach, one shoe on and one shoe off, still dressed like a glitter ball. I put the tea on the nightstand and turned him over. You're safer from choking on your own vomit if you're lying on your front, but I wanted to check if he was still breathing. He groaned and sat up. I put the mug of tea in his hand. 'Momster,' he croaked, 'what time is it?'

'Six-fifteen,' I said, because the clock on the cooker still said so. All this looking after other people was doing my head in. I'm responsible for me and Electra. I'm not anyone's mother, auntie or nan. I don't do the group thing. Sometimes you see bunches of us homeless dossing down together in benders or cardboard cities. For safety, they say. But if you're a woman, and you haven't got a tough boyfriend, sleeping in the middle of a bunch of rat-arsed blokes isn't what I'd call safe. Even for me. They don't call them blind drunk for nothing.

I gave Too-Tall her tea. She was fingering her chin and teeth, waiting to see if anything would fall off.

'It's your own fault,' I said. 'You shouldn't have let him in. I told you.'

'And I told you... ' She squinted up at me. 'It *was* you, wasn't it? I don't like bag ladies.'

The only one who thanked me for her tea was Electra. Dogs are the only people who actually benefit from human kindness and tell you about it. Electra's tail began its slow arc from left to right and back again.

I stroked her while she lapped from her bowl, and I couldn't help noticing that meaty dog food and sleeping indoors for a couple of nights had made a difference to her. Her coat felt smoother and my fingers didn't bump along her knobbly spine the way they had back in Harrison Mews.

'You're putting on weight,' I said. I was pleased.

She looked at me reproachfully. 'I don't run for my living anymore,' she said. 'You don't have to starve me.'

'I *never* starved you.'

'No, but you sometimes forget me.'

'Who're you talking to?' Smister walked in. He'd showered and was wearing a silky pink robe and ostrich feather mules. 'What's wrong with Too-Tall? And why's your bed in bits all over the floor?'

I said, 'Kev hit TT and he bust my bed *and* probably some more of my precious ribs. But TT thieved the front door key off him so we'll be safe for a while.'

He sat down on the other kitchen stool and looked crushed. Electra sympathetically licked his shell-pink toenail.

'You mean he's gone? Did he leave a message for me?'

'Are you insane?' I said. 'He's got a wife and a baby.'

'I may be insane but I'm not stupid. I know he's straight. That's how I'm sure I'm a real girl—I only love straight men.'

There was no answer I could think of. Electra and I stared at him.

Smister said, 'Have you got another white bomber to spare?'

I thought my injuries should take precedence over his need for wall-bangers so I said, 'Don't you think you're taking too many? You could've slept through Kev beating me and TT to death. You could've slept through him choking the life out of you.'

'Am I supposed to take sobriety lessons from a sozzled old cow who talks to herself, looks like something out of a locked ward and wears a rotting rag round her noggin? You whiff something awful. If you want me to take you serious, have a shower.'

'You just want to get your thieving monkey paws on my stuff.'

'I just want to be able to walk into a room with you in it without having to drench a tissue with *Chloe* and stuff it up my hooter. It's not asking a lot.'

'Just pain,' I said. 'Soap and water hurt the stitches. I might slip and fall. I can't get the scarves off. I'm scared of mirrors.'

'Get over yourself,' said sinister Mister Sister, the one who'd never managed to keep her fingers out of my stuff since we first met.

'You even pinched my dog,' I said, giving him a hard suspicious stare.

'I never. I found her, lost, on Brompton Road.'

'That's true,' Electra said.

'Whose side are *you* on?'

'The side of truth and beauty.'

'Truth and beauty, my baggy bottom!'

'What're you bleating about?' Smister said. 'Truth and beauty? You're a hag and you never tell the truth.'

Electra laid her head on my knee and gave me a look which said, 'Disengage—you can't win.' Her advice is so practical and she looks out for me with such care that I often feel like crying.

Smister said, 'Hey, come on—all you need is a shower. I'll sort your hair out for you. Just run the hot water over your head till the rags melt off and use a little of my shampoo. You don't have to rub hard and you don't have to look in the mirror.'

I carted all my luggage into the bathroom, where Electra could keep an eye on it. I kept peeking round the shower curtain to make sure no one opened the door. If you've tried to shower in as many crap hostels as I have you learn to watch the door like a hawk. You don't have any advantages when you're wet and naked. Well, *you* might, but *I* don't.

Electra went to sleep, and in the end I relaxed enough to let hot water work hot magic. The silk scarves peeled off without taking too much scalp with them, and I used Smister's shampoo and conditioner because they promised me 'body and shine'. If there was one thing I needed after my violent encounter with Buzz-cut Kev it was body and shine.

There was a chunk of my head that was prickly with stubble and stitches and mushy with bruises, but I didn't look into the misty mirror. Not once. Satan created too many ways to make a woman miserable without me helping him by looking in mirrors.

I wore Natalie's towelling robe which still felt clean and luxurious in spite of the dog hair.

Before I left the bathroom I ran half a bathful of water, added a good dollop of the soap powder I found under the basin, and dumped everything I'd been wearing into the bubbles. If you leave it soaking long enough all you have to do is get in and tread it like grapes. It has the added bonus that you can remove the black stuff from under your toenails—no small achievement for those of us who sleep rough.

Too-Tall was sitting in a saggy armchair looking frail and superior. Without any provocation she said, 'Seventy-eight percent of rough sleepers are certifiable. It's true. My social worker said.'

'And what's *your* excuse?' I asked nastily.

'I have a physical disability. I'm not a bag lady. I'm in sheltered accommodation.'

'And I'm what they call a sofa surfer,' Smister said. 'I'm homeless but I always have a roof over my head. I'm saving up, see.'

'Oh right. How much did you save last night?' I couldn't seem to help myself. I needed a drink.

'She saved *me*,' Too-Tall said, turning her weepy wet eyes towards him. 'They were picking on me outside Casualty on Goodge Street.'

'Not Goodge Street,' Smister said wearily.

'They were trying to take my prescription off of me. But I need those pills. They stop me getting over-excited.'

'And who's got them now?'

'Well Josepha has.' Too-Tall gazed adoringly at Smister. Her expression made me want to retch. I opened my mouth to put her straight.

'Momster,' Smister said, sounding a warning note, 'do you want me to do your hair or not?'

'A makeover!' Too-Tall clapped her bony hands and stared at us expectantly. She adored Smister. Electra adored Smister. I was missing something.

Or was I? Jody, Josepha, Sister, Smister—some people have too many identities and it never bodes well. Whatever you called him, he was up to something. He was using me, Electra and Too-Tall, and if I hadn't needed a drink and a haircut I might have confronted him about it. As for names, I have one or two myself. I don't use the name I was born with—the one they arrested and convicted even though the cops got it wrongish. Mostly I'm known by a description which amounts to 'that barmy old bat with the dog.' I quite like it. It relieves me of the responsibility of being anyone else.

Smister couldn't make me over. All he could do was to cut and layer my hair so it curled and softened the outlines of my smashed face. He did something clever with a clean scarf, so I looked less like a badly sewn quilt. All I wanted was to seem a little more normal and that was what Smister did for me.

Of course he wanted something in return. 'Breakfast?' he suggested hopefully. 'I usually charge fifty quid for one of my cuts, but from you, Momster, I'll just take a full English breakfast.'

Actually it was well past tea time when we shambled out into the rain. Fortunately South London is the kingdom of the all-day-breakfast and we found a Greek Cypriot caff half a mile away. Smister put away sausages, bacon, eggs, tomatoes, beans and fried bread with great splats of ketchup and brown sauce. He looked like a doll but he ate like a trucker. Too-Tall had spaghetti hoops on toast with chips. I made do with sausages for Electra and scrambled eggs for my sorry teeth. We drank tea the colour of conkers.

We were a weird bunch. We all bore the mark of Kev, but apart from that we had nothing in common. Smister would have nothing to do with me if he didn't want to steal my dog, my pills and my money. TT thought she was better than me and never tired of pointing it out to Smister.

She wanted to whisper with him behind my back as if they were twelve-year-old schoolgirls. I had no idea what Smister wanted with TT unless it was her medication and her benefit money.

Scrambled eggs and tea woke me out of my cosmic daze long enough to ask myself why Kev, employed as security for South Dock High Rise, allowed us to squat in one of the flats he was supposed to be guarding.

Kev fancied Smister in a sick, punitive way. But he wouldn't allow him to import riff-raff like TT and me unless there was a profit in it for him. But why should I care about what someone wanted with me when I was living for free in a horribly costly city?

I was sleeping on a dry mattress and Natalie was paying for the scrambled eggs. Surely I'd be stupid to question gifts like those. I perked up and started to enjoy myself until I realised that it meant I was beginning to sober up and my ribs were screeching again. I should be drinking wine, not tea. I got up to put the matter right.

'Oy!' said Smister. 'Where you off to?'

'What's it to you?'

'Oh let her go,' TT said eagerly.

He ignored her. 'I thought you said we were going to find a cash point.'

'Electra needs dog food.'

'And you need booze.'

'We don't need *her*,' TT said.

'I've got to find a pet shop for Electra's coat.'

'We could all go.'

'Or we could light a fire and sing songs, just you and me,' TT said.

'There's no poxy fireplace,' Smister pointed out, and in the end we all went to find a pet shop as I knew we would. We also stopped at a cash point. I don't know why I bothered resisting Smister. He always got his way. It's what young, pretty people do. But Electra wore a proper coat home in the never-ending rain. It was green with blue straps, waterproof and lined. She looked lovely in it.

All in all, it was a good day—if you don't count Kev walloping me and breaking my bed. After a bottle of red I didn't count anything, even that. I was just happy to go to sleep happy for once.

Chapter 15

Fire!

///

I was dreaming about sitting in the back of a bus with Electra. A famous actor was driving and being very nice to us until he disappeared and left us tearing downhill on a helter-skelter. Electra started barking. 'Let me out, make it stop.' She trod on my face and chest.

I opened my eyes and found Electra standing on top of me barking her head off.

Smoke was seeping under the door and creeping across the floor like spilt milk.

I sat bolt upright on my mattress. I looked at the window. We were eight floors up. It was still dark.

I looked at the door. It was the only way out, but there was a fire on the other side of it. Electra and I would have to walk through fire.

I looked at the wine bottle on the floor next to the mattress. It was empty. I couldn't even drink myself back to sleep and wake up dead.

Electra was shouting at me at the top of her voice. That's the thing about dogs—they can't see the advantage in being dead.

I went to the door. The knob wasn't hot. I grabbed my stuff and Electra's coat. I opened the door.

The blaze was in the middle of the living-room. It looked like a bonfire made of old sofa cushions. They were piled up and smelled like smouldering tires, snorting out black oily smoke. But the rest, the carpet and curtains, was going up like dry hay.

Too-Tall was running up and down wringing her skeletal hands and crying, 'Help! Make it stop. I can't get out.'

I ignored her and dragged Electra and all my stuff into the bathroom.

I turned on the taps. I soaked two t-shirts and Electra's new coat and put them on her. She was rigid with fright and quaking. 'Who are you?' she whimpered, 'and what've you done with my bag lady?'

'I *am* your bloody bag lady, you idiot. This is *your* fault—you're forcing me to save your life, which requires speed, decision and will-power.'

I soaked the towelling bathrobe in cold water and put it on. It was very heavy. I stuffed everything that I'd left soaking in soapy water into the wheelie case with the Louis Hooey bag. It was heavy too.

'What about Smister?' Electra was peeing with fear, but she still managed to remember Monkey-paws. 'He's still sleeping. He'll die!'

'That'll teach him to steal the sleeping pills.'

'You had me to wake you up. He's got nobody. You can't let him die.'

I noticed she wasn't bullying me about TT. Should I try to save the cretin who started the fire?

I left all the taps running. I opened the bathroom door and rushed out.

Electra stayed where she was.

'Come *on!*' I screamed. 'This is your stupid idea.'

'I didn't mean it to get so big,' Too-Tall sobbed. 'Usually the fire alarm goes off and then they 'vacuate the whole wing. It's your fault—you don't have a fire alarm.'

'I'm not talking to you.' I went back and grabbed Electra. 'Come on,' I pleaded. 'Trust me.'

She came; proving once and for all that a bitch in fear of her life will believe anything—even that I am worthy of trust.

The fire, howling and cracking like scarlet ice, cut us off from the door. I rushed us into the big bedroom.

Too-Tall jittered in too and ran straight to the bed where she threw herself into Smister's narcotic arms, crying, 'Josepha, save me! She wants me to die.'

Electra barked and licked his face.

I unpacked sopping wet clothes and stuffed them into the cracks around the door. Then I opened the window.

We were eight floors up so the window only opened three inches. My breath was whimpering in my chest. My lungs refused to expel the thick black air. I stood next to three inches of fresh wet oxygen and retched.

TT was shaking Smister like a duster. He said, 'Fuck off, I'm sleeping.'

'Fire!' she shrieked, 'make it stop.'

'Phone the firemen,' he mumbled, 'and save one for me.'

'Yes, *phone!*' she screamed. 'Phone 999 and WAKE UP.'

He woke up and stared at TT, Electra and me from beneath reluctant eyelids. 'Fire? Really? Proper fire—not burnt toast?'

'Save me,' TT sobbed. 'Someone always saves me.'

Sinister looked at me as if I was the sensible one. 'Haven't you phoned... ?'

'You stole my fucking phone,' I snarled between puking and retching.

'Real fire?' He got out of bed, his silly silky gown swirling around him. It would flare and be gone like swan's feathers in white heat.

A coiled worm of thick smoky phlegm exploded from my throat. I yelled, 'Don't go near that door!'

'What?'

'Just don't open the door. Phone, phone!'

At last he seemed to hear me. He found the phone and punched in the numbers.

TT wheezed and wailed. She smelled of charred cushions.

Behind the blistering door the living room cracked, howled and exploded like fireworks. 'Where the fuck are we?' Smister said, smoke and sleepers sloshing in his brain.

For a panicking moment I thought I was running out of things I once knew. Then, 'South Dock High Rise.' I croaked. 'Eighth floor.'

'*Hurry!*'TT screamed. The lights went out.

'I *told* you,' Smister shouted at the phone, 'Three women and a dog not three men and a girl. *Hurry. Please.* The lights have blown.' He hadn't forgotten he was a girl, and he hadn't forgotten Electra either. I grabbed for his hand and dragged him towards the three small inches of wet oxygen.

'He says we should lie down. He says there's less smoke on the floor.'

I didn't want to leave my three inches of life, but the cold air followed us down and settled with us on the gritty carpet.

At last, I thought, I can go back to sleep. If someone saves Electra, Smister will look after her, and she can look after him. I've performed my last act of hope. I'm done.

Done, I thought, like a cake in the oven; like a piece of meat cooked through. A smoky black giggle escaped—because I would be done, *exactly* like meat cooked through. Would I smell of lamb, beef, pork or venison? Would there be anyone left to make the gravy?

Chapter 16

I Do A Deal With The Devil

///

There's a deep sea diver staring at me through huge goggles.

I try to tell him to fuck off but he has his glass hand clamped over my torn up mouth.

Deep sea diver with a burning sun in the sky above his head. There's something wrong.

I'm lifted bodily out of the burning sun into the cold wet ocean. This isn't right.

I dash the glass hand away from my mouth and yell. 'Electra, she can't swim.'

'Alright, I got the dog.'

A deep sea diver steps off the diving board into the life raft with Electra limp in his arms. She says, 'You saved me, big boy. Hold me in your hard hairy arms.' And a fireman says, 'Steady on, girl, I'm a married man.'

I turn my head and see Smister nestled in the arms of a big sooty uniform. He's wearing one of Natalie Munrow's wet t-shirts over his night gown. His face is dirty, his blond hair's tousled, but he still looks fetching.

Electra sprawls dead at my side. I wrench off my oxygen mask and push it over her snout. I lean on her and force her chest to move. On the other side of the boat someone's doing the same thing with Too-Tall Tina.

'Stop that.' The fireman tries to take the mask back but I'm crying so hard and trying so hard I scarcely notice him.

Smister says, 'Leave her alone. She wouldn't want to live without that dog anyway.'

He's clutching my Louis Thing bag in one hand and a fireman's arm in the other. Now I know why Electra liked him so much. He may be a rotten little thief but he understands.

She asked me to save her and I failed. I'm alive and so are Smister and TT because *Electra* wanted to live. She saved us all and now she's dead. If I could sacrifice any one of us to bring her back I would.

The fireman forces the mask out of my hand and covers my nose and mouth. It smells of sweet dog and sour soot.

Another fireman says, 'We've gotta get down—I'm losing her.'

But I'd already lost her. In a spasm of grief and fear I turn to Smister—but he is snuggling in his fireman's arms and looking at TT. It is TT who is being lost. Take *her*, I plead silently. Take her.

The boat jerks, sways and begins to drop.

Electra spasms. She sits up. She licks my face. I hug her till she squeaks. She licks the salt and charred lashes from my sore eyes. I'm weeping so much I can't see her. I just hold on. Because I didn't save her; she saved me. It's always been that way round.

And I made a bargain with someone—probably Satan: Electra lives only because TT dies. I am killing TT. It is my decision. I am guilty. But my best friend is here and I can't feel anything but glad.

The cold wet dawn smacks my face, and the warm wet dog in my arms rears up on her hind legs to look over the edge of the juddering bucket we're riding.

A fireman tells me to sit down but I want to look too.

I stare down into a sea of light. We are going to land on the surface of the sun.

'Effing Eleanor,' the fireman says. 'We're all going to be reality telly stars.'

It's true. The surface of the sun is really the glare of spotlights. Some belong to the fire crew, but most belong to film crews.

'Where?' Smister cries, standing up. 'Does my hair look a mess? I can't be seen like this.' He rummages in my bag till he finds the little gold compact and a comb.

'Sit the fuck down,' roars my fireman. Smister and I obey, but Electra stands tall until our bucket comes to a halt. I'm so proud of her I would cry if my eyes weren't too sore to wipe.

Chapter 17

Exposure

//

We were celebrities. People clapped and cheered as we climbed down from our giant cherry picker machine. Smister tossed his blond hair as if he was on a red carpet. The fireman who got the most praise was the one who carried Electra down to dry land, because it looked as if he had saved a helpless dog from a burning building. But *I* knew who had saved who.

Then I noticed a little group of South Dock High Rise residents—including the ogre in his white nighty and the little old bird who survived World War Two. They were muttering and booing at the back of the excited crowd. As I watched, I saw a cop go over to talk to them.

Medics aren't nearly as judgemental as cops. They gave us huge lungsful of oxygen, irrigated our eyes and wiped our faces before letting the cops talk to us.

I thought it might be time to creep away into the grey wet dawn. But Smister had other ideas. He never let go of his fireman's hand even when the medics were working on him. 'Craig,' he sighed, still husky from the smoke. 'Don't leave me. I'm frightened. I owe you… everything.'

'Don't you worry,' Craig said tenderly. 'These people will look after you.'

Smister was turned on by the men who made him feel safe. I wondered how often Craig beat up on his wife.

I should have crept away without him, but the hand that wasn't occupied with Craig still gripped my bag, and, with half of London's media watching, it didn't seem the right time for a dingdong catfight.

A lady with a scarlet raincoat and a black umbrella loomed over me and said, 'We'd like to interview the dog and the hero who saved her on GMGB TV. We can transport them in a car straight over there.'

Scarlet and black, I thought, looking at her coat and brolly—the Devil's colours. What if Gram Attwood saw us on TV? Maybe he didn't have to; maybe he knew where I was all along and sent Too-Tall Tina to light the fire that would burn us for eternity.

Smister piped up. 'Can't you see my mum's sick and confused? I'll bring Electra.'

'That's her name? Electra?'

A medic said, 'Do you mind? Nobody's going on telly without they've been checked out at Casualty first.'

A cop said, 'And nobody's going on telly without they talk to the police first and answer a few questions.' He'd crept up on us without our noticing.

I wrapped both arms around Electra and croaked, 'Nobody's taking my dog anywhere.'

'You need treatment,' the medic said. 'Your lungs sound terrible and if that ain't enough, it looks as if you've been in some sort of accident.'

'I'll need all your names,' the cop said, and the lady in the Devil's colours took out her notebook too.

Before I could stop him, Smister said, 'I'm Josepha Munrow and this is my mum.'

'And the tall lady over there?'

Smister and I turned our heads and watched Too-Tall being loaded onto the second ambulance. They hadn't covered her face, but I'd made my bargain with Satan so I wasn't allowed to hope.

'Tina,' I said.

'Tina what?'

I shook my head.

'She was suffering from facial injuries like you two. Care to comment?'

Smister bowed his head and held Craig's hand to his cheek. Craig looked as if the penny was just dropping—maybe he could feel Smister's stubble. Maybe he was about to be associated with something a little too twisted. He withdrew his hand and stood up.

'Craig?' Smister's voice was quavering with sorrow and understanding.

'Gotta get back to work,' Craig said. 'Be lucky now.' He strode manfully away.

I reached over and touched Smister's sooty young hand. He sighed and said, 'Maybe if I'd had a shower, or if I'd been wearing my black teddy set.'

I patted his monkey paw sympathetically, and because he was in love and not paying attention I grabbed my bag back.

The cop rapped his pen against his notebook. 'I'm waiting. What've you got to say about the facial injuries, and I need to know… '

'You'll have to wait a bit longer, mate,' the medic said. 'I'm taking these two to Casualty.'

'Listen to me.' The cop bent down and waved a cold blunt finger in the medic's face. 'We got a fire—probably started deliberately; we got a woman at death's door; we got these two here who know something but ain't telling me doodly-doo. And now, in case my shift ain't been perfect enough already, we got you—obstructing the course of justice. Care to comment?'

'They need urgent treatment.' The medic was young. He looked to his partner for support, but she suddenly got very busy bagging up dirty swabs.

'If I miss my breakfast,' the cop said, sensing his own dominance, 'the breakfast I've been wanting since an hour ago when I got this poxy shout—they won't be the only ones needing urgent treatment.' His cold blunt finger smelled of nicotine and his uniform smelled of boiled eggs. He scared me the way cops always do.

'Five minutes,' the medic said, sulking. 'But I'm putting in a complaint. In writing.'

'You do that, Sunshine.' The cop turned his back on the medics and focussed his pencil-point eyes on Smister and me. 'Names?' he said.

'I don't feel well,' I said. I could hear my voice wheezing and wheedling like it did on the street. I was silently begging Smister to shut up.

He said, 'My mum's been in a car wreck and doesn't remember too much.'

'Names?' the cop repeated. 'The quicker you tell me, the quicker you can go to the hospital.'

'I told you—I'm Josepha Munrow and this is my mum, Mrs Munrow. We didn't really know Tina except we saw her in Casualty when Mum was in for her head. Tina said she was scared her boyfriend was going to kill her so we got sorry for her and went back to her place for the night.'

'Which Casualty?'

'UCH.' University College Hospital is north of the river and outside the cop's patch.

'So out of the kindness of your bleedin' hearts you go spend the night with an anonymous stranger cos she's in danger of her life? Am I hearing you right?'

'We locked him out. We didn't think he'd, y'know, do anything in front of witnesses. But we were wrong. And now look at us—beat up and lost everything.'

'What's the boyfriend's name?'

'I don't think Tina ever told us.' It was Smister's turn to silently plead with me to shut up.

'Kev,' I said, coughing up black slugs of painful phlegm. 'Kev, short for Kevin. I don't know his last name, but he wore a security jacket and I think he worked for the management.'

'And if you locked him out, how come he got close enough to beat you up?'

'We were asleep. Tina let him in. She was scared to death of him but she still loved him and he could wrap her round his little finger. Even after he nearly slaughtered, er, Josepha and me.'

'You think he started the fire?' He was a smart cop—he was going to do all my work for me. And he was nearly right: in an odd way Kev *was* responsible for the fire.

I said, 'Ask him yourself.' I pointed to the edge of the crowd where a guy in a high visibility jacket was standing, drinking tea from the back of a van with some of the South Dock residents.

'That's not him,' Smister said. And then he caught on: 'Oh silly me—course it's him.'

The cop said, 'Don't go anywhere. We ain't finished yet.' We watched him hurry away muttering into his walkie-talkie.

I woke Electra up and dragged myself stiffly to my feet. My joints felt like they had broken crockery in them. I'd coughed so much I thought I'd broken *all* my ribs and perforated a lung or two. But I had to go or the cop would come back and bust me for sure. Then they'd abduct Electra. Because this was serious. It wasn't just Vagrancy or Drunk and Disorderly or me being a Public Nuisance. This was Arson and Death. Huge subjects that made my poor brain tremble.

'Hey,' the medic said. 'We haven't finished. You've got to go to hospital.'

'Sorry,' I said. 'Thanks ever so much for all your help, but I got to find food and water for my dog.'

'About time,' Electra said. 'I'm parched. I was clinically dead, you know.'

'Yeah, we got to go,' Smister said. 'She won't be parted from her dog.'

The medic decided not to argue anymore. He was fed up but he gave us bottled water and told us that it wasn't only Electra who needed plenty to drink. I looked at the bottles and shuddered. It wasn't water I needed for my poor trembling brain. I just wanted to be somewhere quiet with Electra and a couple of bottles for company.

Of course, what I want and what I get are two different countries, thousands of miles apart.

Smister was trailing round after me like a lost puppy. Except it wasn't me he was trailing, it was the crappy handbag. And there was the woman with the red coat and black umbrella who was whispering to him about appearance fees and a 'substantial *per diem.*'

Worst of all, we had to pass by the group of residents which included the ogre in his nighty and the WW2 veteran who had been joined by righteous Nan and her hard hoodie granddaughter.

'Got what you wanted then?' the little old woman shrieked.

Nan, like wrath in a waterproof, folded her arms and barred our path. 'How much they pay you, eh? What's the going rate for making poor folk homeless?'

'Smoke-damage,' boomed the ogre. 'I hope you're happy.'

'You done what the Nazis couldn't—put me out on the street.'

'Losers,' said the hard hoodie, and spat at us.

This was why Electra, Smister and I accepted a lift in Carmel's car. I felt like rats were gnawing at my guts because I was too sober now to avoid the truth. Kev wasn't just letting social outcasts like Electra, me and TT stay in empty flats. No. He wanted us there. He used Smister to recruit us: the weird, the ugly, and the damaged, addicted rubbish from London's lovely gutters, all to make life unbearable for poor but respectable council tenants. The Corruptor wanted to refurbish and reprice the property as luxury river view apartments.

I was garbage from the gutter. I was dirty and drunk and I let my dog pee and poop in the corridor and the lift. Who would want to live next door to me?

I sank down in the back seat of Carmel's car so that no one outside could see me. Nan was right all along—I was an agent of the fat Corruptor.

That's what happens when you let yourself want stuff. All I wanted was a roof over our heads cos it was raining so hard. But I became a player in some other bastard's game. Nobody bothered to explain or give me any choice. Why? Because I was garbage from the gutter and I don't rate any choice. I was there to be used like bog paper and flushed away when I'd served my purpose. When the developers moved in and wiped away ordinary folk's homes, painted fancy desirable residences over the top and sold them to the sad aspirationals who couldn't afford them without huge loans, I would be back in the sewers under London, because that was my place in the economic life of our beautiful capital city.

———

This is a cautionary tale for people who can't control their anger, who have no opportunity to take their pills or have a little drink to calm themselves down. Listen and remember, or one day you might find yourself, a charred wreck, ranting to a camera about social injustice when all the interviewer wants to hear is a story about a heroic dog and the brave firemen.

It began well enough: the studio people had collected more than a hundred pounds to help us out. And the GMGB viewers, who'd seen our early morning rescue and watched Electra standing tall, looking over the edge of our cherry picker, had rung in and pledged a staggering amount to 'help our little family start again.' Bless them all.

My lovely daughter 'Josepha' somehow managed to grab a wash and makeup session in the ladies' room. She looked gamine, tousled and oh so very helpless. Electra looked beautiful, noble and hungry. They didn't interview us on the red sofa in the main studio because we were too dirty. We were in a small anteroom where the chairs were institutional and blue. Carmel sat next to us and said, 'Those of you who earlier witnessed our exclusive footage of our guests' dramatic rescue from a burning block of flats must've wondered about the fate of the family involved. Well, I'm happy to tell you that Mrs Munrow, Josepha Munrow and Electra are all safe and well here at the GMGB studio. Welcome, all of you.'

'Don't forget Tina,' Smister said in his helpless and breathless guise. 'Mum and me, we're praying for her recovery.'

'As are we all, I'm sure,' responded Carmel, who didn't know Tina from a sack of frogs. 'Tina, our thoughts and prayers are with you.'

It was right then that I started to hate Carmel; not just for her immaculately tailored attitude or her golden feathers, but because she too was using us like bog paper to line her golden nest. Tina's death and the homeless from the eighth floor were simply conveniences to get her and her career noticed. But mainly I hated her because we weren't allowed to park our sooty arses on the sacred scarlet sofa.

'And this,' Carmel piped excitedly, 'is Electra, the heroine of the hour.'

'We owe our lives to Electra,' my sweet young daughter said. 'She raised the alarm and woke mum, she even tried to open the window in my room so we could breathe. She's the best dog in the world.'

I suppose it's my fault: it was me, after all, who told him he'd make more money if he looked as if he was putting the dog first.

'And whose idea was it to dress her in a wet shirt? I'm sure none of us will forget the sight of her being carried out of a burning building wearing a Ralph Lauren polo shirt.'

'Was it Ralph Lauren?' Smister said, impressed.

I would never be able to forgive him for exploiting Electra on a blue chair when she should've been guest of honour on a scarlet sofa.

'Nothing but the best for Electra,' he said looking anxiously at me. 'Mum gave us all wet clothes. She knew what to do after Electra got her out of bed. Tina would be here with us if she hadn't panicked and tried to open the bedroom door.'

'So you were all cut off from the exit and trapped in the one room? That must've been terrifying.'

'Oh yes, terrifying,' Smister gasped. 'It was Electra who kept us together. Except for Tina. Then Mum blacked out and I thought we were going to die. It was Electra's faith that pulled me through.'

'And a couple of big strong firemen,' I said trying to stop myself throwing up. 'They pulled you through the window.'

Smister gave me a beatific smile and a vicious pinch on the back of my arm.

'So many heroes,' Carmel purred.

'And a few villains,' I said. 'Who started the fire, and why?' The true answers to those questions were, first: Too-Tall Tina, and second: because she was a lunatic. But that wasn't what I wanted to say.

Carmel started to mither something about an investigation but I interrupted. I didn't have long. I already had the shakes and they were turning into the rattles. The air was creaking in my chest like an un-oiled hinge. And I was very anxious because appearing on national TV isn't the best way to escape police attention.

I said, 'Developers are trying to force the long-time residents out of South Dock High Rise. They're employing so-called security men to fill empty flats with junkies and homeless folk and folk with antisocial problems. And they're trying to scare people by starting fires and making the building unliveable.' I would've gone on but talking squeezed my lungs into wet retching coughs. Electra stood up and whined in concern.

Carmel said, 'You've no proof of that, Mrs Munrow.'

'I do have proof,' I said. '*I'm* the proof. The Corrupter, the Devil, he's used me and Smis... Josepha like bog paper. Get in his way and he'll stomp on you so hard you'll end up a bad smelling smear on his doormat.'

'Cut!' yelled Carmel. She smelled of air freshener. I hate air freshener. It makes me want to hurl.

Chapter 18

More Exposure

//

'I can't believe you did that.' Smister was shrieking. 'You made us look totally insane.' He held a fistful of the money the studio people collected for us before they actually met us.

'Barking mad,' murmured Electra.

'I need a drink.'

Smister glanced at me craftily. 'I'll get you a drink if you give me all the rest of those big white tablets.'

I stopped. Even the rain smelled of soot. I said, 'Did you take Too-Tall Tina's medication?'

'What're you talking about?'

'You know what I'm talking about.' I took the white bombers out of the handbag, and walked to the nearest drain in the road. I popped one tablet out of its plastic bubble. Water gargled restlessly. Rain and shite were hurrying away underground to the Thames. I dropped the tablet down the drain. A couple of hours' worth of pain relief swam away beneath our feet to numb the little fishes. Never, *ever*, say I don't make sacrifices.

Smister ambled casually towards me. 'We shouldn't be here. We're too close to the studio. The cops're probably on their way.'

He was right. I popped another bubble. 'Don't you lay one finger on me,' I said. 'I'm so sick of everyone roughing me up. Are you listening?'

'I'm *listening*. Don't do anything else crazy.'

I took the tablet between thumb and forefinger. 'TT said you took her medication. She was a fire nut. She'd done it before. She said, "The alarms go off and then they come and rescue me." That sounds like a habit to me. And you took her meds. The way you keep taking mine.'

'I didn't,' he said. 'When did she say that?'

I couldn't remember, so I just stared at him accusingly.

'I didn't take her tablets. I swear.' His eyes were so blue and transparent I couldn't believe they hid murky depths. He said, 'When I met her there was a bunch of crusties trying to take her prescription off of her. Those arseholes wanted her scrip *and* her disability allowance. And she was so short of love she was going to hand 'em over.'

'So she gave them to you instead. She's going to die cos she was "so short of love"?'

'Don't say that. She'll pull through, won't she?' His blue eyes were brimming. I couldn't tell rain and tears apart. 'I only took a couple of tabs, I swear. And she gave me some money for food. But she had money left. Honestly.'

Smister was crying for Too-Tall Tina. Which, I have to admit, was more than I was doing. I was rattling, angry and suspicious, but I wasn't in mourning.

Electra stepped gracefully across the puddles to his side. She laid her trusting snout against his hand and he stroked her slim head. She was weeping too.

'Hypocrite,' I said. 'You didn't care when she was alive.'

'I looked after her,' Smister wept. 'I let her stay with us.'

'So that Kev could give her one of his famous whackings.'

'At least he was honest. Those crusties would've been her best friends until she'd given them everything she'd got, and then they'd have dumped her. They'd *all* have whacked her. You know they would.'

I had to admit that was true too. And I knew that some people are so short of love that even a whacking is welcome attention. If anyone understood about that it was Smister. And me.

I couldn't stand it anymore. I had a stabbing headache and my hands were trembling for all to see. 'Come on,' I said, deciding that the truth wasn't worth fighting my only friends about. 'I *got* to have a drink.'

I didn't mention the fact that he'd been pimping for Kev—bringing in trash like me to make life unbearable for the old residents. Which of us hasn't dirtied ourselves for love?

We bought wine and dog food at a mini-mart, and I fed Electra from a paper plate I found near a bin. While she was eating, Smister and I shared a bottle of wine. It was a normal sized bottle and we shared properly, sip for sip.

Smister said, 'Don't get twatted. We've got to lay low and chill. We can't do that if you're rolling around, roaring drunk.'

'I don't roar.'

'I've seen you.'

'He's right,' Electra said. 'I don't feel safe when you binge.'

'I got to admit you were great in the fire,' Smister said. 'I could've been badly singed if it wasn't for the soaked t-shirts. I could've lost my eyelashes.'

He sounded grateful. The headache vanished, and so did the rattles and the nausea. I said, 'Let's go north of the river. I never feel comfortable in South London.'

'Me neither,' Electra said.

So we caught a bus to Liverpool Street Station and went to the concourse to find lunch. I was hungry and looking forward to a burger and beans, but the first thing I saw was an early edition of the Evening Standard on a station newsstand. There was a picture of me on page one. It was under a headline that screamed: '*Impostor!*'

'Shit!' Smister stopped so suddenly that Electra bumped into his legs.

I hissed, 'Keep walking. Don't attract attention.'

But he went over to the newsstand. I put my head down and hurried off to the burger bar. My hands were sweating and trembling. I bought two burgers and went to hide in the ladies' lavatory to eat.

Smister joined us there but was too excited to eat anything. 'My picture's in there too,' he said. He opened the paper and showed me a picture of himself in Craig's arms being carried to the ambulance.

'I look like a waif.' He sighed in satisfaction. 'Miss Angelic Rescue of the Month. Hardly any slap, a strategically placed smear of soot under one cheekbone and look at those legs. Long or what?'

There was a larger photo of Electra, wearing her wet Ralph Lauren polo shirt, standing on her hind legs looking regal. The caption read, 'K-nine Hero-ine.'

'What do they say about me?' I could hardly breathe enough air in to ask the question.

Smister folded the paper. 'You might want a disguise. Your brother's saying you're not his sister.'

Thank fuck it was still raining. I bought an umbrella. Everyone hid their heads under umbrellas.

'It won't always be raining,' Smister said. 'What will you do when it stops?'

But I knew it would never stop. It was one of those years.

We went to a Christian Aid shop. I bought a man's raincoat, a man's fedora and a dry purple velour leisure suit with a hood, all for thirteen pounds. There were no shoes to fit me. Smister made vomiting faces at me, but the sales woman was so old she hardly noticed. She tottered into the back of the shop to fetch a bowl of water for Electra.

Smister turned his nose up at all the clothes. He said he knew an Oxfam in Chelsea that had cast-off designer labels. So we took the Circle Line from Liverpool Street to Sloane Square and I read the Standard.

On the front page was a photo of me, taken off the TV. I think it must've been just before I honked on Carmel's

Monolo Blah-knickers because I have a look of desperation in my undamaged eye. My face is still swollen lopsided. The layers of sopping wet clothing have dried in wads and wrinkles. The words lumpy, bumpy, dumpy, grumpy and frumpy hardly begin to describe me. Even so, I look recognisably human—ten times better than the reprinted picture of me in hospital they inset beside it.

I tilted the brim of my new hat down to my nose and read on about how Natalie Munrow's brother talked to the Standard reporter after the first picture was published. He'd already expressed serious doubts to the police that the woman in hospital was his sister. But he hadn't been able to identify the dead woman either. He couldn't tell who she was. The police were comparing the brother's DNA with the body's, but until they had the results they were hinting that grief plays tricks and he might be in denial.

The headline shrieked, 'IMPOSTER', because it seemed that the reporter from the Standard took a tape of the catastrophic interview with Carmel to show him, and he said it was absolutely, positively not his sister.

He also said that no way, no how, could Josepha be Natalie's daughter. His sister was childless.

Smister, who was reading over my shoulder, said, 'He's right, isn't he? You're not Natalie Munrow. That's why you can't remember your PIN number. You was never a financial executive.'

'Yes I was,' I said quietly.

'Yes she was,' Electra said. 'She was a branch manager.'

'Right!' Smister said. 'And I'm a fairy princess.'

'I'm a *furry* princess,' Electra said.

'You are,' I agreed, stroking her sleek head, 'you can be anything you like.'

'Well,' Smister said, 'I can be a fairy princess more easily than you can be executive material.'

'If I don't have another drink soon, I'll fall apart.'

'You *promised*,' Smister and Electra said together. And I couldn't remember if I had or not.

Natalie's brother told the reporter that a stranger was cavorting round town spending his sister's money—money that was his and his sons' by right as her only living relatives. His name was Malcolm Munrow. But he was lying: I don't cavort; I've never cavorted in my life. Well, maybe once—but the only one who knew about that was Gram Lucifer Attwood. Could the Devil be in league with Natalie's brother?

'Does it say anything about Too-Tall in there?' Smister's voice had a trepidacious shake in it.

I looked, but the article only said that the fire crew had dealt so speedily with the fire that only a handful of victims had been taken to St George's Hospital to be treated for smoke inhalation.

We got off the train at Sloane Square and I couldn't help remembering that I was now quite close to the little mews house with the yellow front door—just a step away from a murder enquiry, from being at best a witness and at worst a suspect.

Traffic ripped by on the wet road like torn Velcro. Chelsea rain smells of smoked haddock, and everyone, whether they're wearing Armani or jailhouse chic, looks expensive.

First Smister went into a chemist where he bought everything a woman needs to look like a proper woman, from glossy head to pink-tipped toe. He bought shampoo, conditioner, sculpting foam, serum, depilatory and all the *et ceteras*. It was this more than anything else that made me realise that he couldn't live on the streets. He needed bathrooms and mirrors. He needed the time and privacy it takes to be a woman. I am what a woman looks like when she has no bathroom, no pride, no privacy and above all no money. Smister needed lots. Being a proper woman is a costly business.

I hadn't really walked for ages, and it felt weird without a backpack and a bedroll. Smister was a pain in the arse: he was acting as if we were two girls out shopping, stopping and sighing at overpriced window displays.

At the end of the Kings Road, just as you get to World's End, is his favourite charity shop. He was right, it was stocked with lightly used designer cast-offs and it wasn't long before he'd spent every penny he had. He was like a little girl—his notion of shopping was to grab everything pink or black off the rails and to squeal.

He had absolutely no idea about how to conserve energy or money. Life on the street is all about having much more time than money or energy. Electra knew, but Smister clearly didn't.

It was time for me to turn my back on him. We would never be fit companions. He would never understand the street or that if you want nothing you'll want *for* nothing. He'd never understand the difference between want and need. And I would never understand why he wanted to cut his genitals off. I could understand being really unhappy about who you are; even to the point of suicide. But I don't see how turning into a Barbie girl by self-mutilation could make him any happier. True, I'd never talked to him about it, but that was because he never actually seemed depressed with the way he was. If you don't count him wanting to be bombed out of his head all the time, he seemed quite optimistic and cheerful.

While he was shrieking, 'Ooh, D&G!' I exchanged the Louis Vuitton for a strong, lightweight, backpack. It was time for me to reject aspirational handbags and become invisible again.

Chapter 19

Electra Needs A Roof Over
Her Head

//

lectra is the only companion I need. We're alike. Neither of us likes the smell of charity shops—even up-market ones in Chelsea. The mould spores made Electra sneeze and the righteous volunteer asked me to tie her up outside in the rain.

'I'm going,' I told Smister. 'Good luck with Barbie Girl.' Because that's how I pictured him after the operations—all pink and plastic with no genitals at all except for a couple of torpedoes sticking out at chest level. But he wouldn't look like that; he'd be a mess of wounds, swellings, bruises and stitches. His nether regions would look like my face when I was in hospital and it would probably be weeks before he could piss without a tube. He'd be one very sick little bunny. And all because he wanted to be a real girl for the likes of Kevin and Craig. Who would beat him till he was a mess of wounds, bruises and stitches again. Because even the most brilliant surgeon in South America couldn't change his taste in men or his need for abuse.

I blundered out of the shop, making the little bell above the door dance in protest.

'Come on,' I said to Electra. 'We can't care about him.'

'No,' she agreed. 'It hurts.' But she turned round and looked at the jangling shop door.

We walked on for a couple of steps before she said, 'But he's your daughter.'

'*He* said she was Josepha Munrow, and you know he's a dirty liar. I don't trust him.'

We walked on. The rain pattered like applause on my umbrella and I knew we were doing the right thing.

A long time ago I trusted the Devil. I had no doubt about him even though I knew he was too good for me. I knew I wasn't loveable and yet I believed he loved me because he told me so. I was that simple. I wasn't about to make the mistake of believing another guy, even if he thought he was a girl.

Electra sneezed again.

'What?' I said. She looked so forlorn that I knelt down in front of her, protecting both of us with the umbrella. Her ears were hot—too hot—and her nose was dry. 'What's wrong? Talk to me.' But she didn't. She stood, her head drooping and her shoulder blades poking up like dinner plates in a drainer.

I hate it when she won't answer—it means I have to work it out for myself—even when I've had a bastard day, starting with a fire and smoke inhalation, going on to being accused of fraud in the national press.

'Oh,' I said, getting it at last. 'You were there too. You nearly died and you've been trudging through the rain ever since.' I blamed myself. I was wasting time and energy thinking about who I shouldn't trust when my true friend was suffering in silence. Obviously she was ill and exhausted and I would have to find somewhere dry for her sleep. Soon.

Gently I ran my thumb along her snout, between her weepy eyes and over her skull. She closed her eyes and leaned against me.

A hand fell on my collar.

'Momster, you great hairy wart,' Smister said. 'What're you up to—running out on me like that?'

'Electra's sick. We need somewhere warm and dry.'

'Like a pub?' He was such a cynic.

'Feel her ears,' I said. 'Look in her eyes. Smell her breath.'

'No thanks.' But he squatted down too and fondled her ears. 'She's got a fever? Should she see a vet?'

If you're a dog owner and you've been homeless for any length of time you'll know that even animal charity vets expect to be paid, and in order to qualify for free veterinary care you need to show that you're on housing benefit; which of course is hard if you haven't got a house. Some people think that it's cruel for the homeless to own dogs. But she'd be dead by lethal injection if I wasn't allowed to keep her.

I said, 'She needs a warm, dry place to sleep and plenty of clean water. If she's still sick in the morning I'll get help.' Because I suddenly remembered that there was a Blue Cross clinic in Victoria that didn't discriminate against homeless dogs. Bless their hearts.

'Okay,' he said. 'I can always find a place. You know that.'

'We can't do abuse anymore,' I said flatly.

'What are you babbling about?'

'Kevin,' I said, 'knocking you about. Electra can't be upset like that again.'

Smister leaned towards me and petted my head as if *I* were the dog. 'Look—I've bought you a present.' He rummaged through one of his bags of pink goods till he found a pair of men's trainers. 'I know they're only Reebok, and the ones you're falling out of are Nike—but they *will* fit and they'll keep you dry. Hey, Momster, what's the matter? I know they aren't Nike or Adidas but there's no need to cry.'

'Why do you want those cruel operations?' I blubbed. 'You're perfect the way you are—even though you're a dirty liar. And you're in love with pain. I hate that. I don't want you to get hurt.'

'It's only a pair of trainers,' he muttered. But we clung to each other, protecting Electra from the rain for at least two minutes.

In the end he said, 'Stay here. I'll find us somewhere. Thank fuck its August and all the students went home to their mummies.' Then he was gone. August? I was gob-smacked. If I'd had to guess I'd have said it was March. So much cold grey rain.

I huddled over Electra in a doorway and fed her clean bottled water from the palm of my hand. When she'd had enough I made a nest for her in my new raincoat and she went to sleep.

I felt alone and unprotected. I had nothing, no bedroll, no layers of clothing, nothing to survive on. All I had was a sick dog and a new pair of shoes. And socks! I found what looked like a brand new pair of white sports socks rolled up neatly in the toe of one of the shoes. I put on socks and shoes. Warm, dry feet made me sleepy and I closed my eyes.

Smister said, 'Wake up. You look corpsified and you made three pounds fifty while you slept.' He put the money into the pocket of his new second-hand jacket.

I climbed out of sleep and onto my feet. Electra stirred and whimpered just once. I fed her more water from my cupped hand. I felt terrible about waking her. Sleep is a dog's best healer. I wondered how I'd feel if it turned out I'd sacrificed Too-Tall's life for Electra's and then Electra died as well.

She limped and I shuffled. We followed Smister up one street and down another, zigzagging into scruffier neighbourhoods until at last we came to a mean, narrow house with dirty windows. There were five doorbells and the front door was wedged ajar with a small piece of cardboard. We slid into a dark, dank hall. Junk mail and fliers crunched underfoot.

'There's nobody here,' Smister whispered. 'All the fridges have been turned off. The flat in the basement's the best—well the driest and there's a door out to the yard at the back for Electra.'

I swallowed hard and said, 'Thanks for the shoes and socks.'

'I didn't know your size,' he said, 'so I asked for a pair of canoes.' He pushed open a door and we went down into a dusty pit. There were three rooms, kitchen and bathroom. I guessed the landlord had been packing tenants in like baked beans because each small room had three beds in it. There was a table, two chairs and a little TV in the kitchen. Nine beds and two chairs; no room for clothes or possessions. This was accommodation for illegal migrant workers or students.

But what might be rotten conditions for them was luxury for Electra and me. She had a bed and three blankets all to herself. I lifted her onto the mattress and she went to sleep without saying a word. I covered her with a blanket. Her ears were still hot and I could hear wheezing when she breathed.

'The roof leaks,' Smister said, 'and so do all the windows except down here. It will be safer if we don't show any light. There's an electric shower so that's where I'm going now. I can't put myself about looking like this, and I smell like an old chimney.'

'I liked you as a nun,' I said.

'Me too.' He sighed. 'I was a brilliant nun. But the blessed habit went up in smoke, didn't it? Listen to me—the blessed habit—I sound like you when you're off on one. Were you brought up by Jesuits too?'

'Everything I know about human suffering I learned from Satan's mouth.'

'Bollocks. You're just a bit barmy is all.'

'And I need a drink.'

'I'll get you one, soon as I've had a shower. Gimme some money.'

This was familiar territory. It was greed, not generosity, and I could handle it without blubbing. As he'd already pinched the money I made on the Kings Road I ignored him and crawled under Electra's blanket, snuggling up to her—just to rest my eyes which were still sore from the smoke.

—◦◦◦—

I woke up hours later. Smister was sitting on the end of the bed wearing a silky frock I'd never seen before and holding a flaming candle. He had a bloody, fishy, alkaline smell which came over quite clearly in spite of his perfume. His eyes were heavy and his pretty lips were smeared and swollen.

He said, 'Don't you want to find out who beat you half to death and killed your friend?'

'I haven't got any friends,' I said. He was squeezing the life out of my heart. I think it was because of the shoes and because he found Electra a house when she needed one. I'm not used to people being nice.

I gave Electra some more water and took her out into the yard. The sky was turning slate grey but it wasn't raining. She did her business among a thousand cigarette butts.

Smister was still sitting where we'd left him staring intently at the candle flame so we took a different bed. But before we snuggled down I blew out the flame and took the candle away. I didn't think I could stand another fire just yet. I pushed him over so he was lying on his side and covered him with a blanket.

'But don't you?' he mumbled. 'Y'know, want to know?'

'I want to sleep. I want to be safe. I don't want anymore violence.'

'Not good enough.' He turned his back on me and lay silent.

Just as I was dropping off again he said, 'You're right I was a brilliant nun. I was a brilliant nun since I was eleven.' He coughed and I could hear the wet weepy smoke still in his lungs. After a minute he started muttering again.

'What?' I wished he'd shut up and take his hand off my heart. But he said, 'I keep asking myself, was he a beastly priest or a priestly beast?'

'I'm trying to sleep.' Why was he hurting me? He had no right. He wasn't my daughter.

Smister turned over and mumbled, 'Either way, he made me feel special.'

'Not good enough,' I said and turned my back on him. I think if I could've been bothered to feel them his ears would've been hotter than Electra's.

Chapter 20

The Doggy Who Burnt Her Toes

//

I had a shower in the morning—if it was the morning—and persuaded Electra to have one too. Both of us were smoke-damaged and we used Smister's shampoo to loosen the grey greasy grime and send it in dark spirals down the plughole. I dried us both off on thin brown blankets.

She was moving stiffly, but she was hungry. I fed her half what she usually ate with lots of clean water. I do look after her, I really do. She eats before me and when there's no wine to be found she drinks before me too. She's quite wrong when she says I forget about her.

Smister had pinched some pills and about ten quid. But as I'd gone back to my old habit of stashing money in my clothes I wasn't broke this morning. My hands were shaking and I badly needed to stock up on the red, but I didn't feel as awful as I'd expected.

I packed a couple of the thin blankets in my backpack, and then Electra and I waited behind the front door till we thought no one was watching. We sidled out into the street. I was coming back but I wanted to be ready in case of emergencies. I wouldn't be ready without a first aid kit, a polythene sheet and a bedroll.

But at the first shop I came to I remembered other stuff like mouthwash, Alto Rica coffee, milk and cornflakes for

Smister because he couldn't start the day without coffee and cornflakes.

I thought, I'll buy this crap for him and I'll share it, but when it's gone, I'll be gone too. By that time Electra will be better and we can lose ourselves on the street again. I won't allow him to corrupt us with soft living and wanting things.

And as Electra still wasn't well, I bought the kind of dog food that prolongs the active life of a pedigree. Because she is a pedigree greyhound from a line that goes back to Henry the Eighth or whichever arsehole started racing dogs for sport.

I bought the first aid kit from a proper chemist. It was expensive because it had a pair of scissors in the box. Outside the shop, I spread one of the brown blankets on the pavement and started to bandage Electra's legs and paws. There were plenty of poor to middling people who are fond of sick animals. For once it wasn't raining. Rain is death to generosity.

While I was bandaging Electra I was sneaking mouthfuls of red to steady my hands. After about forty minutes I'd collected five pounds, seventy-two pence and I was feeling almost normal.

'Thank you,' Electra said. 'You can stop now. I'm beginning to feel like an Egyptian mummy.'

'Never mind that,' I said, 'you're sick. You need good food and plenty of rest.'

'And you need to stop drinking before you spend every penny on more red and get completely hammered.'

'But this is how we live.' It was true. We live one day, one hour at a time. If we have money, we eat and drink. We don't save money for a rainy day because all days are rainy. She should understand this.

'I do,' she said, 'believe me. But that was before life got so dangerous.'

But I didn't feel in danger. I felt we were where we belonged and that in my fedora and raincoat I was as anonymous as an old chip packet blowing in the wind.

But she was right and I was wrong. Old chip packets don't appear on morning TV with their dogs. Old chip packets don't throw up on glamorous TV presenters' shoes. People who didn't wish me well were looking for me.

A little girl said, 'That's the doggy from off the telly.' She dragged her mother over to us.

The mother said, 'Did the poor dog burn her feet? Here let me give you something for the vet's bills. I know what that's like. We had to have our Tommy put down last year. He wasn't eating on account of his bad teeth and we couldn't afford to get treatment for him.' She gave me one pound, twenty-three pence.

The little girl, who was petting Electra, said to anyone who looked even two percent interested, 'This is the doggy who burnt her toes.' She was a cute little pixie in a scarlet plastic raincoat so she drummed up quite a bit of business for us. A hurt dog and a cuddly little Tweety-pie are a killer combination. She petted Electra with her sticky hand. Electra glanced at me nervously. It started to rain again. I packed away all the lovely coin the beautiful people gave us. I took one more swig and packed the bottle away too.

'Oh dear,' Pixie-pie lamented as her mum tried to hurry her away. 'The doggie's bandages are getting wet.'

'They're like shoes,' I assured her. 'When the flood hits us and all the little fishes come to nibble her dying toes, she will be saved.'

The little girl burst into tears. Her mum caught her hand and dragged her away, giving me a look I would have to scrub off later with holy water.

When we staggered home Smister was still in bed, curled up in his blanket. I wanted to tell him about my success so I shook him awake.

'Fuck off,' he said 'I'm sick.'

'No you're not. I got you coffee and cornflakes. You smell horrible.' It was my turn to criticize. He was always telling me I needed a shower. 'Go away,' he mumbled. 'I'm hurt and sick, and it's all your fault.'

Everything's always my fault. I climbed onto Electra's bed and went to sleep. I'd been out earning a living so I'd deserved it.

———⊗⊗⊗———

Smister didn't get up the next morning either. I brought him coffee and cornflakes in bed. He didn't even sit up to eat and drink. He just lay on his side and spilled as much as he put into his mouth.

'Are you Lady Muck?' I said. 'What did your last servant die of?'

'Who the hell are *you?*' Smister said in his weakest little girl voice.

'You know who I am.' I was quite upset by the question so I took a trip to the kitchen for a slurp of wine.

When I got back, Smister said, 'You aren't who it says on your credit card.'

'You nicked my card again?'

'It was never your card.'

'Then whose pocket did you steal it from? You're a thief and a fruit fly.' I stormed out, pausing only to grab a bottle from the fridge.

Electra said, 'Maybe you should've stayed and listened.'

But I wanted to go back to the spot where we'd done well before so I didn't listen to her either and we hurried through the rain to the chemist shop. She was limping and didn't seem very happy, but I knew she'd feel better when I'd bought us some goodies.

Just as I was about to open my bag to get out the blanket and the bandages I smelled the thick layered scent the homeless carry with them on a rainy day. I looked up because I knew then that I'd strayed onto someone else's patch. A pair of granite eyes looked straight into my eyes and out the other side.

I didn't recognise him, but the hair on the back of my head stirred in a cold whisper of warning.

Hiding under umbrella and fedora, I shuffled off as fast as I could. Electra kept up in spite of her poor legs. She was spooked too. At the corner we looked back and saw him watching us, a looming shadow of a tattered man in the rusty remains of a leather cowboy hat.

We hurried on. At the next corner I turned again and he was still behind us. He didn't seem to be walking. He was just *there.*

I wanted to run to the student house and lock a proper door against him. But Electra wouldn't let me. 'You don't want him to know where you sleep,' she panted. 'You can't lead him to Smister.'

Ahead, I saw Fulham Broadway Station. And that's where he caught me.

Well, it wasn't me he caught—it was Electra.

The tattered man in the cowboy hat wrenched her scarf out of my hand. He doubled it and pulled it tight around her throat, choking her till her eyes bulged.

'No!' I cried.

'Yes,' he snarled. 'Gimme what you got or the bitch dies.'

'Heugh!' Electra coughed.

'What have I got?'

'Gelt. Hundreds. I saw you get it on the telly. And you got the brass neck to be out on the cadge again today.'

'But I haven't got any left.'

'Bollocks.'

'My… my daughter got most of it, and I had to pay the rest to the vet.'

'You're lying, you arseholed old sow.'

'Look at my dog. She's sick. Animal doctors cost an arm and a leg.'

'Heugh!' said Electra.

'Fuck you,' he said, twisting the scarf even tighter. 'Gimme what you got. That's my pitch you were going to steal. There's rent to pay, you thieving bitchwhore.'

There was a torn magazine on the floor by my feet. I bent quickly and picked it up. I was completely fed up with being frightened of big blokes. I rolled the magazine into a tight cylinder. Electra was hanging from his hand as if by a noose. He shouldn't have done that.

I stepped up close to him and stabbed him in the Adam's apple with the rolled up magazine while screaming, 'Fuck off!' into his face.

I bet you never thought a gossip magazine was a deadly weapon. It's true that it won't wound you or make you bleed. But, rolled up, a magazine is as strong as a stick. It won't bend. If you attack throat, eyes or droopy man bits you can do a lot of damage.

His mouth opened like a barn door. Nothing came out except a guttural rasp. But he didn't fuck off so I kneed him in the groin.

The tattered man grabbed for his throat with one hand and his nuts with the other, letting go of Electra's scarf as he doubled over. She sprinted away into the rain.

'Electra, *wait*,' I yelled. But she ran out into the traffic. Her bandages trailed behind her, turning grubby and soggy. She may be old, but she's still a greyhound and much faster than me. I only caught up with her because a bandage snagged on a supermarket cart. She panicked, struggling to escape, pulling the cart towards her as she tried to get away. I was trembling too, but with elation. I'd been threatened by a violent bloke— but I won, I won, I won. Chalk *that* up to the archetypal victim!

'Electra,' I said, 'calm down. We got away. We're alright.'

She hardly heard me. She was so scared that the look in her eyes hurt my heart and made me ashamed. She'd been cruelly treated because she was *my* friend.

I gathered her up in my arms and held her till she stopped struggling. This is why I'm glad I don't have a real daughter. Your enemies can get at you through the people you love.

Chapter 21

Smister's Dreadful Story

///

E lectra drank a lot of water and went straight to bed. She wasn't hungry. She just looked at me with those grateful amber eyes, and I thought, What's she got to be grateful for? Because all I'd done was rescue her from the mess I'd made for her in the first place.

'It's for emergencies only,' I promised as I put the rest of the red into the fridge with the milk.

Five minutes later Smister shuffled out of the mouldy shower, clean and without make-up. He looked dejected and cowed; a girlish boy who'd been hurt or humiliated. I was surprised—pain and humiliation were usually what turned him on.

Eventually he said, 'I'm sorry I took your card but I needed to score something I could take to Lou's Club to deal, or share, so that I wouldn't look like some sad loser who'd lost everything in a fire. I can look wistful and winsome, but not like a loser.'

He looked utterly like a loser, so I said, 'Go on,' and sat down opposite him.

'So I used your cash card because the candy-man only takes cash. But the ATM swallowed the card and there was no cash. So either you've gone over your limit or you ain't Natalie Munrow.'

What game was he playing now? He'd read the Evening Standard so he *knew* I wasn't Natalie Munrow. Did he want to take the moral high-ground because he'd stolen something that wasn't mine?

I said, 'What were you going to buy with all that stolen cash?'

'Does it matter? Get your head out of a bottle just for once and try to understand.' He gave me his wounded fawn look and went on, 'I was shook up so I went for a coffee nearby. Cos I wasn't sure they'd let me into Lou's if I wasn't carrying. Real people go to that club, Momster, like barristers and surgeons. Why would they let *me* in?'

'Because you're young and pretty?'

He couldn't meet my eyes. Then he said, 'I'm trash. I'm the slum bum boy when I'm at Lou's.'

'Don't go there then.'

'But they give me presents and take me to parties. And like I said, there are surgeons.'

'Oh Smister... '

'Don't start that again. You aren't listening. *Listen.* I was sitting there having a mocha when two guys in suits walk up. And suddenly it's like—"You were observed attempting to obtain money from the ATM on Shaftsbury Avenue, we're the Fraud Squad, what you got to say for yourself, you cheap tart, and don't even bother talking cos we ain't gonna believe you anyway."

'Cheap tart! I was wearing my Donna Karan. So they want to look in my bag, and I'm, like, "you need a warrant," and they're all, "Don't be a stupid little cow, the more trouble you give us now the worse it'll be for you later." And, "Come with us, we'll show you what rights you got."

'They seemed straight, so we went and sat in their car in an underground car park, and for a while it was okay cos I just said I'd found the card on the ground next to the ATM. And they were saying, "If you're telling the truth, no worries, pretty little thing like you." But then it's, "How did you know the

PIN number?" So I say, "It was written on the card." And they say, "We'll recover the card so we'll know if you've lying." And I say, "It was in ink, it came off in the rain."

'Momster, they were so freaky—one minute it's, "I could really fancy a little doll like you," and then it's, "C'mon, we know you stole the card off of a dead body." Dead body, Momster? I never saw a dead body in my whole life.'

'Too-Tall,' I said. 'You saw Too-Tall.'

'She wasn't dead. Don't say that.'

He suddenly slumped and laid his head on the table as if he was going to sleep. I thought I'd leave him like that because there was an ache in the pit of my stomach that only a slurp of red comfort could fill. But he said, 'Don't go Momster. You gotta tell me, did all that good stuff come off of a dead woman?'

I tried to pretend I couldn't remember. 'I don't know. There was a dead woman but I never saw her, and one time I thought she was me. I know some of the blood was mine.' I didn't want to lie, but I was afraid he'd done a deal with the Fraud Squad cops.

'You said you were Natalie Munrow.'

'No I didn't. Everyone in the hospital told me I was her— even the WPC with fair hair and no arse to speak of. She gave me the house keys. And that handbag.'

'So you thought you were her?'

'I couldn't remember anything. When I went back to the mews house my keys fitted her door, but my feet didn't fit in her shoes. And then I saw you with Electra, and I knew who *she* was. It's the only thing I'm totally sure of.'

Smister ran his pearl-tipped fingers through his hair, trying to understand.

I said, 'How did you get away from the Fraud Squad? Did they charge you? Are you going to turn me in?'

He was so young and transparent I almost believed he wasn't going to make up a story.

'I'd *never* turn you in.' There wasn't a flick of the sweet blue eyes. He shifted uncomfortably though. 'But you were seen on telly pretending to be Natalie Munrow.'

'No I wasn't. *You* pretended to be Josepha Munrow, and *you* said I was your mum.'

'You've got a cracking good memory for someone with amnesia,' he muttered into his coffee. 'The way you drink—it's amazing you can remember your own name.'

'But I can't.' What did he think I was? Simple? He was a thief and a liar. I should never forget that for a moment.

He said, almost in a whisper, 'They tricked me. They'd seen us on the telly. They knew about Natalie Munrow and me calling myself Josepha. They knew right from the start that I was lying about the card and the PIN number. They were playing with me, Momster; they were catching me in lie after lie till there was nowhere to hide.'

I was beginning to feel sorry for him. 'Then what?'

'Then Jerry, the big one, said, "We got you good. We got you wriggling on a hook like a pretty little fish." He was walking his fingers up my leg while he was talking. The other one was breathing heavy and sniggering. And then Jerry said, "Wriggle on *this!*" And he stuck his fingers up... you know... ' Smister paused and chewed some colour into his lower lip. He took a deep breath and went on, 'But of course he found a bit more than he'd expected. Some of them get very cruel when they think you've made a fool of them. They had a torch and a screwdriver in the glove compartment... '

I couldn't say a word; I could only stare at him.

He stared back at me, waiting for me to ask. But I couldn't. So I shared the only comfort I could. I took the bottle of red out of the fridge and gave it to him.

He glugged it down and said, 'Why're you snivelling, Momster? No one raped you with a torch and a screwdriver.'

'Shut up,' I yelled. 'Shut up, *shut up!*'

I ran out of the kitchen. I was going to fetch Electra and leave forever. But she had weepy eyes too, so I took some of the packets of co-codamol and zopiclone and put them on the table in front of Smister. He let them lie. 'They gave me something strong at St Stephens—enough for a week—and antibiotics for three weeks. I've got my own prescription.'

'How did you get away?' I asked in the end. Because, God help me, even though I was crying for him, I was still wondering how much he'd betrayed me. If he hadn't done it for money, maybe he'd done it for mercy.

'I didn't. They dumped me out of the car when they'd finished.'

'You should go back to bed,' I said. 'You heal better when you're asleep.' I was only just beginning to notice how still he was sitting, how blue the shadows under his eyes were, how pale his lips. I'd thought it was because he wasn't wearing any make up, but in reality he was injured and unwell. I never notice the crucial stuff till too late.

Smister lay on his side with his eyes closed. I covered him with an extra blanket. After a while he said, 'I'm not gay. Really I'm not. People like... well, no one understands. I'm not gay, I'm a girl.'

'Okay,' I said, thinking I should stay till he went to sleep. But if he was going to talk about it I'd have to leave.

He said, 'No, you don't understand either.'

'Actually,' I said, standing up, 'you're right. I don't understand a bleeding word. Why would you want to be a girl? There's more to it than wearing pretty frocks.'

'I don't want to be a girl,' he said in a choking voice. 'I *am* one.'

'You think *I'm* barmy? Why do you have to be a girl? Why can't you do the difficult thing and be a woman?'

'Don't go,' he said, trying to sit up but wincing in pain.

'Then shut up.' I sat down again, next to him, and waited till he fell asleep.

Chapter 22

Jerry-cop And
The Mouse Momster

///

I wish I could protect Smister.

Why doesn't God spray-paint cruel people with tiger stripes so that we can all see them coming and take evasive action? And if the meek actually were blessed, nothing frightening or painful would ever happen to Electra or Smister. And when Jesuits say, 'You are the responsible author of your own actions,' are they talking about us suffering mortals who are always broken and battered by those with power, or are they commenting sarcastically on *God's* little actions? Like earthquakes in built-up areas, floods, cancers and cops called Jerry? If you'd told me that Gram Satan Attwood created all that, I'd believe you. But when you tell me that God the *father* was the responsible author I have to inform you that he really must hate some of his offspring. Usually he hates the sweet ones and lets the Jerry-cops off scot-free. This is why I believe in the corporeality and power of Satan. If God exists, either he has no executive influence at all or he doesn't give a shit about suffering mortals.

This was what I was thinking at the chemist while buying one of those post-natal rubber rings so that Smister could sit up without pain.

In the mini-mart I thought about making a healing chicken soup that all three of us could eat. But I couldn't remember how, so I bought a few cans and a can opener instead. I brought bread and eggs as well because I could probably do something with those. It'd been so long since I had a kitchen that I didn't know how to think about food except as something I could cadge or find in a bin. You lose skills like cooking and carpet-laying when you haven't got a home.

Also, if I stocked up the kitchen with things Smister could prepare for himself, I could slip away with a good conscience. You see, Smister might have ratted me out. Plus he was a wounded fawn, and Satan had given Jerry-cop the power of a predator to smell him from afar, to pick him out of a crowd, pull him to the ground and tear pieces of still living flesh from his poor confused little body. He could smell Smister's friendlessness and poverty. There would be no retribution from Smister's solicitors, parents or influential mates.

Smister is not one of God's children because God doesn't exist and therefore has no children. But Jerry-cop is definitely a favoured son of Satan.

I know for a fact that Satan can smell defencelessness because he could smell mine. He picked me out of a crowd and was the responsible author of my actions. He has passed his gift on to his son Jerry-cop. So I don't want to be anywhere in the neighbourhood when he comes calling on Smister. For Jerry-cop is like his dad, Ashmodai, the Lord of Lust and Wrath who rules his circle of hell with whips woven from scorpion tails that he uses to flay you, body and soul. Gram Satan Ashmodai.

I wished I could protect Smister. But I didn't seem able even to protect Electra. And no one could protect me except me—if I was lucky enough to find a gossip mag to roll into a deadly weapon—an insufficient instrument to use against the son of Lord Ashmodai Attwood.

My head was in a plumber's grip, my teeth were loose, sweat dribbled down my ribs, my clumsy hands trembled, my lumbering feet stumbled and my stomach lurched like a ship in a storm. Even so, I made it back to Cadmus Road without taking a single snort of the wine I'd bought for Smister.

I'd had the shakes, and the rattles, now I think I've got the DTs. But still I have to feed everyone, and heal everyone and give them good clean water and red wine. I have to wash and bandage their wounds and then wash and fill their bowls. For am I not the great mother in the sky? The enemy of the Lord Ashmodai and all his minions?

No. I'm the lowliest of all creatures—the humble mouse, feeding on crumbs and scurrying away at the first sign of trouble.

The Mouse Momster—that's me. My children are derelict, drunk, addicted, mad and suffer with arthritic paws. They're outsiders, inadequates, homeless and abused. They are young and confused. They are old and confused. They are dogs with no family ties. They sleep at the bottom of the barrel.

Chapter 23

Torpedoed By A Shock Encounter

//

A fter a few years, I mean days, spent like that—only going out briefly for food, always picking a different shop, sleeping a lot, I found that my now sticky plum-coloured leisure suit hung on me like old man's skin. I'd fed everyone except myself because I'd been too queasy to eat.

'It's not that, dafty,' Smister said, sitting up in bed and looking perky for a change. 'It's all the wine you're not drinking. You'd be amazed how many empty calories there are in cheap wine. What does it feel like to be sober after all this time?'

'Having the DTs does not make me sober.' I could feel the aching spot in the middle of my chest; if I could stick a knife in it gallons of darkness and liquid, writhing insects would come spewing out.

'Well at least you're not babbling about God and Satan.'

'Well *excuse* me,' I said, making for the door. 'I'm going to let Electra back in. At least *someone* appreciates me.'

Electra came in from the yard. Her limp was barely visible, her eyes were bright, her nose was wet, her sides were sleek, but she didn't talk to me anymore. Instead of saying hello she waved her tail and seemed to smile. Then she went back to bed. Nobody ever believes me when I tell them how lazy greyhounds are.

I took one of Natalie's zopiclones and lay down too. It was a good thing she'd been addicted to sleepers and painkillers—I don't know how I'd have lived through the tormented days otherwise. I wondered if her pain and insomnia had been caused by Gram Attwood too. DTs or no, it wasn't too fanciful to call him Lord Ashmodai. Soon he would appear as an angry landlord and throw us back into the street.

We'd been careful about showing light or being seen, but one day, inevitably, he'd come.

It was a schizophrenic street; the north-east end was posher—they had proper curtains and cars with tax discs. The other end, our end, was for the dirt poor and immigrants. Broken down vans arrived in the night and were unloaded into other vans which vanished by morning. There were flats full of single men. There were women who only came out at night and were whisked away in minicabs. There were women who only came out in the day, swathed from top to toe in shadows. There were old, encrusted Londoners who complained they never heard English spoken anymore.

Sometimes there were fights. Sometimes the cops came and removed, for instance, all the Somalis. But by nightfall their house would be full again, whether with the same Somalis or different ones I couldn't tell. As far as I could see, we were all dispensable.

I came and went when I thought I wouldn't be seen. But I got as wet as everyone else and I realised that there were a lot of folk nearby who didn't want to be seen either. The rain poured down on saint and sinner alike, and everyone complained in a thousand languages.

Smister never went out. I put the kitchen telly in the bedroom. It only received two channels. And I brought home a portable radio I 'found'. Sometimes he watched the telly and listened to the radio at the same time, as if the combined broadcasts could drown his own thoughts.

Sometimes Electra lay across his lap like an elegant fur rug. They seemed to enjoy each other's company. It was a wordless, restful friendship, and every now and then I got the impression that I was too noisy and clumsy for them. I thought they blamed me for all their hurts and troubles; and I *was* to blame, especially for Electra's.

Smister went through all of the anti-depressant pills, and the only way I could tell that he wasn't suicidally blue was because he hadn't been neglecting his beauty regime. He cleansed, toned and moisturised religiously, and asked me to bring some honey-coloured hair dye so that he could get rid of the pink and violet streaks. He said they didn't look classy. He said he didn't want anyone ever to call him a cheap tart again.

I can confirm that, tart or not, he wasn't cheap. If I hadn't had a big man's raincoat with deep pockets and ten busy fingers to fill them he'd have beggared me. Except, of course, I was a beggar already. I wasn't a good one anymore—not without Electra—but I managed to hustle a few quid as I shuffled down the road muttering, 'Could you spare a little change, please, for the bus to the hospital, for a bed at the hostel, for a bowl of soup.'

Most people like a reason to give you money, but sometimes someone will say, 'I'll spare you some change if you spare me the story,' and they pay me to shut up. On the other hand one amazing old bird gave me a fiver because she said I was the first person who'd talked to her all week. I tried to find her again every day after that, but I never did.

Money came hard without Electra. For one thing, money was tight for everyone that drenching summer and no one wants to stop in the rain especially when they're feeling broke themselves. For another most people don't see why they should give a grown-up person who's well enough to walk anything at all—which is why a lot of us sit down to make ourselves took small and vulnerable. You don't want to be taller than the person you're asking for money from.

Smister said, 'You never buy us anything green to eat.' We were chomping on the egg dish he called Momster's Mess. I'd even stolen salt and pepper shakers from a nearby caff to make it more palatable, but he was an ungrateful little sod.

'Electra doesn't like vegetables,' I said.

'What're we going to do?' he asked in exactly the same tone of voice.

'I'll buy you a fucking cabbage,' I said because I'd never actually told him that I pinched everything.

'We can't just wait to be evicted,' he said. 'We need another plan.'

I don't do plans. Planning is like admitting you have a future.

'Have you got a driving licence?' he went on, with the persistence of the truly stupid.

'Have *you?*'

'They wouldn't let me take the test. They said I didn't fill in the form properly. You know that bit where they ask if you're a man or a woman—M or F? Well, I couldn't write M. I just couldn't.'

Electra gave him a look that said, 'You shouldn't have to.' I've said this before and I'll say it again: she really is a nicer bitch than I am.

He went on, 'What I mean is, can you drive? You do know all sorts of stuff your average bag lady doesn't.'

'Hey! What's an *average* bag lady?'

'If I find us a car can you remember how to drive it?'

'Why do we need a car?'

'We got to get around.'

'Why?'

'We're going to get tossed. You said so yourself. I can't show my face. I can't find us a roof. But if we had a car… '

'Where'm *I* gonna get a car, poop for brains? It isn't exactly a pair of tweezers and a magnifying mirror.' That had been his latest lady-fying requirement. Didn't he know that there's a kind of nobility if you're caught nicking food to feed your family, but none at all if you're nabbed while stealing tweezers?

'You haven't answered. Can you drive?'

Once I'd had a blue five-door Vauxhall Astra and I used to take Mother to the shopping centre every weekend. We went to Falmouth for two weeks in August to be near my brother. Gram Attwood wanted a sexy little vintage Austin Healey Sprite but I couldn't afford it.

'I had a car once,' I said, 'a long time ago in another life.'

'Great,' he said. 'So *you'll* be legal even if the wheels aren't. You didn't lose your licence, did you? Drunk in charge? Anything like that?'

'What does it matter? We aren't getting a car.'

'And I want you to find me a phone, Momster—something disposable. But black and silver would be nice.'

'See what I'm dealing with?' I said to Electra. But she just smiled at me indulgently.

'Don't talk to her,' Smister said. 'She's only a dog. Besides, if she could talk back she'd beg us to get wheels—to save her poor paws and her arthritis.'

'Electra doesn't beg; she's too dignified.'

'Well I'm not. Momster, *please*. Find me a phone and I'll find us wheels.'

So I shuffled off to Chelsea where I was a long way from Cadmus Road. I took a phone from an obnoxious young man who was so busy boasting to his mates about how much his new flat cost his father that he didn't notice me sliding his phone out of his pocket. He was too stupid to realise how many people with nothing there are on the street these days, and that it's both insensitive and risky to advertise wealth.

Smister said, 'That's way cool. Pity I can't keep it.' He was still traumatised by what Jerry-cop did to him, but he was losing the sour, sickly smell. Youth and chocolate were beginning to reclaim him.

'Go away,' he said. 'I'll be phoning my friend and I don't want you listening in.'

'Well if he's a total loser like…'

'You promised you'd never talk about Kev or Too-Tall... '
He gave me his hurt kitten look. Then he relented. 'I met
Pierre in the clubs. He's on the Diana Ross circuit but
he works in a garage by day. He knows I'm saving for the
operation, so he's bound to want to talk about it, and if you
were listening you'd go all righteous.'

'I do not go all righteous.'

'Well mopey then. Or weepy. And I really wish you
wouldn't. It's my body and my decision.'

In a huff, I put Electra's coat on her, tied a salmon pink
scarf round her neck and we went out.

It was a long time since she and I had been out together
but we fell into step with each other as if we'd never been
apart and I realised how lonely it was on the street without
her. In spite of the rain she was enjoying herself too—sniffing
at walls and lamp-posts, shaking herself so that water drops
flew off her ears like a halo.

People hurried home from work without noticing us. I
avoided the chemist shop where we'd first seen the mean guy
in the cowboy hat, and Fulham Broadway Station where he'd
attacked us. But we asked for change from people waiting for
busses because they couldn't walk away without losing their
places in the queue. With Electra by my side I earned more
money than abuse.

I was just about to accost a new bus queue when Electra
stiffened, tugging at the salmon pink scarf. I looked down. Her
tail was tight between her legs and the hair on the back of her
neck lifted in a stubbly ruff. I spun round.

'Thought it was you,' Georgie said, stepping up so close I
could smell the burgers he'd had for tea, while Joss crowded us
on the other side.

Chapter 24

Threats, Thieves And Pierre

///

Joss twisted my arm behind my back.

'Don't yell,' Georgie said. 'We don't want to hurt you—we only want to talk.'

'Then tell Joss to let go. I haven't got over the last time you didn't want to hurt me.'

'That was a mistake,' Georgie said. 'Joss was freaked out.'

'There was a fucking dead fucking body in there,' Joss said. 'I knew you'd fucking think I topped her. I figured you wouldn't say nothing if you was dead too.'

'Ow-ow-ow,' I said.

'Don't yell!'

'Then stop hurting me.'

'That's logical, I suppose,' Georgie said, and Joss let go of my arm.

I crouched down beside Electra and smoothed the panicking hair on the back of her head.

'And then,' Joss said, as if he'd never been interrupted, 'Georgie here said maybe you fucking did it.'

'Did what?' I straightened up and we moved into a shop doorway.

'Killed the dead body—aren't you fucking listening, cloth ears?'

A wave of rage started at my ankles and rolled up my legs till it hit me in the guts. '*I'm* not the violent one here. I don't kick dogs or friends in the ribs and break their teeth and give them concussion and amnesia. *I* don't beat up business rivals and stuff them down manholes. And I don't have the brass neck to track you down and accuse you of... ' But the sentence was never going to end well, so I said, lamely, 'How did you find me anyway?'

'The Lone Ranger said he seen you round here.' Georgie had the grace to look embarrassed. 'What's the matter with you? Yorking on telly, making a freak show of yourself when everyone including the law's looking for you.'

'What did you do with the fucking dosh?'

'What dosh? I'm cadging off bus queues cos I'm an eccentric millionaire, right?' I was trying desperately to remember what I'd told the 'Lone Ranger', the mean guy in the cowboy hat. Electra licked my hand.

'Electra nearly died in that fire,' I said, gratefully stroking her head. 'The vet's bills were horrendous. And Josepha took the rest.'

'And how come you never mentioned you had a fucking daughter?'

'She lied. Everyone lies on telly. Don't you know that by now?' I couldn't go far wrong by appealing to Joss's paranoia.

'So that blonde bint lied about them taking up a collection for you, people fucking phoning in, an' all?'

'Bingo! You don't think anyone gives a toss about the likes of us, do you?'

'Fucking A right!' Joss said, and Georgie rolled a skinny cigarette, lit it and passed it round. The smoke hit my virgin throat like sandpaper but it seemed as if we were nearly friends again.

Then Joss said, 'What about the dead fucking body? If I didn't kill her and you didn't kill her, who did? She didn't fucking kill herself, did she? No one batters themselves to death.'

'I don't know. I was too busy dealing with you battering *me* to death.'

'Stop whinging,' Georgie said, handing me the roll-up again. 'You're all right now, aren't you?'

'Well, don't blame me for thinking Joss did it—two women smashed up the same way, at the same time, in the same place.'

'She was fucking dead before we got there.' Joss squinted at me angrily. His mucky beard smelled of alcohol and hot dogs. 'I didn't even need to bust the door in. I think she was dead before the first time I saw you there. Remember? You was already outside that ritzy little house. That's why I thought *you* done it.'

'So you just wandered in, found her dead and then stole from her?'

'He thought you were on to something,' Georgie explained. 'He thought you wasn't sharing.'

'You know what I fucking do to people who don't share?'

'Yeah,' I said.

Georgie was giving me the crafty eye. He said, 'So did you tell the filth about us being there?'

'Did *you?*'

We all stared at each other. Joss broke first. 'Know what, you arseholed wrinkly old moo? We could of. We could of made a few quid turning you up. People been asking.'

'Who?'

'Dunno,' Georgie said. 'Word comes down the line—you know how it goes. We thought it must've been the cops cos we kept hearing from people who think we're your friends, and they pretend they're your friends too. Only we know for a fact you don't got no friends except that poxy dog. And another fact is they're the sort as would grass you up for a jar of marmalade.'

I crouched down next to Electra. 'What do I believe?' I whispered to her. 'I've spent weeks thinking Joss was a killer.'

'For fuck's sake!' Joss looked ready to kick my head in again so I stood up quickly.

'Gimme an answer or I really will do you this time.'

'I haven't talked to the cops,' I said. 'Would I be here if I had? Would *you?*'

'Cos you know what I'd do if you talked?'

'Same as you did when I hadn't?'

'Too fucking right.' He bristled and flexed his shoulders.

I sat down with a bump and buried my face in Electra's neck. Joss was insane, paranoid and violent. I used to be quite pleased to see him. I used to think he was nearly normal.

'Now turn out your fucking pockets,' he snarled.

So I gave him the seven pounds 86p I'd collected that afternoon. What was I going to do—fight both of them?

'Sorry,' Georgie said, 'but you did make us come all this way three days in a row to find you. You owe us the bus fare at least.'

They stole my Trilby hat as well, but they left me the umbrella so maybe they were budding humanitarians after all.

After they'd gone I stayed sitting with Electra in the doorway for a long time. If I'd got up then I would've gone to the nearest offie for a couple of litres of red. A body can only stand so much threat and insanity without comfort. A few swallows of red would stop my guts from churning and my brain from twitching. A couple more and maybe Electra would talk to me again and tell me what to do. I might even be able to sleep without pills.

I hate being on the wagon. It's very bad for my nerves.

Perhaps it's better for my memory though. I began to remember that Joss didn't cause all my injuries. Some of them happened when I fell over in the bath. Someone screamed and I fell over. What on earth was I doing having a bath in a stranger's house with a dead body in the living room?

If you've never been completely wankered you probably won't have to ask yourself a question like that. And not be able to answer it.

I remembered seeing Gram Attwood with a woman. He caught a cab to Harrison Mews. She went to the theatre. The next day I saw the same woman leave the house in Harrison

Mews. It was the same woman. I'm sure it was. And it stands to reason she was Natalie Munrow.

Then I went off for a beer with Joss, and later there were guinea pigs, chocolate biscuits, and a little kid who called me Big Foot. That happened. Didn't it?

I was sleepy when I got back to Harrison Mews so I don't know what happened until Georgie came running out of the yellow door with bags full of stolen stuff. Then Joss gave me a terrible kicking.

Some time before that, Natalie came back to her house and got herself beaten to death. I screwed my eyes tight shut and tried to see her leaving the house. I remembered her looking back because she'd left Gram in bed. Gram would have been there. He'd have been gorgeous and sleepy. He never got up early. She brought him coffee with cream, and muesli with slices of banana. Afterwards he went back to sleep. That's what happened because that's how Gram liked it, and what he liked he made happen.

Don't tell me I'm wrong. I know I'm right. I was there: I sliced the banana. I squeezed his luxuriating thigh before I left for work. And sometimes I rushed back at lunchtime to see if he wanted a nice sandwich. Or even me.

Was that when he killed me?

'Was it?' I asked Electra, but she blinked and sneezed at me so I knew I should take her back to Cadmus Road before she caught another chill.

Luckily there wasn't an off-license on the way home. Because, I can't promise I'd have had the strength to pass it by. I was still shaking from the memory of Joss's staring, bonkers eyes as he said, 'If you blabber I'll mash your skull into your stinking brain. You won't have any face left at all. And your brain will be all scrambled up with egg shells and fag ends. Bye-bye.'

Bye-bye? Maybe the scariest part was Joss thinking he could finish off a threat like that with a harmless 'Bye-bye'.

Joss batters people. That's how he is. He breaks eggs but there are no omelettes. He's the logical suspect. Except he isn't logical, and nor am I. I used to be, and then when my heart died my brain went on the sick list too.

If it wasn't Joss and it wasn't me who killed Natalie, that left the one I used to call Gram Attwood—otherwise known as Lucifer, the Devil, Satan and Ashmodai.

Except he isn't interested in death. He may kill your heart, your mind and your spirit, but he leaves your body alive to feel the pain. Pain is his gift—even in bed when, hurt and degraded, you still want him. In the end you crave the hurt and humiliation because it's the only time he touches you. You have no other proof of his love.

Or has he changed and added death to his repertoire? I can't believe that: death is sometimes merciful and Gram is not.

Or did he love Natalie more than he loved me? Did he kill her to spare her years of pain and madness? Whereas with me, his indifference was so manifest that he couldn't even be bothered to come to court or prison and watch me suffer.

I turned my face up to the streaming dark sky and let the rain irrigate my tear ducts. Electra whimpered.

'Okay, sweetheart,' I said, and we took the last few steps to our home.

Music greeted me as I walked down to the basement. It was a song called 'Tainted Love' and it fitted my mood so perfectly that I almost forgot that Smister only ever listened to talk radio.

I stopped on the stairs, but Electra went ahead confidently, her tail waving a gracious hello. I followed with more caution.

Smister, now honey-blond and funky in red, was dancing with a tall bald guy in overalls. He had black almond-shaped eyes, skin smooth as polished wood, and forearms like Popeye's.

'This is Pierre,' Smister said, all dimples.

'Hi,' Pierre said, holding out a hand the size of a hubcap. 'I hear you've been looking after our girl here.'

'Isn't he just gorgeous?' Smister said. 'He's from Detroit, you know.' He was glowing, relaxed and slightly stoned. I couldn't see any wine, but the heavy scent of blow was making Electra sneeze. At least I hoped it was the weed and not a chill.

I dried her off. The temperature of her ears was normal and her eyes were clear.

There were plates on the tiny table with brown cake crumbs on them. Pierre caught me looking and said, 'My girlfriend sent brownies, but we got the munchies... sorry.'

Smister said, 'Something happened. What happened, Momster?'

I looked at Pierre.

Smister said, 'Don't worry about him, he's solid.'

I sighed. 'The guys who broke my face—they found me. I was going to bring us back some fish and chips, but they took all my money.'

'Fuck the fish,' Smister said, pulling up a chair for me to sit on. 'Are you okay?' He turned to the smooth wooden man in overalls, 'They killed her friend and then kicked her brain into cake-mix so she can't remember anything properly. Also she was heavy on the sauce, but she gave it up a few days ago. It hasn't made much of an improvement that I can see. Except she doesn't do her God and Satan piece so often—that used to be quite annoying.'

'Going cold-turkey screws with your body chemistry,' Pierre said. 'It's hard. You should maybe cut her some slack.'

'Isn't he the cutest?' Smister said. 'You should see him do "Can't Hurry Love". I swear there isn't a dry seat in the house.'

'It's the transforming power of a big wig.' Pierre dipped his shiny dome modestly, and I thought, at least he told Smister he has a girlfriend. I was prepared to like him, but there were too many confusing sexual signals wafting around. I'm a beat up old broad and easily confused these days.

'Did they hurt you?' Smister pulled the other chair close. Pierre sat down and Smister sat on his knee looking small and fragile.

'See, that's what makes me wonder if I got it all wrong,' I burst out. 'They twisted my arm and thieved my money, but that's like shaking hands for them. If Joss actually killed Natalie, and he went to all the trouble of tracking me down, he would've killed me too; no argument.'

'Then why did he bother?'

'Cos he wanted to know if I'd grassed him up to the cops. And also everyone who saw us on TV told him I was in the money. Everyone wants a piece.'

'But how did he know where to find you?'

'Remember I told you about a mean bugger in a cowboy hat at Fulham Broadway Station? Well *he* told them.' I could see that he didn't remember—he'd been so whipped by his own woes he hadn't even listened to mine.

Nevertheless he said, 'This is why we need transport. We should never have gone on TV. It's brought us nothing but trouble. I thought it'd open up the world of show-biz but all the wrong people were watching. We need to be able to change location quickly. We got more enemies than a debt collector.'

Pierre was eyeing my lopsided haircut with disbelief.

I was embarrassed. I said, 'Georgie stole my hat.'

'You surely do need something to escape in. Good thing there's no lightning around—you'd be struck by that too.'

'You *do* understand.' Smister kissed the top of Pierre's perfect scalp and wiped the lipstick off with his wrist. 'I *knew* you would.'

Pierre brushed Smister off his lap as if he were a week-old kitten. He stood up. 'Tell you why I'm doin' this, girlfriend. It's because you've finally wised up about those assholes you always fall for. See, you got a blind spot for abusive guys and I can't help you till you wanna help yourself.'

That explained something: Pierre was far too kind to be Smister's latest hump. He went on, 'I got something you could be interested in. Give me till tomorrow evening. And in the meantime do something about your friend's hair.'

'I lost my scissors in the fire.'

'Then get her another hat.'

'I told you, I haven't been going out lately.'

'So start now before you lose your oomph.'

I wondered, if I paid him, whether I could persuade Pierre to be my friend too. It'd been years since I'd met anyone with even the tiniest motivational bone in his body. No wonder he could convince audiences he was Diana Ross even though he was six-foot-three with wrists like a riveter's.

Chapter 25

The Last Straw

///

S mister got up the next morning and dressed conservatively as a Catholic schoolgirl in a yellow kilt and black tights. He swathed my head in a scarf patterned with black and pink kidney shapes and I couldn't argue him out of it. Pierre had spoken: we were going out and that was that.

I scraped together all the money I could find in the various secret places in my layers of clothing and we celebrated with breakfast at a Polish café. We had hot sweet tea and sausage sandwiches. The owner, a round woman with no eyebrows, made a big fuss over Electra.

Just for once it wasn't raining so I couldn't hide behind an umbrella. I felt exposed. I thought everyone must recognise us and I could almost hear the click of mobile phones automatically dialling 999.

'No one can even see you when you're with me,' Smister said tossing his honey hair. Today he looked more sassy and less trashy than usual. It seemed as if Jerry-cop had taught him a very hard, unfair lesson.

He found me a trilby on a stall, and paid for it by exchanging the fatal pink Donna Karan dress. I wore the hat over the pink and black scarf which made him giggle. The stall-holder called him 'love' and 'doll' and made him feel confident enough to steal a pair of scissors from a hairdressing salon when he went in to 'make an appointment'. He was much better at stealing than I was.

He went into an office building to ask if he could use the loo. I watched through the glass doors as he flirted the guy on the desk into submission. He was only gone ten minutes but he scored nearly seventy quid. He told me that all he'd done was to trawl one open-plan area for carelessly slung jackets and bags.

Sometimes it can take me two hours to scrounge seventy pence.

But anxiety bathed my viscera in acid, and in the end I said, 'Smister, have you ever been to prison?'

'No,' he said. 'Have you?'

'You know I have. So you'd better let me do the stealing.' Because I could see men's predatory eyes follow him everywhere, and in chokey there are loads of bastards as bad as Jerry-cop.

'You?' he said. 'But Momster, everyone can tell you're not a consumer or a spender. You look street. You smell street. You walk like you're on the cadge. Even Electra looks like a beggar's dog when she's with you. When she's with me she looks like a fashion accessory.'

'And yet you thought I was rich,' I said bitterly.

'You had money, a Louis Vuitton bag and an iPhone. What did you think I'd think?'

'So I was good enough for my dog when I had an iPhone?'

'Of course,' he said blithely. 'If you're not young and pretty, you've got to have the sexy product.'

'You must be the shallowest person I know.'

'Sorry if the truth hurts.'

'The truth about chokey's gonna hurt you too.' I grabbed Electra's scarf and stomped away.

'You were more fun when you were smashed,' he shouted after me.

'Remember Jerry-cop and get stuffed,' I shouted without looking back. Electra looked back. She even looked sorry.

'You're a sentimental fool,' I said, and without thinking I went into a con store and bought a bottle.

I tore the cap off, stuck the neck in my mouth and took one giant swig.

Oh the *relief*. The iron claw that was clamped round my head released its grip. Sweet relaxation hit the lining of my gut and was absorbed instantly.

'You're disgusting,' a lad told me. He had expensive trainers and the blackened gums of a crystal meth user. I sneered at him and walked away. I had my salvation in my own hands. It isn't often that I know with absolute clarity that I'm doing the right thing.

What's the point of having a friend if all he does is wind you up? A home is useless if it makes you scared of the landlord. Seventy pounds won't help you if it can send you to prison.

Why would I want any of that if I can live free at the bottom of the heap? I ask for money, yes of course I do, but you can walk away. I'm not the taxman; no one's forcing you to give me a handout. And you're perfectly right—I *will* spend it on drink. Because drink is reliable: it keeps me warm, it helps me sleep, it gives me the moxy I need to get through another day without jumping off a bridge.

'I could quite fancy a bowl of Pedigree Chum around now,' Electra said.

'It's yours, my friend.' We turned, walking companionably side by side to Cadmus Road.

I packed everything into my new backpack. Then I fed Electra and gave her clean water. I was ready to go. I took a look round the bedroom we'd shared and at the girly clutter that followed Smister everywhere. I shrugged.

'I don't care how much dye and conditioner he puts on his hair,' I told Electra. 'It still smells like boy's hair to me.'

'Me too,' she said, 'but it's very sweet boy's hair.'

'Come on.' I wanted to get out before she made me think twice.

We walked away.

It was oddly quiet for a dry day. Usually, when the rain lets up, people, especially the Somalis, come outside to eat, drink, smoke and chew qaat. The street becomes everyone's front room. Today it was as if a storm was brewing and everyone had boarded up the windows. I looked up at the bruise-coloured sky. 'Prepare for a wetting,' I told Electra.

'Prepare for a roasting,' she replied, stopping dead and crowding into my legs for protection.

A car door slammed.

Chapter 26

In Which The Cops Catch Up

//

'**A**ngela Mary Sutherland?' A man in jeans and a brown leather jacket faced me. Too close.

'Angela Mary Sutherland?' the cop repeated. Of course he was a cop. Who else accosts you in the middle of the street with your full name as if it were a crime? And gets it wrong.

'Scuse me?' I said.

'Are you Angela Mary… ?'

'You made a mistake.'

'… Sutherland?'

'Never heard of her.' My real name is Angela *May*. But don't tell anyone.

'Oh I think you have.' He was round-faced and comfortable looking. A little cushion of paunch curved above his belt. 'Did you just come out of a house down there?' He pointed.

I turned my head to look. Electra stared at his finger.

'No,' I said. 'I can't afford no houses.'

The cop was pointing straight at Smister who had just arrived at the front door of the squat.

'Of no fixed address,' I blathered. 'The woman with no name from Nowhere.'

'What?'

'I hurt my head, see,' I confided. 'And now I talk to the animals.' I knelt down and put my arm round Electra. 'Pretend he isn't there,' I said, 'and then he'll go away.'

'No he won't,' the cop said. 'I need to ask you some questions about an incident that took place a couple of months ago.'

'It was either yesterday or a year ago,' I said. 'There's nothing in between.'

'You might want to watch that mouth of yours,' Electra whispered. Over her shoulder I saw an ambulance draw up outside the squat. Beautiful inspirational Pierre got out. Smister flew from the front door and flung himself into his arms.

'Sub me to a cup of tea and I'll tell you everything,' I told the cop. 'I do terrific confessions, when I'm not hungry. Buy one, get one free.'

'I'll take you to the station... '

'No you won't. You buy me proper tea from a proper caff or I'll confess to another animal. Who are you anyway? And get it right this time. You've a terrible memory for names. In fact I think you're half man half machine and I don't want to confess to either half.' I got up and walked away. He had to follow me, and while he was following he had his back to Smister and Pierre. I picked up the pace.

'Where are we going?' Electra panted.

'Oy!' said the cop. 'Slow down.'

But I swerved across the road and dived down a side-turning.

'This man's pestering me,' I shouted to a couple of guys on some scaffolding.

'Police,' the cop called. He had his warrant card in his hand now and was waving it around for all to see. The guys on the scaffolding hooted.

'Enough,' he said. 'Stop or I'll arrest you.'

When we were out of sight of the squat on Cadmus Road I stopped.

'I'm DC Anderson,' he said. 'I want to talk to you about the death of Natalie Munrow of 15 Harrison Mews, South Kensington.'

The sound of her name and address coming out of an official mouth nearly made me faint.

'Are you ill?' he said.

'I need a drink.'

'No you don't,' chorused Electra and DC Anderson.

I unscrewed the bottle top and guzzled as huge a mouthful as I could before he snatched the bottle.

'That's it,' he said. 'I'm calling for the car.'

'You're violating my human right to drink legally purchased wine,' I screeched, trying to grab the bottle back.

'You're resisting arrest,' Anderson said.

'Are you arresting me? You never said.'

'If you stop resisting I won't arrest you.'

'That's not fair.'

'Nor is beating a woman to death and fraudulently taking her identity for material gain.'

I dropped down on one knee next to Electra. 'Our only chance is to run away. Are you ready for a sprint?'

'Not with another cop in a car coming round the corner,' she said. 'I'm not a drag-racer.'

The car stopped by the kerb next to us. Anderson said, 'Get in the car. We only want a chat at this stage.'

'Chat away,' I said, 'but do it here and now. Electra gets sick in cars.'

'Get in the effing car you silly old bat.'

'Is he trying to be charming?' I asked Electra.

'Get... in... the... car, or I'll formally arrest you and leave your dog out here in the road.'

'Please get in,' Electra said. 'I'll try not to be sick.'

So we got in the car and Anderson's mate drove us to Earls Court Road nick. So much for Habeas Corpus and Human Rights. I was scared. I didn't know if the cops really thought I'd killed Natalie and I hadn't drunk enough red to deal with it.

'Or too much,' Electra said. 'It only takes half a bottle before your judgement toddles off down the Swanee, babbling. This is not a babble-friendly situation.'

'What?' said the sergeant, 'Speak clearly for the tape.'

'And that's another thing,' Electra said. 'You should have a lawyer.'

'I don't want to piss them off.'

'Louder,' shouted the sergeant. 'Stop mumbling.'

'I was talking to Electra.'

'Why's that?' he asked. 'So that you can give yourself time to think up a pack of lies to tell me, and then blame it on the bleedin' dog?'

'Electra doesn't lie.' I was offended. 'She never lies. Have you ever known a dishonest dog?'

'Dogs steal,' Anderson said. 'My brother had a lurcher once... '

'Oh well, *lurchers*,' Electra said.

'But the dog didn't *lie* about stealing, did he?'

'Well, no,' Anderson conceded.

'Shut the fuck up, both of you,' yelled the sergeant. 'Natalie Munrow. Remember her? She's dead.'

I couldn't think of anything to say to that.

The sergeant went on, 'You were observed lurking in the vicinity of 15 Harrison Mews close to the time of the murder.' He waited for my comment. As instructed by Electra, I waited for his question.

'Nothing to say?' he asked. 'We have your fingerprints, your DNA and your property recovered from the murder site. Would you care to explain?'

'Not really.' I said. 'I don't remember much.'

'What do you remember?'

'Well, crawling across a floor. Drinking wine with a gravy baster because my mouth was all smashed.' I gave him my best smile to show off the damage.

He looked disgusted and stared at the tabletop instead. 'Why were you there anyway?'

'I didn't see a dead body. I don't know what you're talking about.'

'Start from the beginning,' he said, pretending to be a patient policeman. 'Why did you go to Natalie Munrow's house?'

'I followed the Devil. That's where he said he was going.'

'The Devil told you he was going to 15 Harrison Mews?'

'Don't be silly,' I said. 'He didn't tell *me*; he told the cab driver.'

'The Devil took a taxi?'

Electra closed her eyes in despair. 'Don't blame me,' I said to her. 'It's not my fault they can't tell what's true even if it turns up floating on their coffee.'

'Sit on your chair and leave the dog alone or I'll have it forcibly removed.'

They think they can treat me like dirt because I don't have an address and telephone number. They said they just wanted to confirm my identity. But it isn't true. I am not Angela Mary. Angela Mary has been caught in their computer system for years and they'll never let go of her. It's a case of mistaken identity.

'And stop fucking mumbling to yourself,' the sergeant yelled.

'Don't you think... ?' Anderson began, 'that maybe the duty medic... ?'

'Is away on an emergency. Anymore bright ideas?'

He turned to me. He smelled of stale Scotch and breath-freshener. The interview room smelled of vomit and disinfectant. It reminded me of hospital. And it reminded me of the story that Smister believed. It was worth trying on again.

I took a deep breath and said, 'I'm sorry. I can't remember things. I had brain damage. They cracked my skull. I had loads of stitches. My hair's grown back a bit but you can still see them.' I started to remove my hat and scarf but the sergeant stopped me.

'We've seen the hospital report. Who cracked your skull?'

'I don't know. It might've been the Devil. I think he killed Natalie.'

The sergeant looked at me craftily. 'Did the Devil tell you to kill Natalie Munrow?'

'He hasn't spoken to me for years.' All of a sudden a wave of sorrow broke in my chest. He circled Natalie with his possessive arm outside the National Gallery but he couldn't remember my face, my name or the sound of my voice.

Anderson handed me a box of tissues.

'Why did you say you were Natalie?' he asked. 'Was it guilt? Were you "keeping her alive" by pretending to be her?'

'I didn't say I was anyone. *They* said I was Natalie.'

'Who said?'

'The doctors and nurses. The police lady with no arse.'

'That's because you stole her handbag,' the sergeant said.

'No I didn't. Someone gave it to me.'

'That would be the Devil too, I suppose?'

'He wouldn't give me anything.' I grabbed another handful of tissues to hold to my streaming eyes. 'He just took and took and took.' I was beginning to get a headache. 'You said I could have a cup of tea,' I said to Anderson, 'with lots of sugar.'

'Shall I fetch her one, sir?' Anderson said. 'And doesn't she need an Appropriate Adult?'

'Oh why the fuck not? Get her a sticky bun and a financial advisor too if you think it'll help. Interview suspended at 5.47.' He strode out of the room as if he had far more important things to do.

'I need the bog, and Electra needs to pee too. We've been in here for hours.'

'Wait while I call a female officer.' Anderson made for the door and I followed.

'I said "wait".'

'But I'm bursting.' Electra and I crowded him in the doorway and pushed out into the corridor.

At the same moment, the door to the next room opened. Two senior policemen in uniform came out. With Natalie Munrow.

Chapter 27

I See Natalie's Ghost

//

I shrieked.

The undead Natalie Munrow swung quickly away.

The senior cop said, 'That was *not* supposed to happen.'

Anderson said, 'I'm sorry sir. She was bursting for a pee.'

I said to Electra, 'We've seen a ghost. I think I'm going to shit myself.'

'Don't be disgusting,' Electra said. 'I don't believe in ghosts who smell of *Rive Gauche* and truffle oil.'

'Does she?' I was shocked. 'You're dead!' I shouted to Natalie Munrow. 'Your brains are scrambled on the Persian rug. The Devil smote you dead.'

'Shut up,' Anderson yelled.

'But that's Natalie Munrow,' I said. 'She's dead and encorpsed.'

'Stop screaming,' Anderson said.

'Calm down, you're getting hysterical.' Electra looked anxious.

'She isn't Natalie. She's a witness.' Anderson was overheated and undercooked.

Suddenly I understood what was going on. 'You're all lying to me,' I said. 'Natalie Munrow has never been dead. You tricked me. It's a conspiracy.'

'Why would we trick you? Come to the canteen. You said you wanted a nice sweet cup of tea and a bun.'

I shouted at him, 'I'm homeless and amnesiac but I'm not a child. This is about fraud, isn't it? It's a life insurance fraud and you're all in on it.'

'Steady on,' Electra said. 'Breathe. You're changing colour.'

'Pick another fall-gal. I'm buggered if I'll let you do it to me again,' I said.

'Don't shout,' Anderson pleaded. 'I'm sorry sir,' he called to the retreating senior cop.

'*Deal* with it, Anderson,' came floating back down the corridor.

'You can't accuse me of murdering someone who isn't dead. But you can find out who would benefit if she *had* died. I bet the brother's in on it too. Watch the brother. He breathes anger like a dragon breathes fire. He's a minion of the Devil.'

'I don't understand. You garble everything. But please believe me—you haven't seen a corpse. Natalie *is* dead. The woman you saw was a friend of hers and she's very much alive.'

'That's what you all want me to believe. That woman is Natalie Munrow. If you want stolen identity, it's her. She's taken her friend's identity *and* the life insurance payout for her lover—the Devil.'

'Why would the Devil want an insurance payout?' Anderson asked.

'Cos that's how he operates. He offers love for riches. He tempts, then he withdraws love, and when you can't stand it anymore you give in.'

'Er, didn't the Devil tempt Eve with an apple?'

'You're not very clever, are you? I'm talking about insurance fraud, not fruit. And I need a pee.'

Anderson caught a passing uniformed cop by the sleeve and said. 'Can you stay with this lady for a sec while I find out what's happened to the duty s-h-r-i-n-k?'

The young cop said, 'Sorry mate, can't,' and Electra said, 'I *told* you. You've *got* to start listening to me.'

'You're all talking at once,' I said. I grabbed Electra's scarf and dragged her at top speed down the emergency stairs. The sound of thundering cop boots chased me all the way but I started shouting, 'I need a wee, I need a wee,' at everyone I met and they all stepped aside as if I were a leper.

On the ground floor I changed my shout to, 'My dog's got diarrhoea,' and a cop even held the door open for me.

When I got to the front desk I stuck my face right up close to the glass and said, 'I want a bed for the night. You can't just kick me out. My dog needs a pooh.'

'What do you think this is—a hostel?' The cop looked disgusted and buzzed me straight out. Electra and I were bounced out onto the pavement. We turned left immediately and scurried into the crowds on Kensington High Street.

'They're so predictable,' I said to Electra. 'If you're running away they'll arrest you, but if you say you want to stay they can't get rid of you fast enough.'

Electra didn't reply. She was having a long relieving pee outside a bookshop. When she'd finished she said, 'All in all you managed pretty well, but in the future I'll thank you not to use my bodily functions as part of your strategy.'

'What makes you Lady Muck?' I said. 'I didn't notice you clamouring to go back to Battersea Dogs Home. It's where they'll send you if I get sectioned.'

'Stay here and quarrel if you like,' she said, 'but isn't that Natalie Munrow over there on the other side of the road?'

Natalie, in her beautifully cut linen suit, her ankle-slimming pumps, her carefully styled hair, was talking into an iPhone which would've made Smister drool. It was the woman Gram Lucifer Attwood touched. His lips kissed her cheek, his lovely hand held her elbow and stroked the small of her deceitful back. His perfect tailoring was her gift. I waited outside a theatre to warn her, but she sent me packing. I was already too late—I was warning a dead woman.

What did she say to the cops when she sat watching me on CCTV in the next door interview room? 'She's the nut job who was stalking me that night'? Because of course there was a CCTV camera. She could see me, but I couldn't see her. They were all in league against me.

She stood at the corner of Kensington High Street and Phillimore Gardens, talking on her phone. She knew that Gram Lucifer Ashmodai was a murderer but no one was chasing her. Or him. Why not?

No one believed me. No one understood what I was saying. And *I* was the one who left bodily fluids at a murder scene even though I didn't know there had been a murder.

The cops had my DNA, but how can I trust them with complicated science when they can't get my name right?

The Devil lured me there to take the blame. Ask yourself, why did he turn up and show himself to me just before a murder? He found me and led me to the scene. There was malice in his forethought.

'Are you going to stand here all afternoon muttering?' Electra asked. 'You're barely a hundred yards from the police station, and you're letting Natalie get away.'

'What am I supposed to do?'

'Well, follow her, dip wad,' she said, giving herself a shake. 'And while you're at it, get as far away from the Earls Court Road as you can. I'm pretty sure you were going to be arrested and formally charged.' She gave me a pitying look and set off east along the High Street.

Natalie stayed on her side of the road and we stayed on ours. She was in no hurry, but she walked purposefully. Her posture was terrific—confidence oozed from every pore. I walked like that once; before I started carrying my home on my back and a dirty great void where my heart should be.

'Look at her,' I said. 'She's got everything.'

'She's meeting someone. She's checking her watch every thirty seconds.'

161

'It's a diamond watch. I bought Gram a Rolex so I couldn't afford anything like that for myself.'

'He's gone up in the world since then.'

'It's not like you to be cruel.'

'It's not cruelty,' Electra said. 'It's reality.'

Just before Kensington Gardens there's a stone and glass swank house called Kensington Palace Hotel. Natalie walked up to the entrance and a man in white gloves and a top hat held the door open for her.

We stopped.

'We need Smister,' Electra said. 'He could go in. We can't.'

'We dumped Smister.'

'What do you mean, "We"?'

'Anyway, he'll have gone off with his best friend Pierre. He doesn't need us. We don't belong in the same world.'

'You're an idiot. What do you want to do? Hang around till Natalie comes out? There's nowhere to wait.'

'We could sit in the park.'

'Good idea,' Electra said, and we wove our way through screeching, honking traffic to Kensington Gardens. Electra had a lovely roam on the grass and I had a lie down on a bench. But I couldn't see the hotel entrance so it was a waste of time. It was getting dark and I needed to witness Gram with Natalie once more so that I could remember my hatred and rage.

Without rage I would never be able to contemplate revenge.

'Anger never goes unpunished,' Electra warned, nosing round my bench. 'Well, *yours* doesn't. Give it up. Go and find Smister.'

But I didn't listen. I trailed up and down outside the hotel until she stopped talking to me and my back started to ache like a rotten tooth. I didn't see Gram Attwood, or Natalie Munrow again, but I did see a matching pair of cops striding purposefully in our direction.

'Oh fuck,' I said and we took off at top speed. I thought I was heading back to the squat, but somewhere along the way night fell and we got lost. Did I mention that Electra has a very poor sense of direction?

We ended up hidden behind some rubbish skips. I wrapped us both in the blankets I'd swiped from the squat. It started to rain again but we were protected by some overhanging planks and polythene so we should have been quite comfortable. Electra sighed a lot. When did she get too good for this life? She should know better than to get used to a bed.

Chapter 28

I Become An Ambulance Driver

//

In the morning I couldn't quite shift the crust gluing my eyelids closed. I fed Electra and let her drink from a puddle. My back was the shape of a coat hanger and my chest squealed like a nest of rats. I set off to find a caff. I knew I'd recover once I got warm and fed. A café owner can be surprisingly generous when he wants you to move away from his door so I had a day-old sausage roll and a cardboard cup of weak tea for breakfast.

Even so it took me nearly two hours to find Cadmus Road. I was cold and wet when I arrived but I still circled the area keeping my eyes peeled for cops or cowboys. The road was busy with people leaving for work and reluctant school-aged kids weighed down, like me, by their backpacks. No one seemed to notice Electra and me sliding stealthily into the squat.

The musty old basement smelled of shower gel, body lotion and hairspray. Smister was alone, curled on his side with one hand under his cheek. He looked so young and smelled so clean that I couldn't bear to wake him. Electra jumped onto one of the broke-back beds. I lay beside her and within two minutes we were asleep.

'Where've you been?' His voice was high with indignation, but he handed me a mug of hot coffee. 'You've been sleeping in a garbage bin. Admit it. I won't *speak* to you till you've had a shower.' He stormed back to the kitchen, his heels chattering like angry jackdaws, leaving a trail of perfume so strong it was visible. Electra sneezed and jumped off the bed to follow him, her tail waving gently.

I sat up to drink my coffee. Smister had made it strong, with milk and five sugars—just the way I like it. My back was being stabbed by rusty knives, my hips felt bruised and my neck sounded like broken glass. Pavement isn't the world's softest bed but it never hurt me like this before. Maybe I'd twisted into a weird position. Or maybe I needed a proper bedroll instead of a couple of thin blankets.

'Or *maybe* at your age, you need to sleep on a mattress, dim-wattage,' Smister said. 'Or maybe you need to stop bingeing and falling down instead of falling asleep. But while you're clean I'll cut your hair. Pierre's right—you look like a total lunatic.'

I was headachy and surly. 'I saved your scrawny little neck yesterday only you were too dumb to notice. The cops took me in.'

'They never!'

'They did. And it was all because I was leading them away from you.' I avoided Electra's reproachful eyes.

'Did they hurt you? Was it... the same ones? Were they looking for me?' He turned so pale his lips looked blue.

I relented. 'It's not all about you. This was about who killed Natalie Munrow. Oh crap!' Because I suddenly remembered the cops were setting me up for Natalie's murder. I was the easiest target within a hundred miles. No wonder they didn't want to believe she was still alive. If they'd believed me, they would have to re-identify the body they had in their morgue. They might have to do a little work, instead of extracting the confession of a bag lady to do the job for them.

'You're paranoid,' Smister said, snipping away at my wet hair.

'I'm serious. I'm in a lot of trouble and I'm scared. If they catch me, will you adopt Electra? I couldn't stand it if she was locked up too.'

'They're not going to catch you.'

'They were in this street. They took me to Earls Court nick. They're trying to pin Natalie's death on me. And they found me not fifty yards from our front door. You'd just come home and Pierre turned up in an ambulance.'

'Oh *crap*,' he said.

'Smister?'

'What?'

'I fell off the wagon yesterday.'

'You didn't fall—you jumped from a great height—with enthusiasm.'

'But you were... '

'Taking risks? Stealing? Get over it. You kept me alive the last two weeks. You stole and begged to feed me. But I don't care how hard you try you'll never make enough to buy an ambulance.'

'You bought an ambulance?'

'It's got beds and cupboards, and there's a water tank and heater the hippies put in. It won't go above 27mph but it's got four months left on the road tax. And Pierre threw in a new battery.'

'But where will you go?'

'We, you soppy old fruit bat. I can't drive. And don't start snivelling again. Hold still. If you're going to drive you'll have to look less like a soak or you'll be breath-tested every two minutes. The point is *not* to attract attention.'

That's how I became an ambulance driver.

Chapter 29

I Drive Back To Where I Started

//

Why couldn't he have allowed me one little drink before throwing me into London traffic? I was a nervous wreck, driving an ambulance in the pouring rain after not driving at all for nearly five years. He has no pity. He's too young to feel pity.

The traffic was horrible so no one was going faster than 27mph, and that gave me time to get to know the cumbersome beast I was driving. The ambo groaned in first gear, squealed in second and wallowed round corners like a drunken camel. It smelled of weed and patchouli oil. Cute little rainbows, moons and stars were sticking to the dashboard. Smister tried to pick them off with lacquered fingernails.

But the windscreen wipers worked and we were warm and dry. Electra curled up between us and slept contentedly.

I said, 'I want to go back to South Dock High Rise.'

'Why?'

'I want to find out what happened to Too-Tall.'

'Well, *I* don't,' Smister said. 'Why can't you forget about her? You got the contrariest damn memory in the whole world. Why can't you remember useful stuff like what happened the day Natalie died instead of something glum and useless?' He turned the radio on. It seemed to be stuck on

KissFM and he could hardly hear it because of the squealing engine. 'We're running *away*, remember?'

Stuck on North End Road I switched off the engine because I couldn't stand the noise anymore. I said, 'I followed Natalie to a posh hotel. You could've gone in after her but you weren't there.'

'Stop blaming me. I don't understand—if she's still alive how come I was nicked for using a dead woman's plastic?'

'Because Gram battered Natalie's *friend* to death so that she'd be unrecognisable. They convinced everyone that the friend is Natalie and Natalie's the friend. The classic switch. Natalie took out loads of insurance on her own life which she and the Devil want to collect. Or maybe Natalie made the friend the beneficiary of the policy.'

'Or maybe your old mate Gram was *married* to Natalie so he'd benefit automatically.'

'What?'

'What did I say? *Don't go!* You can't leave me in the middle of a traffic jam!'

'You have no pity,' I yelled. 'You're too young and you want to torture me as well as yourself.'

'Shut up.' He grabbed my arm like he was drowning in a rough sea. 'Please stay. I've got a little red wine in my handbag.'

'How little?'

'Enough for a pick-me-up.'

So I stayed and had a mouthful of red which settled my nerves and steadied my hands on the wheel.

When he saw I was alright again, he said, 'One day you're going to tell me why you call this guy the Devil and what he did to you.'

'No I'm not,' I said and I meant it. I didn't want to reveal my shame and humiliation to someone so young and pretty— so without pity. Besides, he wouldn't be interested in a story that didn't revolve around beatings and mutilation of body parts.

'Okay,' he said, without the grace to hide his relief. 'But we have to find Natalie or the Devil—what's his name when he's off duty?'

'Gram Attwood. You can't find him—he finds you.'

'Short for Graham? I'll start with the phone book.'

I snorted. 'You can't just look up Satan in the phone book. He manifests himself when he has plans for you, but not otherwise.'

'You never actually tried to find him, did you?'

'I don't have to—evil is all around, all the time. You should know—you're the one who was tortured with a screwdriver.' I stopped talking to him till we found ourselves facing west on Western Avenue near Wormwood Scrubs Prison.

Then I realised we were on our way to East Acton where I used to live with my mother.

I panicked.

I wanted to turn round but there was too much traffic.

I wanted to stop because I couldn't breathe.

The ambulance smelled of hot metal and battery acid. How many people had died in it and been dragged away to hell?

Electra stroked my hand with the top of her head.

'Breathe,' Smister said. 'What the fuck was *that* about?'

The ambo was in a pub car park and I had no idea how it got there. We raced through the pelting rain. I could only move because we were running towards red wine.

Smister left us at a table in a dark corner at the back. I tried to dry Electra with my scarf and the sleeves of my leisure suit. She sat close to me with her head on my thigh, protecting me from the waiting waking nightmares.

Smister came back with two glasses of wine but he wouldn't give it to me till I'd drunk some water and had a wash in the cloakroom.

'It's the last you're drinking till we've stopped driving.'

'Then *you* drive,' I said. But he ignored me and read a phone book instead.

After a minute he looked at me curiously. 'What made you come here?'

I didn't know. 'Maybe it's because I've forgotten how to turn right—across the traffic.'

'Bollocks.'

'You don't know how intimidating it is. You can't drive.' But after a mouthful of wine I admitted, 'I used to live near here with my mum. She's dead now.'

'Is that right?' he said, 'because there's a Mr G S Attwood living at 17 Milton Way. Does that ring a bell?'

I died from the pain. Graham Stephen Attwood was still living in my house.

My mother died and has no grave. I died and have no home. But Gram Satan Ashmodai de Ville is living in my house.

This is the house that he 'sold' to pay my legal fees and bury my mother. Except my lawyer is still unpaid, and my mother was kept in the morgue until there were enough other unclaimed bodies to make it worth while for the council to dig a big hole somewhere.

This happened because, stupid shameful old bag that I am, I appointed the Lord of Vermin as my legal representative here on earth with unlimited power of attorney.

Smister was crushing my hand and pinching my arm at the same time. 'You're making a scene. Shut *up*.'

'Smister,' I said as clearly as I knew how, 'I need a drink.' I leaned across the table and took his glass which was half full. Before he could protest I tipped it down my throat and felt the warmth surge from my guts to my poor cracked heart that let the icy wind blow in and freeze me to death. Smister got up, walked away and left me.

I poured water into the palm of my hand and gave Electra a drink.

'You should've known you'd end up back in East Acton,' she whispered. 'It's Karma.'

'You know I don't believe in predestination.'

'Well I do,' she said simply. 'My life was written in my blood. I was bred to be fast. But every career ends in failure.'

'But your failure shouldn't mean your death.'

'It didn't. You were my second chance.'

'And you were mine.'

'Don't be stupid. I'm a dog.'

'You're still my salvation.'

'You can't find salvation in a dog or a bottle. It's in your own hands.'

'No it isn't.'

'Scares you, doesn't it?' She raised her muzzle to the ceiling and gave an imperious sniff. 'You might have to think properly and start taking responsibility instead of going, "Oh it's not my fault—I was weak and feeble and I loved too much." And then finding a bottle of red and getting twatted again.'

'That's just vulgar.'

Smister said, 'Why are you telling your dog off in public, making scenes? You're lucky I've got an honours degree in charm and diplomacy.'

'Who's to charm?'

'The landlady, sponge brain. She's allowing us to park up here till tomorrow. I told her my "mum" had a nasty turn and needs a good sleep.'

'Why do I always have to be your mother?'

'If you were anything less than a mother everyone would wonder why I didn't dump you. But if you're my mum I get points for loyalty even when you're trollied off your tits.'

'Why *don't* you dump me?'

'I already told you.' Sinister sighed loudly and turned his pretty eyes up to the ceiling.

I wouldn't miss him telling me something crucial like that, would I? Half the time he complains cos I remember things. Now he's taunting me cos I don't.

'You're going for a lie-down,' he said, with his evil charm. 'I'll find you one of your sleepers. But I don't want another squawk out of you till you're sober.'

I lay down on one of the bunks in the ambo. It was a lot softer than the pavement and better for my skeleton than the broke-back beds. Smister fed me sleep from the palm of his hand.

When I woke up it was because I heard the Devil calling. Smister and Electra were gone.

Chapter 30

Called By The Devil

///

S mister left me with only a bottle of water. What am I supposed to do with that? Water's no good for anything but washing.

Rain drilled holes through the ambo roof and into my skull. My poor brain winced and shuddered but the bastard hadn't left me so much as one mouldy aspirin. I put on my coat and hat and snuck out into the dark wet night.

There were no lights on in the pub so it must've been well after closing time. But I knew where to go—the Devil was calling me home.

The High Street was grim, shuttered and half familiar. At one end Sherrie's Nail Bar had been turned into a Halal butcher and at the other a fancy French patisserie had replaced Ron's Electrical, but it too was up for sale or rent. Claire's Hair, where my mother went for her wash and set and her bi-weekly top-up of bilious gossip, was still there.

At the Pizza Place you turn right and walk to the end of a residential street. Turn right again and the first turning you'll see is Milton Way. My mother's house, my house, Casa Ashmodai, is a hundred yards up on the left. It is semi-detached and a low wall divides its front garden from the garden of its conjoined twin on the other side. Its face is ruddy with Edwardian bricks. A concrete path runs round the detached side to a gate which protects the tiny back garden and kitchen door.

My mother and I kept the gate locked except once a week when it was opened for the purpose of expelling rubbish bins. When Gram moved in I became less concerned with security. Evil no longer lurked outside, trying to get in. It now had a key of its own and was sitting with its feet up on the coffee table waiting for dinner. I called it Darling. My mother took to her bed. I took to crime. Gram took everything.

The Devil doesn't fear attack; the gate was unlocked. I opened it and slithered my scaly way to the kitchen door. The neighbour's security light went on and skewered me, hand already grasping the doorknob. A grey cat stood, petrified, on the fence. We stared at each other in a rictus of alarm. The garden was bathed in white light and the rain shone like crystal rods. The door wouldn't open.

I bent and felt for the spare key under the tub that once held a bay bush and scarlet geraniums. My back was hard as steel, my joints clanked like unoiled cogs but my robot self remembered. The key was still there but it was too crusted with lime-scale and the corpse of the dead earth to turn in the lock. I should have known—nothing living thrives where the Devil walks, nothing but his creatures, the rats, bats and cats. Green turns brown, nature withers and women rot in chokey, undead, with freeze-dried hearts.

I looked at my mother's garden—at the bare fence where the dog rose used to ramble. The cat hissed and jumped down to defecate in the bed where once pure white lily of the valley rang its tiny bells and nodded to the grape hyacinths. If ever I needed proof that Ashmodai, Master of Corruption, lodged here, this was it.

Fear made me dither, and while I stood trembling the kitchen door swung open of its own accord.

Horned and hoofed, red eyed and yellow fanged, the Devil raised his tyre-iron to strike me dead…

———

Electra licked the rain off my face.

'Get up and shut up,' Smister whispered. 'You'll wake the neighbours.'

'I knew it was you,' I said. 'The Devil doesn't use a tyre-iron.'

'Yeah-yeah, that's why you shrieked and fainted.'

'I slipped. What're you doing here with a tyre-iron?'

'I thought you were Graham Attwood coming home.'

'How did you get in?'

'Unlatched kitchen window.' He pointed to the one above the sink. 'I stepped in the washing-up bowl. I think I broke a plate.'

My mother, standing at that sink, used to boast that she had never in her life broken a plate, cup or glass. She said I was always in too much of a hurry. I could see my mother now—mid-height, mid-weight, hair washed and set every two weeks—as she complained, 'Rush, rush, you're sloppy about everything, and I'll never know where you got those great clod-hopping feet. It wasn't from my side of the family, that's for sure.' She'd look down at her own neat shoes. 'No wonder you're so clumsy.'

I couldn't get to the office early enough or leave late enough to escape her harsh tongue. So I did well at work. Banks love busy, industrious little bees. Or they do until the bees help themselves to some of the honey. A bank will only tolerate thieves if they're on the board of directors. Yes, if you want to steal, steal big. Gobble up entire insurance companies and pension funds.

'Momster!'

'What?'

'I asked you where he would keep his papers, his laptop, personal stuff?'

Of course, I was in Satan's stronghold with an unbeliever.

We followed the signs of decay and neglect up to my mother's bedroom where the sight of her white sheets stained with carnal ichor and tumbled in disorder made me retch. He killed her and stole her bed. Of course he did: it was the biggest bed in 17 Milton Way. Mine had been the smallest. It was gone. Like me it had been used, abused and discarded. In its place were a computer table and a Posturistic office chair. There was a desk under the window. It supported the latest tech toys, monitors, mice and keyboards, games, three phones plus chargers. He hadn't lost his taste for gadgetry.

At the top of the house, my brother's room was now a well-appointed home gym. My whole family had been wiped out to meet the corporeal needs of Ashmodai.

Electra whimpered. Her ears were pinned flat against her narrow skull. She knew she was cowering in the shadow of true evil and she'd heard something...

Just before Smister switched off the light I saw the three of us reflected in a floor-to-ceiling mirror—Electra, pressing against my legs, me, in coat and hat looking like a deformed man, and Smister, sassy in slim denims, boots and a frock-top, head cocked, listening to the sound of a front door slamming. He flicked the switch. We disappeared into the dark.

A woman's voice called from the bottom of the stairs, 'Darling, is that you?'

I clutched Smister's hand and we backed away from the door into an exercise bike.

Footsteps on the stairs. I heard the creak of the fourth step from the landing. I tried to disentangle my coat from the bike pedals. Smister and Electra melted away.

The voice came from my mother's bedroom door directly below us: 'Are you asleep, sweetheart?' A hideous breathy coo. She said, 'Gram, baby?' And I heard her open the bathroom door.

Then the smell of *Rive Gauche* and truffle oil—the scent of a spectre—wafted up the stairs. My wet coat caught around my legs, tying me to the exercise bike. How did the ghost know I was here? How did she know *anyone* was here?

The light blinded me. I threw up my arm to shield my eyes. The exercise bike suddenly released my coat and I stumbled forward.

The ghost of Natalie Munrow shrieked like a dying seagull. It staggered back and tumbled in slow motion down to the lower landing, bouncing off every other step, somersaulting and showing lacy knickers the colour of ashes of roses.

I just had time to think that I never knew ghosts were allowed to have elegant undies when Smister yelled, 'You didn't have to threaten her,' and pushed past me.

Electra joined us and looked down on the heap of arms and legs that lay at the bend of the stairs.

'Are you insane?' Smister said. 'You rushed at her. You were going to hit her.'

'No, no,' I protested. 'I stumbled.'

We crept down the stairs to the pile of parts. I was thinking, a ghost can't die—it's already dead.

Then the ghost sighed. Which is what ghosts are supposed to do.

'Thank fuck,' Smister said. He bent over Natalie, straightening her arms and legs, supporting her head. 'Ring for an ambulance, doofus. Don't just stand there muttering.'

So I stepped over the two-time corpse and went to the bedroom. A space age remote handset stood on the cabinet by the Devil's bed. I rang for an ambulance.

'17 Milton Way,' I said. 'There's been an accident. A woman fell down the stairs.'

'Is she breathing?'

'She shouldn't be, but she is.'

'Slow down, Madam. I know you're upset but please speak slowly and clearly.'

'She's breathing,' I said, and at last I started breathing too. 'She isn't properly conscious. It was a very hard fall.'

'On no account try to move her,' the expert on the telephone told me.

At that moment I saw Smister, supporting Natalie Munrow, coming across the hall.

'Right you are,' I said, feeling light-headed.

'Get out the way,' Smister said, and let Natalie down onto Satan's bed of corruption. Her head rolled back like a cabbage on a kitchen floor. Her eyes were unfocussed. The impeccable grey-green eye shadow was smudged. I liked her better that way.

'Ma'am?' the expert on the phone said, 'Ma'am, are you there? Did you hear me? It's vital that you don't move the victim till the ambulance crew gets there.'

'Don't move her,' I said. 'Right.'

'Oops,' said Smister.

'Make sure she's covered and doesn't get cold.'

'Covered,' I said. 'Right.'

'You're doing fine. The ambulance will be with you in about five minutes. Not long to wait now.'

'Five minutes,' I said. 'Right.'

'Fucking hang up!' Smister hissed. He snatched the phone out of my hands, rubbed it all over with the Devil's dirty sheet and dropped it on the bed. I grabbed a blanket and covered Natalie up to her chin. Her skin was spectral grey.

We rushed downstairs. I shut the back door and put the key in my pocket. We escaped by the front door which Smister left ajar for the ambulance crew. On his way out he picked up a black umbrella.

'It was *you*, bird turd,' I said. 'I knew it was you.' I led us at a cracking pace up Milton Way in the opposite direction from the High Street which was where the ambulance would come from.

'It was me what?' he panted.

'You left your sodding wet umbrella in plain sight. That's how Natalie knew someone was in the house. She thought it was Ashmodai and came looking.'

'Ash who?'

'If she hadn't thought Gram was there she'd have gone away.' I turned the corner at the end of the street and dropped down in a crouch. I needed to catch my breath. I opened the bottle of gin I'd swiped from the kitchen and took three enormous gulps.

'Gimme that.'

We had a short undignified tussle which Smister won.

'Oh lord,' Electra sighed. 'Not *both* of you!'

'We had a shock,' I told her. 'We're stressed out.'

'No shit,' Smister said. 'Why the sodding hell did you push her downstairs?'

'*I did not!*'

'Shut up! You'll wake the neighbours. You *always* go for maximum fuck-up and you *always* succeed.'

'Now who's shouting?' I whispered. 'I did not push, threaten or harm her in any way. If anyone's to blame it's you for leaving your umbrella where she could see it. *And* moving her when any fool knows you're not supposed to.'

'Both of you be quiet,' Electra warned. 'The sirens—listen.'

I peeked round the corner as the ambulance sped up Milton Way and stopped outside number 17. Lights went on all up and down the street as the neighbours woke up with their nosey noses twitching. That was the Milton Way I knew—everyone watching everyone else from behind the curtains.

A few minutes passed and then the ambulance crew came out carrying Natalie. I think she was wearing a neck brace but it was hard to see from the distance and through the rain.

'They haven't covered her face,' I said.

'She isn't Too-Tall,' Electra said, leaning against me sympathetically.

'I'm telling you, she was alright when we left,' Smister said. 'If anything happens to her it'll be medical malpractice.'

The ambulance U-turned and roared away.

'I'm cold and wet,' Electra said. 'What're we waiting for?'

'We should go,' Smister said. 'She's bound to tell the cops there were strangers in her house.'

'It isn't her house!'

Electra slid away and hid under a low hedge.

'Go away, both of you,' I said.

'You're never thinking about going back in?' Smister said. 'Listen, you sad old souse, the cops are coming. It's suicide.'

'I'm not going back inside.'

'Then what're we waiting for?'

'Ashmodai.'

'Who the freaking hell is Ashmo-whosit?'

'He's a member of the fiery circle,' I said, 'the Lord of Lust and Rage.'

'Oh for fuck's sake—where do you get all this shite from?'

'Same place as you get your stupidity and carelessness,' Electra said from under her bush. 'Take a long look at yourselves—you're both catastrophes waiting to happen. And I use the word cat advisedly.'

'Cats are minions of the Devil.'

'Oh, give it a rest,' said Smister and Electra together.

'Go away,' I said. 'Leave me alone.'

'You've got to promise not to go back in,' Smister said, and Electra crawled out from under the bush and nodded.

'All I need is a little support,' I said. 'But all you ever do is tear me down.'

'What're you talking about?'

'Always going on about how clumsy I am—how I drove our dad away with my neediness. Is it any wonder I turned to Satan for affection?' I took another swig of gin.

Smister snatched the bottle away. 'You are so totally marmelised I can't understand a sodding word you say. I'm taking Electra and if you've got a single brain cell left you'll come too.'

But I wouldn't. They didn't get me. I *had* to wait for the Devil. It's what I always do.

I studied the cars on Milton Way and there it was—the cat I'd last seen crapping in my mother's garden appeared on the pavement. It crossed the road and sat sheltering under a little red German car. I had one of those lodged in my memory like a speck of dust in my eye. It was irritating but I couldn't get to it. It was a sign. I approached with caution. The cat hissed and climbed into the wheel arch. I put my hand out and touched the hood of the car. The cat spat and slithered away. But it left the mark of Satan—the hood was warm.

I know what Electra would've said. She'd have said that the engine was warm and that's why the cat chose the little red car for shelter. She'd have said the engine was warm because the car had been recently driven not because the cat transferred its demonic energy to whatever it touched.

But Electra's just a dog, she doesn't understand signs and symbols. The corporeal world, with its sights, sounds and smells, overwhelms her. She has no room left for alternative dimensions. Although sometimes she can sense them. Then her hackles go up and she trembles.

But tonight the hair on the back of *my* neck prickles and *I* am trembling. For Gram Satan Ashmodai sent the cat to me as a message.

He is coming.

Chapter 31

I See The Devil's Feet

///

I awoke to the sound of his voice, to the smell of truffle oil and *Rive Gauche*.

He said, 'But you're only going to be there a few more hours. Can't you... ?' He sounded angry, but not thunderous. It was that complaining, impatient dissatisfaction I'd learned to avoid at all costs.

My head was on a pillow and the pillow smelled of Natalie. My eyelids creaked. I woke up in my mother's room and Gram Attwood's bed. How the hell did I get there? Gram Attwood was downstairs talking on the phone.

He said, 'Well, I need a shower first and coffee... I've been up half the night with you, in case you've forgotten.'

He needed a shower. He was coming upstairs.

I got off the bed. I grabbed my hat. I fluffed a pillow, tried to straighten a sheet.

There was nowhere to hide. I went down on the floor and scrambled under the bed.

He said, 'The sooner I can shower and have breakfast, the sooner I... No, I'm not trying to... No, I'm not threatening you... now that's just paranoia... no I did not hire them—you're raving mad.'

I could see his feet in hand-tooled black loafers and midnight blue silk socks. Then I saw his naked feet. I could've reached out and stroked them.

He said, 'If I was going to put the frighteners on you I wouldn't hire a derelict old man and a blonde bimbo to do it, would I? No, I'd do it myself, wouldn't I? And we'd both enjoy it.' He was almost laughing. His voice was caressing but his bare feet paced impatiently. The Devil, oh the Devil.

I buried my face in my hands and tried not to breathe. He was blaming me again. That's why I was here. I came when he called. As always.

And yet… I couldn't hear her but I knew she was accusing him. I knew she was crying and begging for comfort. She was not happy in love. She was nagging and demanding and he wouldn't like it.

She was accusing him of sending two people to hurt her. Why? Had she threatened him? Did she know something he didn't want known? Was she holding it over him? On maybe *she'd* done something bad. She'd offended him in some way. She thought he was punishing her; that he sent for me and Smister to punish her.

He cut the phone call short. I turned my head and saw his heels going away to the bathroom. I saw his silk shirt rumpled on the floor, his trousers, like empty snake skins, beside it. I heard the sound of running water and the screech of the shower door.

I rolled out from under the bed. I stopped myself from picking up his clothes, folding them and burying my nose in them. They wouldn't smell of him anyway.

I crept away, down the hall, down the stairs and into the kitchen. There was no more gin. I tried all the cupboards. There was nothing in the fridge but milk and white wine. He didn't cook. There was only bed, wine and pain when you took the Devil for your lover.

I picked up an already opened bottle and necked it.

I couldn't put it back in the fridge empty, so I looked round for a rubbish bin to hide it in. I opened the cupboard under the sink and grabbed the first black plastic bag I saw.

The weight surprised me. I dropped it on my foot and stifled the yell of pain.

Inside the bag was a little stone lion with a broken leg. The lion's head was stained rusty red. I put it back.

From upstairs, I suddenly registered that the shower water had stopped running. I stuffed the empty bottle in my pocket and let myself out by the kitchen door.

The rain was misty in the air. I tipped my hat down over my eyes and shuffled as quickly as my headache would allow down Milton Way. Last night I had a plan, but I couldn't remember what it was. I had seen the Devil's feet, his cloven hooves. I was terrified and now all I wanted was to escape his wrath.

I dumped the wine bottle in the bin outside the Pizza Place on the High Street. Then at Mother's old hairdresser, Claire's Hair, I remembered my plan. I used to call Claire 'Hairy Clairey' because she was a malicious gossip and I hated her. But I could use her.

'What're you doing up at this time?' Smister snarled. 'It isn't even seven o'clock.'

Electra smiled at me sleepily and thumped her tall. She was warm and didn't want to get up.

I was wet and cold but I had to tell them my plan before I forgot again.

'You're going to the hairdresser,' I told Smister.

'Like fuck, I am. I had a whole restyle a week ago. I'm perfectly happy with it.'

'Say you've got split ends or something.'

'Split ends? *Me?*' He was outraged.

'I don't know what you do at a hairdresser anymore, but you've got to go and talk to Hairy Clairey. She lives next door to Mother and she's the World Champion gossip. She knows all and tells all.'

'If you think I'm going to let someone called Hairy Clairey within a million miles of my head you're even more demented than you look.'

I suddenly caught up with what Smister said about the time: it wasn't even seven o'clock. No wonder Gram had been in such a foul mood. He hated getting up early, and after spending half the night with Natalie he'd want to sleep till noon. She didn't know how to treat him. She wasn't a worthy handmaiden for him.

I turned Electra out into the car park to do her business. Smister snuggled back into his sleeping bag with his back to me.

I said, 'I'll make coffee.'

'Don't even *touch* the Primus. You'll break it.'

So I had to sleep till Smister woke *me* up with a mug of coffee at eleven.

Chapter 32

What Hairy Clairey Said

//

Smister was in a rancid strop when he got back from Claire's Hair. 'I will not say one single word to you till I've washed out this suburban crust. Momster, I swear to God there were old age pensioners in there waiting for their monthly blue rinse.'

'He's such a snob,' I said to Electra.

'Too *right*,' Smister said, bending double over the tiny sink and turning on the water. '*Nobody's* allowed to make my hair feel crusty. She's made me look middle-aged. It's unforgivable.'

I had to agree. Hairy Clairey only knew one style, and what was fine on my mother looked like shite on Smister. I should know—it was shite on me too the few times I let Mother bully me into going.

'Okay, she's a rubbish hairdresser,' I said, starting to help him rinse. 'She's a world-class gossip though.'

'Oh she's that, alright.' Smister wound a towel into a turban around his head. He examined his face in the mirror. 'D'you think I should get my cheekbones done when I get my new boobs?'

'Never mind your boobs; you should get new brains.'

'You just don't get it, do you?'

'You're trying to wind me up, aren't you?'

'And it's so easy.' Smister sighed. 'No wonder that arsehole dumped you. You're no challenge. Boring.'

186

'You want the body of a woman but you'll never lose the instincts of a bitch.'

'I'll have the body and instincts of a *goddess*, thank you very much.' He yawned and stretched. 'Don't blame me for what your mother told her tragic hairdresser. Her words; not mine.'

'Boring? Easy?' My mother was dead, but she could still hurt me.

'If you're going to go all whiney I won't tell you anything.' Obviously I'd seriously annoyed him by sending him to Claire's Hair. I said, 'Let's go to the pub. I'll buy.'

'No! I'm so fed up with you making trouble for me. We'll have coffee here. And I'm not saying another word till you take the pledge and swear on Electra's life you'll stop getting twat-faced.'

I didn't answer but I let Electra out into the car park. It had stopped raining.

Smister went on, 'I don't understand you. Claire said you were quiet and *ladylike*. You hardly ever had a drink except at Christmas. And then you started making cow's eyes at a man half your age... '

'I didn't.' I could hear my mother's voice coming out of Smister's mouth. 'There were only eleven years' difference. That's nothing these days.'

'Plain, unpopular, never one to run around—in fact as far as Claire knew you'd never been out with a lad even as a teenager. Then you took up with a toy-boy and broke your mother's heart.' He was deliberately imitating Claire, who I knew had been mimicking my mother.

'You're so cruel.' I was sobbing.

'How am I being cruel? *You* forced me to go there and ask questions. You shouldn't ask questions if you can't take the answers.'

'I wanted to know about now, not about years ago.'

'She was filling in the background. I was expecting some great doomed romance but it was just banal and grubby.'

'She was telling it wrong then,' I shouted. 'My love, my passion, is *not* banal and grubby.'

'*Nor was my hair*,' he shrieked.

'Your hair is not as important as my life.'

'It *is* my life.'

'Don't be so fucking stupid.'

'You *totally* don't get me. You'll never get me.' He was so upset his eyes filled with tears. That hadn't happened even after Jerry-cop abused him. 'You haven't even said you're sorry,' he wailed.

My throat tightened. 'I'm sorry,' I said, 'I'm so, so sorry. Claire's a horrible person and a worse hairdresser. I shouldn't have sent you there.'

'That's all you had to say,' he sobbed, gripping my hand. 'And I'm sorry I said you were easy.'

We sat quiet for a minute. Then he started putting gel onto his damp hair, teasing it, drying it and keeping an eye on its progress with two mirrors. I couldn't deny that it mattered a lot to him. But his life? I may be barmy but I'm not *totally* clueless.

'You're beautiful,' I said, when he turned off the diffuser and could hear me.

'One drink,' he said. 'Only one. I mean it. And you've got to eat something. You haven't eaten anything since we left the squat.'

So after he'd prettified himself to his own satisfaction he tidied me up too and we took Electra to the pub. Electra had already made friends with the landlady. She's my ambassador. Maybe she represents my human side. The landlady, Abbie, let us into the pub as long as we sat by the door. 'Your dog has the most beautiful eyes,' she told me. 'I used to have a boyfriend with exactly the same colour eyes.'

'So did I,' Smister said. And they giggled together like a couple of schoolgirls.

We had shepherd's pie and peas. Smister was persuaded to give Abbie a makeover and I promised to sweep the car park so we ate for free. But we had to pay for our own wine and coffee, and Abbie watched me like a hawk while I sipped from my glass and tried to look 'ladylike'. I'd fallen so far away from Acton's idea of 'ladylike' that I didn't know what it was anymore. Would I ever recapture it? Would I want to?

Smister said, 'I told that hair-butcher that I was staying a few days with a friend and I'd been woken up in the dead of night by an ambulance at number 17. She said she had as well, cos she lives at 15 which is next door. She said she couldn't get to sleep for ages afterwards worrying about that poor Mrs Attwood.'

I started to protest but he interrupted. 'Don't gulp. You're only getting the one glass so don't look at me like that. Eat your peas or I won't tell you anymore.'

I gulped my coffee instead and burnt my tongue.

'Anyway the butcher said that she'd met "Chantelle Attwood" one day last year when she was bringing the milk in and Chantelle was brushing leaves off the windscreen of that swanky little red Porsche. She said, "She wasn't fooling anybody. She didn't even wear a ring. If you ask me she deserves everything she's going to get from that slimy little snake." She meant your Ashmo-Devil. That's when she started filling me in on what happened to you and your mother. I shouldn't have called it banal. I'm sure it was totally horrid.'

'Why's she calling that woman Chantelle?'

'Cos it's her name?'

'She's Natalie Munrow.'

'How do you know?'

'I saw her with Gram outside the National Portrait Gallery and I followed them to Haymarket. Gram took a taxi to her house in Harrison Mews. Then I saw her leaving the theatre with her friend. The next day I saw her leave the house in Harrison Mews. She was picked up by someone in a little red… oh!'

'What?'

'The little red Porsche was outside 17 Milton Way last night.'

'Why wouldn't it be—if it's Chantelle's car and she went there to see Gram?'

'But… ' I couldn't think of anything else to say. A structure was falling to pieces in my head and all I could hear was smashing glass.

'I don't understand why you think Chantelle's Natalie and Natalie's Chantelle,' Smister said, stirring the debris in my head with a giant spoon.

I said, 'Because why would Gram kill anyone unless there was money to be made? So it has to be a life insurance scam, or something to do with inheritance. Natalie's pretending to be Chantelle.'

'But who said Gram killed anyone?'

'He's Ashmodai, Lord of Lust and Wrath. Evil is his game.'

'I don't think that would stand up in court,' Smister said.

Electra got to her feet and stretched. She laid her head on my knee and gave me the sweetest, most sympathetic look I'd ever seen.

'You agree with me don't you?' I said. But she shook her head till her ears flapped.

'Listen to me,' Smister said. 'You've got to stop all this devil crap. You don't believe it yourself—you don't even believe in God.'

'I see no evidence for God in this world but the Devil's work is everywhere.'

'Bollocks. And who cares anyway? What I want to know is where's the evidence that a weaselly saddo like Graham Attwood ever got the guts to kill anyone. According to the hairy butcher he's just an old fashioned fanny-hound who lives on women and has the hots for high finance. She said every single woman she saw him with, including you, was something in a bank.'

'No!'

'You've got to hear this, cos it seems to me you've let a pile of crow droppings ruin your life. He grew in your head until you turned him into a ginormous figure and called him Satan. But he isn't, Momster, he's just little. Small. Nothing.'

'He… '

'Don't start yelling. If you start yelling, the landlady'll kick us out.' He covered my depleted wineglass with one hand and snatched his own out of my reach. Electra whimpered.

'You don't understand,' I whispered painfully. 'You're talking about something terrifying and mysterious as if it's… '

'Just ordinary? Listen, Momster, somewhere, sometime, you got broken. You can survive out on the street, you can save me from a fire, you can nurse me back to health after *I* got broken, but for some reason you can't look up Graham S Attwood in the phonebook. Why? I think you knew where he'd be all the time.'

'I didn't… I can't… ' I couldn't get my tongue to work. Suddenly my glass was empty. I said, 'You don't understand. I'm his servant. In the beginning I took the blame because he wanted me to. Then he called and I went to a house with a dead body in it, and now the cops are looking for me. He called again. I answered and Natalie Munrow fell downstairs and nearly broke her neck. It isn't just *ordinary*. He has powers.'

'Not over me, he doesn't,' Smister said. 'I went there because I was looking for something to hold over *him*. See, if he gave your house back *I'd* have somewhere to live. Okay?'

Then he stopped. 'You're not okay, are you? I'm an idiot. Let's go for a walk.'

Outside, the pavement was still wet and shiny. Electra's claws clicked by my side. The world smelled of rain and carbon emissions. It was as it should be except for the emptiness and fear in my heart. For if Smister was right, and the Devil was as irrelevant as God, then I'd really have to be afraid of the police who couldn't even get my name right. I'd have to be afraid of laziness, ignorance, cruelty and bigotry. *Ordinary* evil.

Electra and I shuffled into the rhythm of long-distance walking, and it soothed us.

Smister said, 'Chantelle worked in the City for Griswold and Brown—they nearly went bust but the government bailed them out. The crappy crimper said Chantelle was let go when Lloyds took them over, but she got a humungous golden handshake.'

'How does Hairy Clairey know that?'

'It was part of a bigger scandal about bonuses and payoffs. The media went in for naming and shaming. Chantelle was named.'

'What about Natalie?'

'Forget Natalie.'

'I can't. There are two women: one's dead and the other's hurt. I don't know which is which.'

'I suppose that's progress.' Smister sighed. 'Can we go home now?'

Even in Acton the streets smell of life—the bins whiff of curry, the gardens of syringa and wet grass. There are recycling boxes out on the pavement which smell of soggy newsprint, old milk and cola. Electra's scent is warm and zooey while Smister's is salon fresh. Life smells sweet'n'sour. Non-life smells of nothing—except maybe battery acid.

Smister said, 'Are you sure the woman you saw with Gram outside the National Portrait Gallery was Natalie? Did you even see her face properly?'

'Not then, I was behind her. But later when she and her friend left the theatre I was as close to her as I am to you. I could smell her. She smelled of *Rive Gauche* and... oh.'

'What?'

'Truffle oil.'

'So?'

'That house, in Harrison Mews, I sat at her dressing table. I sprayed myself with... She didn't have any *Rive Gauche*, did she?'

'I don't know.'

'You've smelled it. Natalie… Chantelle reeks of it and you practically carried her to bed.'

'Oh, *that* smell. Momster, surely if Natalie was involved with Gram, Hairy Clairey would've known about it? I mean Natalie was in the papers, probably on TV when she died. If she was known as Gram's squeeze he'd have been crapped on by the cops and the whole of Milton Way would've known. The hair butcher would've mentioned it.'

'Maybe nobody knew.'

'It was a secret shag? He was humping Natalie behind Chantelle's back? But they were friends so Chantelle must never find out?'

'Maybe,' I said.

'Or maybe she still had a job—Natalie I mean. Maybe he'd spent all of Chantelle's golden boot and was moving on to the next meal ticket.'

'How could I get it so wrong?' I said.

'You were pissed?' Smister suggested, patting my shoulder sympathetically.

'But they were friends,' I protested. 'Friends talk to each other about their boyfriends.'

'Not if you're bonking your friend's number one shag you don't. In that case you lie like a stair carpet—up, down and sideways.'

We walked back to the pub car park and the ambo. But I wasn't happy. Yes, I get pissed and, yes, I may have the odd memory lapse or a rare error of judgement. But this sounded incomplete. It was the sort of reconstruction Smister would indulge in when he was tired and wanted a nap; when *an* answer was preferable to *the* answer.

'What do you think?' I asked Electra, but she just yawned.

'Natalie Munrow had Issy Miyake perfume on her dressing table,' I told Electra. 'I couldn't smell it because of the Draino.' But when I turned over to look, both she and Smister were asleep.

Chapter 33

So I Remembered

///

In the morning Smister took Electra with him when he went to the pub to give Abbie her makeover. I was supposed to sweep the car park but my hands were shaking so badly I could barely hold a coffee cup let alone a broom.

I put on my hat and coat, and walked through the rain to the High Street. I wanted money. I sat down outside the Pizza Place with my hat on the pavement in front of me. The hat collected more water than money; people don't like stopping in the wet to juggle with bags and brollies just to give you a little something. It didn't matter much. I needed the space around me and my familiar worm's eye view of the world. I needed quiet because of the shakes. I couldn't handle Smister or Electra pressuring me.

They simply don't understand—you need a drink before you can even consider trying to give up drink.

I'd lived in Acton for years but no one recognised me. Not even Claire who peered at me suspiciously through her windows over the road.

Nor, fortunately, did Ulysses. After about an hour and a half he stormed out of the Pizza Place shouting, 'Wha's the matter wit chew? What I ever done to you? You're killing me here. You want I call the cops?'

He also gave me a big slice of pepperoni pizza, a cardboard cup of coffee and a ten pound note. He's a kind man with a loud voice. I knew that. Why d'you suppose I chose his place to sit outside?

In Speedy Mart I bought Cocoa Pops for Smister and Yum-Chum for Electra as well as a bottle of red for me.

I drank just enough to calm the shakes and stop them from turning into the rattles. I hid the rest behind the driver's seat of the ambo. Then I had a sweep round the car park with the stiff bristle broom Abbie thoughtfully left out for me. All the abandoned glasses went on the bar with the beer bottles, and all the snack packets went into the bin. I did a good job.

The rain stopped and Electra came out to join me, rummaging around the picnic tables in the little garden and staring in astonishment at two life-sized plastic fawns in the flower bed. Although it was a fairly modern pub, Abbie's taste in décor ran to coach house twee, with blackened lamps, faux beams, horse brasses and copper bed-warmers; and of course plastic wildlife in the herbaceous borders. There's nothing as authentically rustic as a 1950s pub in the suburbs.

I had a blinding flash of *déjà vu*—Electra's astonishment; my snobbery; something out of place and time.

And then Smister called me into the saloon bar and my thought vanished while the landlady twirled and showed off her new self.

She said, 'You know, your daughter has a very special talent.'

'Um, yes,' I said, 'and you look ten years younger.' It's always safe to say that, but actually it was nearly true.

'You must both have lunch and a drink on the house,' Abbie said, beaming.

Smister was too pleased with himself to argue about me having a drink. We sat at our table near the back door and Smister said, 'It was like Abbie had been to a fancy-dress shop and said, "Dress me up like a brassy blonde barmaid and don't spare the push-up bra." I just told her she had too much class and was too young and pretty to settle for clichés.'

'A *very* special talent,' I said, stroking Electra's ears.

'Oh shut up.' But he was in too good a mood to mind, and we ate green Thai curry with chips.

Because I'd had a drink earlier and knew I could have another when I went back to the ambo, I sipped my wine in a ladylike fashion. Electra relaxed and lay down under the table. No one was pressuring me, hassling me or accusing me of anything.

So I remembered.

I sat up straight. Electra raised her head, her ears like exclamation marks.

'What?' said Smister.

'I have to go back to South Kensington.'

'Why? Aren't they still looking for you there?'

'Make me look more like a man and they'll never recognise me. Anyway it won't matter. I can probably prove that Gram killed Natalie.'

―――※※――

Neither of us wanted to risk me driving the ambo into the middle of London so we took the Central Line to Notting Hill Gate and the Circle to South Kensington. I don't know why the non-believer wanted to come unless it was because he thought I mightn't come back and he'd lose his personal chauffeur and litter sweeper. Obviously his heart and mind were with Abbie because he spent the journey giving me a blow-by-blow account of the alchemy by which he transformed her from a stereotype into a pretty woman.

All he did for me was to get rid of the headscarf and the belt to my raincoat, alter the tilt of my hat and hoik my tracksuit bottoms around till they sat low on my hips and trailed their hems on the wet ground. He spent exactly three minutes on it. That's all. It was the stupid, time-wasting bit of femininity that interested him—the bit that cost a fortune and was out of style in two weeks.

'Why do you want to be *that* sort of woman?' I asked in exasperation.

'I *am* that sort of woman,' he said firmly.

'There's no point to it,' I said. 'You're either a woman or you're not.'

'You wouldn't say that if you were forced to grow up acting like a boy while watching your older sister learn to act like a girl. It was when she got to puberty that I finally understood.'

'What?'

'It was to make her like honey to the bears. I couldn't believe it. She was just my snotty, snooty sister but she became something magical to the boys. I thought, "Why doesn't anyone look at me like that? Why don't they follow *me* or try to touch *me*?" It just wasn't fair.'

'You were jealous of your sister?'

'No one could be arsed about me,' he said.

'Except the beastly priest,' I reminded him.

'But he was a just an old pervert. He wasn't one of the handsome young guys who hung around Celia. I was so envious of her, I wanted to be her.'

'For the attention?'

'For the desire. I wanted to be wanted like she was wanted. Girls don't want like boys do. They just want to be wanted.'

'Rubbish,' I said, thinking about wanting Gram Attwood. 'What happened to Celia?'

'Last time I saw her she had three babies under six and she was fat as salami.' He looked down at himself in his sassy short kilt and coloured stockings. Every man in our carriage had scoped him out when we got on the train. He seemed self-satisfied.

I was annoyed with him so I said, 'Well maybe babies are the whole point of being wanted. Ever thought of that?'

'Maybe you don't know sod-all. Ever thought of that? So where are all *your* babies?'

'Maybe I'm one of nature's failures.' I shut up then because I had a lump the size of a watermelon in my throat and I didn't know if it was for him or for me.

'You don't know what it's like,' he muttered, 'wanting to be wanted and not being an object of desire.'

Don't I though? I was thinking again about wanting Gram Attwood, of doing anything to keep him. He asked me to steal, so I stole. I wondered what I would've done if he'd asked me to undergo mutilating surgery to hold his attention. But I didn't want to compare my tragedy to Smister's. We didn't talk again till South Kensington.

Chapter 34

Smister Takes A Stupid Risk

//

I wished now we'd brought the ambo.

I kept thinking about the half bottle of red I'd stashed behind the driver's seat. If I could have a sneaky sip of that, I thought, my hands wouldn't be shaking as we walked from South Kensington Station to Harrison Road. I wished it was raining so that I could hide under an umbrella. But Smister, being a real girl, skipped along at my side tossing her blonde hair and attracting attention and responding to it. She had Electra on a leash made from a vintage silver disco scarf. Electra looked rather fetching in sparkly silver but she'd stopped talking to me when my hands had started to shake— just when I needed her most.

'I wouldn't mind living here,' Smister said, surveying the entrance to the mews.

'See that house down the end with the yellow door?' I pointed. 'Well I'm going down there to look at the... ' Suddenly I noticed that I wasn't the only one with the shakes. Electra's ears were flat against her skull, her tail had disappeared under her belly and she was shivering like a stripper in an east wind. She hadn't forgotten.

'Stay here,' I told her and Smister.

I hadn't forgotten either. I thought I had, but when I watched Electra sniffing the life-sized plastic fawns in the flower bed outside the pub it came back to me. I knew I'd

watched her before—sniffing at a little stone lion perched on
the edge of a rustic stone water trough outside a mews house
with a yellow door.

I walked slowly down the cobbles, and yes, the water
trough was there, but the lion wasn't. There were pale marks
where paws had rested, telling me that I hadn't imagined it.
But where was it now?

'What's up, Momster?' Smister said, sneaking up behind
me quietly enough to make me jump.

'There used to be a stone lion here, and I know exactly
who took it. It was the Devil. He smashed Natalie's head into
a pulp with it and then hid it in a plastic bag under his kitchen
sink in Acton.'

'Oh for fuck sake!' Smister brushed past me and knocked
sharply on the yellow door. Electra and I clung together,
backing away towards the shelter of hanging clematis. I
couldn't believe he'd take such a stupid risk. Natalie's brother
had seen us on TV.

The door opened slowly and a man peered out. He was
bald and bespectacled.

Smister said, 'I'm looking for my friend Natalie… '

The man started to close the door. He didn't seem to
recognise Smister at all.

'Hey?' Smister cocked his head to one side and the door
stopped moving.

The man said, 'My sister's dead. You can't be much of a
friend or you'd know that.'

'But… ' Smister took a step back in shock. 'But she was
supposed to come to Dublin for a long weekend. She never
showed up and I haven't been able to get in touch since.'

'Dublin?'

'They were going to stay with me.'

'They?'

'Nat wanted me to meet her new boyfriend.'

'You'd better come in,' the man said, opening the door
to Smister who was drooping with shock and sorrow. I heard

him say, 'This is terrible, terrible news,' as he stepped into the house with the yellow door.

'Is he a total moron?' I asked Electra. 'I know he's changed his whole image but… ' Electra said nothing. She gave me a pleading, unhappy look and I hurried both of us out of the mews. I was very unhappy too but, given that we'd had gorgeous Smister standing squarely in front of us, I didn't think Brother Munrow had noticed Electra and me at all.

We sat down on the steps to one of the big houses in Harrison Road which had a view of the entrance to the mews.

After five minutes the front door opened and a young woman in an apron appeared. She shook a broom at us and said, 'Shoo. Missus gone call police. You go now.'

Missus *never* talks to us herself, and nor would I if I had a maid to do it for me.

We moved further down the street. I didn't really know what to do. Suppose Missus actually did call the cops? What would she tell them? That I was a man or a woman? That she'd seen me before? In the mews? In the paper? On telly?

I'd got what I came for—I hadn't dreamed the lion; it had been there, and now it wasn't. I couldn't risk attracting attention by waiting for Smister anywhere near the house.

Electra and I went to wait at South Kensington Station. But first I bought a small bottle of wine from the same shop where Joss and I bought the beer—how long ago?

'What the hell does he think he's doing?' I asked as soon as my hands stopped shaking and my heart lay down to rest.

Electra sighed. 'Trying to help.'

'Help? He's put us all in danger by going into that house.'

'And you can't wait to hear what he has to say when he comes out. Put the bottle away.'

She's so righteous. I stuffed the bottle into my raincoat pocket.

We went to a public loo. It was the one I went to that terrible day with Joss. I remembered weeping at my reflection.

Now, when I looked in the mirror, what I saw was in some ways better, in some ways worse. Then my hair had been a mop of wire wool escaping from a beanie, and my skin was rough and purple with veins. I was huge and hulking in layers of clothing, and bent from the weight of worldly goods on my back. Now, I was sleeker and smoother but I had on my face two visible jagged scars, still healing, and I didn't dare open my mouth because of the broken teeth.

Electra, on the other hand, was as beautiful as ever: no bags under her eyes, no scars or wrinkles. 'Of course,' she murmured, standing on her hind paws and waiting for me to turn on the tap so that she could drink. 'It's humans who screw up. Dogs are blameless. *We* all go to heaven.'

'There's no such place.'

'There is for dogs.'

It was drizzling again so we waited by the photo booth inside the station. When people started to look at us we went inside the photo booth to hide, until, abruptly, someone tore the curtain aside and a woman with a large pink face pushed her head in.

'I was right—it's you,' she crowed. She was wearing a brown felt hat and a raincoat. 'Jolly good show. Never forget a face.'

'Excuse me,' I stammered, 'I don't think… '

'Not you,' she snapped. 'Her. The heroine of the burning tower block. I saw it on TV. You, as I recall, merely vomited. She saved lives. I'd like to award her a prize.'

'She'd love that,' I said hopefully.

'What's her favourite charity?'

'Me.'

'Don't be more obtuse than you can help,' the woman said. 'Where did you find her?'

'Battersea Dogs Home. She's a rescue… '

'I can see what she is—and, frankly, I'd like to rescue her from you. In lieu of that, however, I'll donate one hundred pounds to the Battersea Dogs Home.'

'I'm sure she'll be jolly grateful,' I said, 'but a little lunch would go down well too.'

'Liquid lunch, I've no doubt,' the woman said, thrusting her nose close to my mouth and sniffing noisily. 'I thought so. If you weren't already three sheets to the wind you'd know that it's supper time. Lunch was hours ago.'

'Oh,' I said humbly. 'We must've missed that.'

'Here's what I'll do—I'll put some coins in the slot, I want a photo of the heroine. What's her name?'

'Electra.'

'Ah, revenge. Good name. But I don't want you in the picture. Think you can manage that?'

'What do you think?' I asked Electra. 'I mean she's rude but… '

'She seems to like *me,*' Electra said.

'Everyone likes you if they've got a single brain in their heads.'

'Absolutely true,' the rude woman said. 'Well?'

To tell you the truth I don't really mind rude women like her. They look you straight in the eye while they insult the shit out of you. Better that than the miserable bastards who won't even look at you.

So Electra had her passport photo taken in her silky, spangled scarf. She looked elegant and gentle, and her eyes shone. So lovely, in fact, that the rude lady gave us two pounds for a can of dog food. What a philanthropist! But I'd bet you any money that she was as good as her word and donated a ton to the Dogs Home.

'Who the hell was that?' Smister had been standing in the shadows watching. 'You gave her your photo. Are you crazy? You're wanted by the cops.'

'Who's calling who crazy? Who walked into Natalie Munrow's house with her angry vengeous brother? Who's also wanted by the cops for using her stolen credit card? You're not crazy, you're fucking insane.'

'Have you been drinking again? Momster, you promised.'

'You're too trusting,' Electra said, waving her tail at him and nudging his hand with her nose.

We went through the barrier and down to the platform without speaking to each other. I really must get myself together, I thought, and leave him. He doesn't understand me at all and he's hopelessly needy and meddlesome. Also he has to have four walls around him and they don't come cheap. Whereas Electra and I can live on nothing at all. I'll go soon. I've given him too many chances already and it's not like he's at all grateful.

Chapter 35

A Quarrel On A train

///

'**A**re you going to listen?' Smister said, 'or are you totally bladdered? Cos I'm not going to waste my breath telling you something you won't remember.'

'I'm not bladdered.'

'Hmm,' Electra said. She was leaning against my legs. She doesn't like the underground—it's too rickety and rackety.

'And you can shut up too,' I said. 'I just had a few gulps to stop my hands shaking. It's very hard to give up just like that. I need a little something.'

'Talk to *me*,' Smister said. 'Don't just mumble in her ear. I know what Pierre said. I agree, you do need something, but you mustn't sneak behind my back. We've got to help each other.'

'With what?'

'Don't tell me you haven't noticed—I'm not necking pills anymore. Well maybe one or two to help me sleep.'

'Of course I've noticed,' I said.

'Liar,' Electra murmured.

'I just didn't want to jinx you.'

'Very bleeding thoughtful.' Smister didn't seem to believe me either but he went on, 'Still, I suppose it *is* easier when I have Abbie's makeover to think about, or your problems.'

'They're your problems too. You profited from Natalie's death. You got caught with the stolen credit card.'

'Oh for fuck's sake!' Smister exploded. 'Do you want to know what I found out or not? Honest, you'd make a marine weep, so you would. Is it any wonder I needed all those happy pills? Have you got anything left in that bottle you're not quite hiding in your pocket?'

So we shared what was left and calmed down even though a busybody pointed out that it was illegal to booze on the train. After that we were both in a friendlier mood and Smister told me about Edward Munrow.

'Pervy old sod,' he said. 'He spent all the time leching my legs and boobs. He's that sort—fingers you with his eyes but doesn't have the nerve to make a move.'

'Don't knock it—it's what got you through the door.'

'Are you stone blind? It was when I mentioned Nat's "new friend". That's what got him jumping. And you know what else you're completely wrong about? He and his two kids cop for her whole estate and her life insurance. No one else, not Graham or Chantelle, gets a look in.'

'And you know that because… ?'

'I asked him if there was any little thing, an ornament or a photo, I could take away to remember her by. And he gave me a load of twaddle about safeguarding her nephews' inheritance. Tight old bugger. He said only the family was mentioned in her will. Not even Chantelle, who was her best mate apparently. He's met Chantelle—he called her a high-flyer; said she and Nat were like "peas in a pod".'

'They looked alike?'

'Well, you saw them together.'

'Sort of, but… '

'You were guttered. *I* saw a photo. They didn't actually look alike—it was more that they had the same hairdresser, went shopping together and developed the same sense of style.'

'And fancied the same man.'

'Edward didn't know anything about that. No one did. The police asked everyone if there was a boyfriend—because the boyfriend's always a suspect, right? But even Chantelle claimed she didn't know of anyone.'

'Well, she would, wouldn't she? She's lying.'

'How do you know? What makes you so certain Chantelle knew that Nat was boinking Gram?'

'I'm trying to remember.' I was ploughing back through the mud in my mind to the night I saw Chantelle and Natalie coming out of the theatre together. I warned one of them about Gram. Beware of Gram Attwood. But I'd said, 'wee bear'. Sometimes I do get my words the wrong way round. Maybe I got the women the wrong way round too.

'I don't know which one of them I warned, but they were both there. They both heard me.'

Smister said, 'If Chantelle heard you warning Nat about Gram, *her* boyfriend, wouldn't she want to know why?'

Of course I would. I mean of course she would. She'd be crushed. And jealous. Murderously jealous?

'On the other hand,' Smister went on, oblivious, 'Chantelle told the cops about this mad homeless woman who accosted them that night. But she couldn't understand a word the woman said. And then she thought she saw a couple of vagrants in the area when she picked up Nat the next day on her way to work.'

'But she's unemployed. You said…'

'Hairy Clairey said.'

'She's never wrong.'

'Says who?'

'Says my mother.'

'Oh well, that proves it then.' Smister sat back with his arms folded and the familiar mute mule expression on his pretty face.

Then I wondered if Chantelle was the secretive sort, who would never admit, even to her best friend, the humiliation of having been made redundant. No one fails faster than a perceived failure. No one becomes invisible and friendless faster either.

But the Devil would know. The Devil shoves his lethal beak into every corner of your soul.

I said, 'It doesn't matter anyway. It was the Devil who killed Natalie, and I can prove it. The murder weapon is under his kitchen sink.'

'I hope there *is* something worth looking at in 17 Milton Way,' Smister said, still sulky and mulish. 'Because I told Brother Eddie about Nat's new boyfriend.'

'No!' I cried. 'Are you crazy? The Devil will strike us dumb and sentence us to eternal damnation in the land of ice.'

'Strike you dumb? I *wish*.'

'Why are you so upset?' Electra asked, pushing even closer to my knees. 'If the police find the murder weapon it'll let you off the hook.'

Smister said, 'It's got bugger-all to do with you anyway. Edward doesn't know your name. He doesn't even know mine. According to Old Fanny the only suspects are vagrants—you and your mates. They think it might've been a burglary gone wrong. But *Edward* thinks the cops are ignoring less obvious leads. That's why he was so keen to hear about the boyfriend.'

'Yes but Old Fanny knows my name, well, most of my name. And they've got my DNA from the mews house. If they go poking around Milton Way they'll find it again. We were bloody *there*, Smister—only two nights ago.'

'But it was your house, you eejit. Yours and your mum's.'

'Years ago.'

'Luckily the slit-hound and his fancy piece are piss-poor housekeepers. Besides, they can get DNA from prehistoric monsters these days. What's a few years?'

'It's the coincidence, sludge for brains—my DNA, my old house, my ex.'

'It *is* a bit leery,' Smister admitted, 'but what you gonna do, eh? How else're you going to clear your name and make sure your old Devil gets what's coming?'

'I was going to keep my head down and hide. But you got caught with Natalie's credit card and then you broke into 17 Milton Way and stuck your big nose in where it didn't belong.'

'My nose is fucking perfect. How're you going to keep your head down, you loser, when you and your dog were on TV?'

'And whose brilliant idea was that?'

'And whose genius idea was it to drive to sodding Acton and wind up in a pub car park fifteen minutes' walk away from the chief suspect?'

'*I couldn't remember how to turn right, you son of a bitch.*'

'*Daughter of a bitch*, you sexist pig!'

'I don't appreciate your use of the word "bitch" as an insult,' Electra said softly.

'Fuck off, both of you!' I yelled, but then I noticed that all the other passengers had moved away and were huddled at the far end of the carriage.

We got out at the next stop and waited in silence on the draughty platform for the next train. The last thing we wanted was to attract attention from the Transport Police.

In the end I said, 'I'm the softest target in the whole of London. The Devil always wins because there's no blessing for the meek in his system.'

'It's a good thing you aren't all that meek,' Smister said. 'In fact, you're a bolshy cow, and I don't understand why you rolled over and gave away all your bolshiness to Gram Attwood.'

'You haven't met him.'

'I've met lots of him—using and abusing buggers.'

'And you lapped it up. Or have you conveniently forgotten Kev? Because it seems to me you gave up membership of the "Told-You-So Society" the minute you took a whacking from him and came back for more.'

'Kev.' Smister sighed. 'I haven't thought about him in yonks. You know what Momster? We're a couple of love's bitches, for sure.'

'The Devil never beat up on me.'

LIZA CODY

'No, he just pounded your emotions into gravy granules to spice up his meat.'

'I'm not going to fight with you anymore. It's just I think that you and your mouth have put me deeper in the brown stuff.'

'But if I'm right about Brother Eddie he'll insist the cops go and talk to Gram. He'll tell them how odd it is that the man Nat loved never came forward when she died. And then they'll see how bogus he is and search the house.'

'Or we could run away to Cornwall. We could take Electra for walks by the sea. She's never seen the sea.'

'Sounds good to me,' Electra said.

'Fantasies,' Smister said.

'You could buy a cute little swimsuit and a sarong and prance around on a Cornish beach. We could rent an old fisherman's cottage... '

'And a young fisherman... '

'And sleep with the sound of waves to soothe us. We could both get well. Sea water and salt air heal wounds.'

We passed the rest of the journey musing about our dream getaway, and nobody mentioned that we could afford neither the petrol nor the cottage. But we were friends again and warm from the wine.

When we got back to the pub car park there was a note from Abbie stuck to the door of the ambo. It invited Smister over to the pub for a drink. I wasn't invited, but I didn't mind because I still had a few gulps of wine hidden behind the front seat. I fed Electra and then settled down to drink my sleeping draught.

I was dreaming about skating effortlessly down a snowy street towards the sea when something hit the door with such a crash that the ambo rocked on its axles.

Chapter 36

Drives Badly Bradley

///

'Open up!' roared the monster, making the black air quake with fear.

Electra let out a tiny, 'Help!' and cowered down.

'Police, open up!'

I reached over to comfort Smister but his bunk was empty.

'Open the door,' Electra whimpered, 'before they turn the ambo over.'

But I didn't have time—the back doors were wrenched open, metal screaming against metal, and a huge shape stood silhouetted against the car park lights, looming, lowering, glowering and wielding a crowbar.

Electra gasped with horror and fled. I wasn't quick enough.

The black shape said, 'Show me your driving licence.' He smelled of cigarettes, beer and fried onions. 'Don't just sit there like Piffy on a pillar. Do as you're told—driving licence.'

I couldn't believe my ears. He came in like the SAS in the middle of the night because he wanted... '*What?*'

'Get up,' he thundered. 'You've been driving without a valid licence, begging and making a public nuisance of yourself. Drunk and disorderly. Get your clobber together. We're going for a little ride.'

I didn't have any clobber and the only thing I'd taken off before going to bed was a pair of shoes. I put them on, but I left my hat and raincoat behind as a message to Smister: I'd been abducted by a cop with a rock hard face.

I stood in the rain waiting for Hard Face to open his patrol car door. There was no point running because the bastard had cuffed my hands behind my back. The rain pelted like gravel on my head. I couldn't wipe my eyes so I could hardly see. Even so I peered around for Electra. I couldn't believe she was going to abandon me.

'Electra,' I called, 'Smister, Abbie. *Electra!*'

'What're you shouting for?' Hard Face said. 'No one can hear you. They're having a lock-in.'

I squinted through the torrents of water at the pub. I thought I saw a curtain move and a face look out at the car park.

He pushed down on my head and shoved me into the back of his car. He wasn't gentle about it and I tipped over on my side. He tried to slam the car door on my foot.

'Ow-ow-ow,' I shrieked, because I don't believe in going quietly. I drew my knees up to my chin and lay, foetal, on the back seat. I could feel my foot swelling up. My ribs and shoulder were howling. My hands were puffy and trembling. My head was drumming and my brain went into spasm.

'Shut the fuck up.' Hard Face was angry with me already—and we'd only known each other five minutes. 'It'd be your own fault if I drove you out to the motorway and left you to stagger around till some truck driver mowed you down.'

Too late, I remembered that the remaining painkillers were stashed in Smister's sleeping bag, and any money I had left was in the pockets of my raincoat. Even if I got away from Hard Face I wouldn't be able to get back to the pub without scoring a few quid.

Hard Face took all his corners too fast, on purpose—to throw me around on the backseat. I was glad now that Electra skedaddled. Lurching on the back seat always makes her…

'Oh you disgusting old troll,' Hard Face screamed. 'You're going to clean that up.' He stopped the car and I rolled, fell, and lay wedged behind the front seat. He couldn't even drag me out or turn me over to remove the cuffs, so he had to drive on. He went on driving too fast and I went on throwing up. I couldn't help it.

Misery multiplied: pain, carsickness, shakes becoming rattles. Kill me now, Mr Hard Face, end my sorrows. Or are you too the Devil's little helper, sent to big up my torment?

At the cop-shop an immense woman with the nose of a bare-knuckle fighter hauled me out of the squad car. 'Bradley, Bradley, Bradley,' she said, 'you're an arsehole. I know you think only women have the cleaning gene but this time you can sluice out your own unit. I'll look after the prisoner because I know you so it probably isn't her fault.'

She almost carried me to the women's cloakroom— my foot was in agony and my guts ached from heaving. I was a straw doll to her and she said quite cheerfully, 'I don't suppose you'll be asking me why they call him "Drives Badly Bradley".' She wasn't gentle, but she wasn't unkind either. She filled a basin for me and helped mop me down with handfuls of paper towels. All I could smell was my own vomit.

She uncuffed me and brought a cup of sweet tea to the cell. I asked her to phone the pub so I could find out how my dog was. I wanted to talk to Smister but I didn't want the police to find out about him. So I asked to speak to Electra.

'Electra?' she asked. 'Ducky, I wouldn't talk to anyone at the damn pub if I was you—they all know Bradley there. What you need is a solicitor. Unless you're just going to plead guilty and get it over with.'

'To what?'

'I don't know.' She shrugged. 'Vagrancy? What're they going to do, anyway? Couple of hours in here? An exclusion order from the pub?'

She went away and I didn't see her again. But when it came time for it they didn't charge me with anything. They fingerprinted me, took my DNA, photographed me and stuck me back in the cell to 'sober up'. In the morning a squad car came and took me all the way from Acton to the Earls Court Road nick.

Chapter 37

Back With The Man In The Machine

//

'**A**ngela Mary Sutherland?' The custody sergeant stared at me over his half-glasses and wrinkled his nose. I smelled strongly of puke.

'That's not my name.'

'What? Speak up.' He consulted his list again. 'What is your name then?'

'Mad Old Bat With Dog,' I said. But Electra wasn't there anymore. She ran away.

'There's nothing to cry about,' he said crossly. 'Just tell us your name, okay?'

'I hurt my head. I can't remember.' Everything ached, especially my head. I couldn't put any weight on the foot Bradley smashed with the car door. I was hollow inside; emptied out, except for jagged, writhing worms of hurt.

'Well, Angela Mary Sutherland, I'm afraid you're going to have to stay with us for a while.' The custody sergeant picked up a phone and barked, 'Get the quack down here, ASAP.' He read out a list of charges which included assaulting a police officer and absconding from police custody.

I lay on a plastic mattress and realised that there would be no absconding on one foot. Electra was gone: there was no friend to guide me, scold me, hold me. An empty place opened like a chasm where my hand should rest. She should be curled up sleeping behind my knees. Where was she? Was she curled up behind Smister's knees, sleeping warm in the ambo? Was Smister even in the ambo? Maybe he'd moved in with his friend Abbie to a cosy bedroom with a cupboard for his frocks and a dressing table with a mirror for his make-up. She'd take him to her doctor so that he could renew his prescriptions for hormones and sleepers. She'd understand completely why he was the sort of woman he needed to be; because she was the same sort.

I was holding him back. If he'd ratted me out to Hard Face Bradley I'd understand, really I would.

They took me to the medical room to see the doctor. He was part of the machine, the grinding cogs and pistons of police procedure. He was imposed upon me like everything else. But he bound my foot and told me to keep it elevated. He told the custody sergeant that it should be X-rayed as there might be a couple of bones broken. He wanted to take a blood sample because he thought I could have a chest infection as well as severe alcohol withdrawal symptoms.

I wouldn't let him take any blood. Once they've got your blood they never let go of it, so next time they needed a rough sleeper to accuse of murder they'd have a huge 'clue' to plant at the scene of crime, all ready in a glass bottle. With my wrong name on it.

'Okay, then?' the custody sergeant asked.

'I'm not happy about it.' The doctor was a good six inches shorter and looked like the brainy kid who got swatted in the playground.

'It's just a super-size hangover.'

'Her foot?'

'She isn't going anywhere on it. Just give us some aspirin.'

'I might have to do a bit better than that.'

Fairy tales do come true. He made the sergeant fetch some water and then he gave me two white bombers that looked mighty like max-strength co-codamol. 'Keep drinking lots of water,' he said. 'I've instructed them to give you two more tablets in four hours. Have you had any breakfast?'

I didn't feel like breakfast, but he insisted I ate some toast and drank more sweet tea. Nice doctor. I never saw him again because after that my old friend DC Anderson came to fetch me.

Anderson didn't look very pleased to see me. He said, 'You nearly got me busted back to Uniform. If you try to abscond again I'll personally chop your other foot off.'

He made me wait in a grubby white interview room. I laid my head on the table, facing away from their spy-camera, and went to sleep.

'Conducting the interview is DI Sprague with DC Anderson in attendance. Also present, Ms Kaylee Yost, duty solicitor, representing the prisoner.'

Kaylee Yost looked about twelve years old. She was stooped and skinny, self-conscious of her acne, and unsure of herself. She reminded me of Too-Tall. I'd be absolutely okay with a firecracker like that on my side.

'Angela Mary Sutherland… '

'That's not me.' I was going to have to stick up for myself. I'd had a short kip and a white bomber. I wasn't feeling too bad.

'No?' said DI Sprague. 'Then enlighten us.'

'T-tell them your name,' Kaylee muttered turning rose red. She was embarrassed that I'd made her open her mouth. This was going to be fun.

'Just Bag Lady. I hurt my head. Do you want to count my stitches?'

'Don't play games with me,' Sprague said. 'You're Angela Mary Sutherland, and we have your fingerprints and DNA to prove it.'

'Never heard of her.'

Blah, blah, blah; I tell them something important to me and they take no notice—not the basis for a relationship of mutual trust and respect.

Drone, drone, drone, like an annoying fly—'... your denial notwithstanding... later you rely on in court may be used in evidence against you.'

'Do you understand?'

'No,' I said. 'Do you?'

'You've just been c-cautioned,' Kaylee informed me blushing hectically. 'Wake up. Pay attention.'

'Where's Electra?'

'Who's Electra?'

'Her dog,' Anderson said, sounding softer. 'A greyhound. Maybe she's still at Acton nick.'

'She ran away.'

'I wonder why,' Sprague said. 'What were you doing in Acton, anyway?'

'I couldn't remember how to turn right. So either I had to go straight or keep turning left. Acton's where I ended up.'

'That's interesting,' Sprague said, 'because Acton's where you started out. Isn't it, Angela Mary Sutherland?'

'I can't remember.' I let my head fall onto the table and pretended to pass out. The worst had happened—the police computer had put the bits together. Bag lady, public nuisance, drunk and disorderly, barmy as a fruit bun, was actually a thundering great thief and a fraudster. She was worthy of their notice. She was wanted for murder.

Smister told Natalie's brother, Edward, about the Lord of Lust and Wrath, Edward told the cops, the cops went to 17 Milton Way and His Satanic Maggoty did the rest. All the carrion feeders were coming home to roost—black flapping birds, white crawling grubs—settling for an endless night of fun and frolic in the hollow centre of my being. If they hadn't stolen my shoelaces I could've hung myself from the doorknob right then and there.

Someone shook my elbow.

'Ow-ow,' I said. '*Assault.* They aren't allowed to touch me. You're my witness.'

'It was me who touched you,' Kaylee said. 'S-sorry. They need you to answer some questions.'

Sprague said, 'I'll cut to the chase, shall I? Samples of your DNA were recovered from 14 Harrison Mews, scene of the murder of Natalie Munrow. Later, you went to 17 Milton Way where a woman called Chantelle Cain was assaulted two nights ago. On both occasions someone of your general description was witnessed at the scene, at or around the appropriate time frame. Care to comment, Ms Sutherland?'

'No,' I said, 'I don't know any of the names you just said.'

'Yes you do,' Sprague said calmly. 'Last time you were here you were questioned with regard to Natalie Munrow's murder and afterwards you saw Chantelle Cain in the corridor where you claimed she was Natalie Munrow's ghost.'

'No I didn't. That must've been someone else.'

'It was you,' DC Anderson said. 'I was there. I wrote it all down in my notebook.'

'You're making it up.'

'D'you want to see my notebook? I'm a working copper not a novelist.'

'You can't tell me coppers don't make stuff up.'

'Sh-shut up,' Kaylee hissed.

Sprague said, 'It's all there, dated and in sequence. Give it up, Bag Lady… '

'Lady Bag to you.'

'… and let's have a proper interview for a change—one where you don't pretend to be demented. Now… ' Sprague consulted my case file, my story as told by the Fraud Squad and the Serious Crimes Unit, the story I told after the Devil wept salt tears from his dead eyes. It represented the pit I dug for myself after he handed me the cold steel shovel. I wasn't innocent by any means, but I wasn't wholly and solely guilty either.

LIZA CODY

'I'm never going to condemn myself to please Lord
Ashmodai ever again.' I said. 'I haven't killed anyone or
assaulted anyone. I always seem to go where Satan calls me—I
can't help that—he has manipulative charisma. But his mouth
is full of scorpions and venom. There's a crack in my head... '
I fingered the longest scar, '... that's where the horror seeps in
and the names drop out. I meet many people in my walk of
life—walking *is* my walk of life in case you don't know. I may
have met all the people you say. But I get very fuzzy without a
drink.'

'And even fuzzier with one.' DC Anderson sounded bitter.

'What is the name of the man you call the Devil?' Sprague
asked.

'Ashmodai, Lord of Lust and Wrath.'

'I told you,' Anderson muttered. 'Didn't I tell you?'

'The name in his passport,' Sprague said.

'Must never be mentioned in the presence of the Law; that
is *His* law. Break it and he will cut your heart into a thousand
slices and drag them out from under your toenails with his
sharp silver claws.'

'Isn't it Graham Attwood, currently residing at 17 Milton
Way? The same address where you used to live with your
mother?'

'My foot's broken,' I told him. 'The doctor said I should
have more pills for the pain.'

'When I say so. Now, what is the current relationship
between you and Graham S Attwood?'

'None,' I said. 'But I'm a good dog—I come when I'm
called.'

'Don't cry,' Kaylee said. 'Here.' She rummaged in a
briefcase and handed me a wodge of tissues.

'He used to be your toy boy, didn't he?' DI Sprague was
unmoved. 'In fact you were obsessed with him, weren't you?
You threw away your previously unblemished career in order
to finance the kind of lifestyle you thought would attract a
young man, many years your junior.'

220

I couldn't answer. His words were tearing holes in my skin.

'In fact,' he went on, 'isn't it true that you are still dangerously obsessed and that your obsession and jealousy are responsible for the death of one woman and Grievous Bodily Harm to another? To say nothing of burglary, identity theft and fraud—but we'll deal with the details later.'

'I-I-I must insist,' Kaylee said, 'that we take a break so that I can seek medical attention for my client. She's in no fit state... '

'In a minute,' Dl Sprague said. 'I don't know why she won't give us a decent account of herself if she has nothing to hide. This... ' he smacked my case file with his hand, '... says it all. She's homeless and he's living in her house. That could be motive for murder. Attwood is the connection between three women, Angela Mary Sutherland, Natalie Munrow and Chantelle Cain. Natalie is dead and the others won't say a word against him, even though this one here thinks he's the Devil incarnate. Angela, do you *want* to be charged with murder and locked up for life?'

Maybe I do. There's always a roof over your head in prison, and a bed, and three square a day. There's medication— you aren't on the treadmill of finding money to score wine, drinking wine, finding more money. If you keep your head down no one bothers you much. No one breaks your heart or betrays you. You don't have to find a place to sleep at night. You're safe.

'That wasn't supposed to be a hard question,' Anderson said. 'Listen, you may not give a shit what happens to you, but what about Electra? At best she gets homed with someone else. At worst she roams the street till she's knocked over, injured and destroyed.'

'You're a clever one.' I said. 'What are you? Satan's mouthpiece?'

'Why would Satan want me to encourage you to tell the truth? Isn't he the Lord of Lies?'

'You're playing games with me.'

'How does it feel?' Sprague sneered. 'Let's stop wasting time. We have witnesses, physical evidence, motive, history of mental instability—I don't know why we're bothering to get a statement… '

'You don't want a statement,' I said. 'You want a confession. You want me to do your job for you. Well I won't. I didn't kill anyone. And I bet you've come up with something that makes you doubt it yourself. Haven't you?'

Anderson just stared at me but Sprague said, 'Interview suspended at 11.13.' He stacked his papers and marched out of the room followed by a hangdog Anderson.

Kaylee said, 'W-why are you so antagonistic? Don't they hate you enough already?'

'They hate me whatever I say. Why don't you go and talk to them? Ask them what they found in the Devil's lair. You know there must be something or they would've charged me already.'

'Why do you talk so barmy? You've not stupid.'

'Go and talk to Old Filthy. Or are you scared of them?' She did look scared. But she wasn't stupid either in spite of being prejudiced. Why don't people accept that you can be barmy and intelligent at the same time? Being barmy doesn't make you stupid unless you were stupid in the first place.

When she'd gone they sent a constable in to sit with me but I laid my head down and tried to sleep again. My heart was racing from the peril I was in and my foot was throbbing in sync with it. I didn't think anyone could hear it but me. Electra would know, but she was living with Smister and Abbie in a *ménage à trois*. There's no room for a fourth in one of those.

All I was thinking about was a bottle of red wine. I could almost feel it trickling down my throat—acting as a disinfectant and killing the crawling things in my chest, becoming the anaesthetic that would hush my throbbing foot.

Was there anything I could tell Old Filthy that would make them let me go?

The only thing they'll believe is a confession: bless me Inspector, for I have sinned, now hand over the communion wine? I think not.

Kaylee Yost came back into the interview room. 'H-how're you holding up?'

'It hurts.'

'What does?'

'Foot, head, everything. I need a wash. All I can smell is puke.'

'I'll see what I can do,' she said without any confidence at all. 'Meanwhile I'll find you some tea.' She went to the door and had a muttered conversation with the constable.

When she came back she said, 'I think maybe you're right. They've only just picked up on the connection between you and Mr Atwood, and when the Acton police went to his house they found something at his address that might or might not be a murder weapon.'

'They don't seem very happy about it.'

'That's because they thought they had you all sewn up, and they don't want to start again. Before, they just wanted to know who was with you when the murder was committed, and who struck the fatal blow. Now they have to think again.'

I laid my head back down on the table. It was the old Georgie and Joss conundrum. Am I a snout or am I not? If the cops caught them Georgie and Joss would make trouble for me. Then they'd try to kill me. It didn't seem fair.

'What isn't f-fair?' Kaylee asked. 'Please would you sit up and concentrate? I can only understand one word in ten. Who's Georgian Joss?'

'Nobody.'

'Is he one of the men who were with you the day Ms Munrow was killed?'

'No,' I said. 'Everyone I know hurts me. I can't deal with it anymore.'

'I can't advise you, I can only represent you.'

'How about getting me something to drink, eh? I can't think. My head can't handle the possibilities. I have to choose between death and damnation. The Doc said I should elevate my foot but there's sod-all to elevate it on. So it's hurting and I need more pills—and a little drink to calm my nerves.'

'I'm not allowed to bring any a-alcohol in here, and frankly, Ms Sutherland, it sounds to me as if you've had too many pills already. You really do mumble, you know.'

But she must've spoken to someone, because when Sprague and Anderson came back they were followed by a uniform who carried in tea and an extra chair for my foot.

I put my feet up, tipped my chair back and very nearly fell flat on the floor.

'Are you going to answer some questions?' DI Sprague said, 'or are you going to play silly buggers forever and ever amen?'

'There are impediments,' I said, but Kaylee interrupted, saying, 'M-my client would like to be helpful, but asks you to remember that she suffered severe head trauma which has affected her memory and her personality, reports of which are, I believe, in your possession.' She stopped, breathless at her own bravery. I patted her knee.

'Just do your best,' Anderson said.

DI Sprague cleared his throat. 'We have it on tape from last time you graced us with your presence, that you claimed to have followed the "Devil" from Haymarket to Harrison Mews. Please continue your account of events from there.'

'I didn't follow. He took a taxi, and gave the driver his address.'

'What number Harrison Mews?'

'I can't remember numbers.'

'Alright. Then what did you do?'

'I waited.'

'What for?'

'To warn the Devil's doxy that she would be destroyed and burned in icy flames while her brains and viscera…'

'Enough!' DI Sprague glared at me. 'In other words, you threatened her.'

'You see,' I said to Kaylee, 'I say "warn", he says "threaten", let's call the whole thing off.'

'No, do continue with your account,' Dl Sprague snarled.

'So Electra and I waited outside the theatre for the play to end. But it was a cold night and when she came out of the theatre there were two of her. I'd had a little drink and I thought I was seeing double.' I don't know why I said that. It wasn't true. It came to me; I thought it was funny so I said it. Now it was part of my statement. I hurried on, 'I told her to beware but I think it came out all wrong and she didn't take a blind bit of notice.'

'Then what?'

'Then we went to sleep.'

'Where?'

'Can't remember. Oh, except for Floating Outreach—Lemony Melony—then we had to go somewhere else or she'd have done me some good.'

'Who?' DC Anderson said.

DI Sprague leaned forward. 'Are you claiming that you spent the night in the West End, and you've a witness to prove it?'

'Floating Outreach?' Anderson said. 'Is that an official agency? Or what? Church?'

I covered my face with my hands. The light was too bright. There were eyes making holes in my brain for the words to spill out of.

'I suppose it'll have to be checked,' DI Sprague said. 'So when did you get to Harrison Mews?'

'I can't remember. I haven't got a watch.'

'Try,' Anderson said, 'it might be important.'

I screwed up my eyes. Someone going to work gave me his coffee, no shoppers on Oxford Street, hardly anyone in Hyde Park except dog walkers. So it had to be before eight or nine in the morning. The bins hadn't been emptied—that's where I got my breakfast. Then it might've taken me an hour to find Harrison Mews.

'Speak up,' Sprague said. 'What're you chuntering about?'

'I-I-I think she said, "Nine or ten",' Kaylee whispered.

'Do-do-do you?'

'*I haven't got a watch,*' I shouted at Sprague. 'I'm doing the best I can, and so's she.'

'You're taking the piss!' Sprague shouted back. 'A woman is dead.'

'A lot of women are dead.' I couldn't help myself. 'Needle Jane in a toilet—poisoned junk; Old Mary, Hungerford Bridge of pneumonia; little Svetlana, Soho—some bastard ruptured her spleen and I don't think she was even fourteen; Too-Tall Tina, in a fire—she wouldn't have been there if some bastards hadn't been beating on her for her prescription and her benefits. Where were you then? What's so special about Natalie? Oh yeah, I forgot about the one-law-for-the-rich, one-law-for-the-poor police.'

Sprague leapt to his feet, picked up his files, raised them above his head and brought them down on the table with such a crack that even DC Anderson jumped. Then he swung round and left the room.

I said, 'Maybe he should try anger management.'

'The one time you choose to be articulate, clear and understandable...' Anderson sighed.

'I don't choose. I live in the Devil's machine by the Devil's rules, and so do you. We're all his pawns. But some of us, like your Mr Sprague, are his minions. I haven't made up my mind about *you.*'

'Sometimes she makes a twisted kind of sense,' he said to Kaylee, 'and then I begin to worry.'

'Perhaps the Detective Inspector should just listen,' Kaylee said, pink and panting. 'P-perhaps if he worried about the details later...' She broke off, twisting a button on her neat black jacket.

I finished my tea. It didn't help. I needed Electra. She was my best friend. Kaylee was no substitute.

DI Sprague came back. He said, 'I've taken my tranquiliser. Now, can we get on with it? You were saying you got to

Harrison Mews at some time between nine and ten in the morning. What did you do then?'

'I waited for him—Ashmodai. I might have dropped off for a moment. He was sleeping under scarlet satin, taking more than half the bed. That's what he does. He takes all your life and leaves you with a tiny corner of your own duvet.'

'You went in and *saw* him?'

'I didn't know which house he was in. I don't have to see him. He lives forever in here.' I tapped my head and my heart.

'Then what?'

Then I had a problem: Joss. Should I save myself and tell them about Joss, or save myself and *not* tell them about Joss? I said, 'I want round the clock police protection.'

'You'll have round the clock prison protection if you don't tell me who was with you. You were seen with two other people so don't lie.'

'I can't be seen. I'm invisible—when I ask for *my pills*. There was someone but I can't tell you his name cos he'd kill me, I mean really kill me with boots and scrambled brains.'

'C-calm down.' Kaylee patted the back of my hand.

'He's one of the big, strong and violent ones who always do Satan's bidding. When he stamps on me with his massive boot my skull breaks and they have to stitch me up. My teeth crumble and I can't afford a dentist. What can you do compared with that?'

'You don't want to find out.' Sprague too was big and strong. He had a violent smile which showed all of his blood-stained teeth.

Back in my cell, they gave me two more pills, a glass of water and a ham sandwich. Then they left me alone.

Chapter 38

It Gets Worse

//

'Where's Kaylee?' I said.

'She was held up,' Anderson said. 'She'll be here in a minute.'

We were in the same scruffy white room with the grey plastic-topped table, four chairs, recorder and camera. The other chair on my side of the table was empty. I put my foot up on it so the cops could see the strapping and remember I was injured. It works with Electra—bandaged paws earn me points for caring. Why doesn't it work on the cops?

Dl Sprague said, 'When you went to Harrison Mews you were with two friends. Correct?'

'I want to wait for my legal advisor.' I was tired, so very tired. I don't know why. The pills had knocked me out for two solid hours so I wasn't short of nap time.

'She'll be here. Now answer the question.'

When they woke me up I was dreaming about being pegged out in the desert for the scorpions to eat. I was stretched so thin I was nearly transparent and the ants were beginning to carve little fingernail-shaped scallops out of my edges, as if I were a leaf, and carry them away to a hole in the ground. My skin felt raw and paper-thin and my throat hurt from the dry desert air.

I said, 'I'm not well and everything hurts. Also, the first time I went to the mews I was alone. And then this bloke came along. But if I say his name I'll die in a horrible way. He'll stick me down a hole in the ground for the ants to eat. But first he'll kick my head into chutney and spread it on his burger.'

'Is he homeless?' Anderson asked. 'Is his name John Farmer?'

'Showing the witness a photograph of John Farmer,' Sprague droned into the recorder.

I stared down at a police photo of Joss. He looked grim and cruel. I was horrified. 'If you know all this,' I said, 'why are you making me commit suicide?'

'We need to confirm witness statements,' DI Sprague said. 'Is this John Farmer?'

'Never heard of a John Farmer.'

'But you do recognise the face,' Sprague said. 'Is this one of the men you took to Harrison Mews?'

'I didn't take anyone anywhere except for Electra. She's the only one I trust.'

'You took two men, one of whom has a record for persistent theft, burglary and assault, to the home of Natalie Munrow.'

'I went there because the Devil told me to. I didn't know Natalie. How would I know where she lives?'

'Lived,' Sprague said flatly.

'Are you sure? Couldn't you have got the doxy duo mixed up?'

'Like you did?' Sprague sneered.

'We're absolutely sure,' Anderson said. 'No doubt at all.'

I sighed. 'Then why did the Devil do it? He does evil for gain as well as pleasure, and a nice fat insurance policy would be a gain. Except he doesn't gain; the nephews do, so it doesn't make sense.'

Anderson said, 'How do you know about the nephews?'

I was so tired I almost didn't recognise my mistake. When I did, I let my head droop down to my chest and said, 'Lord Ashmodai sometimes lets the *few*, the chosen *few*, gain. It encourages them to obey him.'

'For God's sake!' Sprague spat. 'Let's get back to John Farmer before global warming kicks in and fries us all. Do you recognise the man in this photograph? And was he in the vicinity of Harrison Mews on the day in question? You don't have to say a fucking word; just nod your head.'

So I nodded my head because Anderson was still looking at me with a peculiar expression on his face. If we got into how I knew about the nephews I'd be putting Smister into the frame. Morally, it's better to rat out an enemy than a friend—though physically it's the other way round, especially if your friend is a lady-boy and your enemy is Joss.

I said, 'I don't know the name you know, and I won't use the one I do know. But he decided there wasn't a mission in the mews and we left.'

'Where did you go?' Sprague asked. But I was wondering if I'd get into more trouble if I told him that was when I saw Natalie come out of the house and be picked up by Chantelle in the little red German car. On the other hand I'd already proved to myself that I couldn't tell which doxy was which, and I couldn't remember if I'd actually seen who was driving the red car. On the whole, I thought, it'd probably be best if I only dealt with what Old Filthy actually asked.

'Are you even listening?' Sprague barked.

The door opened and Kaylee scampered in looking harried.

'Interview commencing at 16.49.' DI Sprague hurriedly pushed the button that started the recorder.

'Are you okay?' Kaylee said as I slowly and painfully started to take my feet off her chair. 'No, no, I'll stand.' Which was great strategy because the cops, who wouldn't break a sweat fetching me an extra chair, immediately ordered one up for her.

'Okay,' Sprague said, 'we've established that you and John Farmer left Harrison Mews together. What did you do then?'

'There's an offie near South Ken Station and we went halves on a six-pack.'

'And then?' Sprague made cranking signs with his hand.

'And then I went to the bog for a wash and when I came out J... Whatsisname had got into a punch-up with another guy so we left... And then,' I said, because bastard Sprague was still cranking, 'we wandered around looking for a quiet place to sit down.'

'When you say "we"?'

'Electra and me. We'd been on our feet all morning and she gets twinges.'

'So?'

'So we had a nice little kip in a graveyard.'

'Where?' Sprague was so damn pushy. 'What time?'

'I still don't own a watch, and I don't know where we were except there was a nursery school in the chapel and they gave us milk and chocolate biscuits when we woke up. One of the kids called me Big Foot.'

'That can be checked,' Anderson said, making a note in his little book.

Sprague started cranking again, so I said, 'And then I went back to Harrison Mews.'

'Why?' Anderson said.

'I don't *know*. The Devil called me and I came running. He hadn't called me for years but there he was, dragging me back, with his icy hand burning my arm.'

'You saw him again?' Sprague said. 'You saw him at Harrison Mews?'

'I saw him here.' I put my hand on the place where my heart should be.

'I-I think it was a metaphor, sir,' Kaylee said, glowing pink under the strip lighting.

'And don't keep doing that air-cranking thing,' I added. 'It's annoying.' I wanted to give Kaylee time to recover.

'Oh, *I'm* annoying *you?*' Sprague said. 'Anderson, take over or I'll throttle her.' He got up and went to stand in the same corner as the camera.

Anderson stared at me and I stared at him. He had a pleasant, potato face which was only just beginning to bake hard.

'Okay.' He smiled. I think he might've had custard for his pudding. Something smelled of custard and it certainly wasn't me. 'You went back to Harrison Mews. What happened then?'

'I think maybe we went to sleep again. This is scary and confusing. Someone tried to kick Electra and she ran away.'

'Was it John Farmer?'

'You've got to say I never mentioned their names.'

'I will,' Anderson said, 'I promise. Now, you said "their names". So more than one man attacked you?'

Another mistake. It was like there were two parts of my brain and they were both playing bebop but in different keys. I started to shake.

I said, 'One man kicked me. I don't remember.' My hand went up of its own accord and fingered the scars round my mouth.

'T-take your time,' Kaylee whispered. 'You're doing well.'

But I wasn't—my joints ached and my clothes had been woven from threads of razor wire.

Anderson said, 'I'm showing the prisoner another photograph. Do you recognise this man?' The photo he put on the table between us was of Georgie looking cross and pathetic. 'All I'm asking you to do at this stage is to nod your head if this man was also in the mews the day Natalie died.'

He waited patiently and in the end I nodded. I'd already dobbed Joss in so there wasn't any point protecting Georgie.

'How did they know which house to break into?'

'I didn't see. Maybe the Devil left the door open for them. They certainly left the door open for me. The Devil wanted me to go in.'

'Did the Devil order them to burglarise the premises?'

'For he is the Lord of Chaos, Confusion and Muddied Waters.'

'And why did he order you to enter 14 Harrison Mews?'

'I am the agent who protects him from earthily justice. Being called is my calling.'

Dl Sprague stepped out of his corner and said, 'Are you telling me that Graham Attwood murdered Natalie Munrow and set you and your two friends up to take the blame?'

'Did I say that? You're stuffing my mouth with words nobody said. I've named no names. I've been out in the rain and winderness for forty days and forty nights…'

'I'm f-formally requesting a break for my client,' Kaylee said, distressed.

'*When I say so*,' Sprague roared.

'This is being *recorded*,' Kaylee said, bravely. 'M-my client hasn't been allowed a proper wash or a hot meal. Sh-she's been in custody going on eighteen hours. And her AA sponsor's been waiting in reception for over an hour.'

'She's in AA?' Anderson asked. 'Not a huge success, is it?'

I said nothing, but I was digging my fingernails into the palms of my hands, hoping Smister hadn't been dumb enough to come and poke his head into the lion's mouth. Then I hoped against all odds that he'd smuggled a drink in for me. Yes, I might've sacrificed Smister and even Electra for a little snort just then. But Smister wouldn't come unless Abbie allowed it. Maybe she sent him with a poisoned drink. Then she could have him all to herself.

My aching teeth came loose in my mouth and started chattering to each other.

'One more question,' Dl Sprague said. 'Answer it properly and I'll authorise a little break for you. Fart around and you can rot here for as long as I like.'

Anderson got up and joined him in the corner where they whispered urgently to each other.

Anderson came back and sat down. He said, 'When you went into 14 Harrison Mews, who was there and what did you see?'

'I didn't see anything. It was blurry. The door was open and I crawled in. On hands and knees. I thought there might be a drink inside. I wasn't feeling too well.'

'Was there anyone else in the house except you and Natalie? Was she already dead?'

'I don't know,' I wailed. 'I keep asking myself that.'

'And what do you keep answering?'

'That's three questions,' Kaylee said.

I said, 'I didn't see Natalie. I don't know why, except maybe Satan clouded my vision.'

Dl Sprague loomed towards me saying, 'So you thought you'd just pop upstairs for a scented bubble bath? The floor was covered with blood, there was a body on the couch, and you're trying to tell me you didn't notice?' If I hadn't known better I would've thought he was genuinely perplexed.

'That's about f-five or six,' Kaylee said, standing up. 'I must protest.'

'I thought the blood was mine,' I said, touching my mutilated face and head. 'I don't understand either. The Master of Gore and Scattered Brains must've had a purpose. But he never tells me anything.'

'Don't cry,' Kaylee said, handing me some tissues. 'DI Sprague, I will make a complaint to… '

'Interview suspended at 17.23.' Sprague looked disgusted. 'We're never going to get anywhere if she keeps breaking down every five minutes.'

'You've seen the medical reports,' Kaylee said. 'Respect them—otherwise I'll get a court order and have her removed to a… a c-care facility.'

'If you mean, "Have her sectioned and s-s-sent to a l-l-loony bin", just say so.' He swung away and slammed out of the room.

Anderson looked at Kaylee and shrugged. 'I'll see what I can do,' he said, leaving rather more quietly.

When we were alone, Kaylee said, 'I-I-I think you'll have to tell them everything. You need to give them a reason not to charge you. B-because the detective inspector really, really w-wants to. He's got so much evidence against you and those two men. If you did nothing else, you all stole from the dead woman. It's beyond question.'

'Everyone said *I* was Natalie. They *gave* me her bag and her keys.'

'They d-did what?'

No one had told her that. So I did. I more or less told her the truth—about amnesia, confusion, concussion. All I left out were the moments of clarity. And Smister—of course I left out Smister.

Chapter 39

Just A Little Comfort...

///

My "AA sponsor" sent in some nice soap and shampoo so they let me have a shower. They threw all my clothes in a bin bag and sealed it tight. There was a clean black track suit for me to put on, underwear and a new pair of men's socks. The smells were of soothing lavender and all the sizes were correct. This was the work of Super Smister. He even sent me a small bottle of mouthwash. It was alcohol-based but I rinsed my mouth thoroughly before swallowing.

When I was ready they took me to a small waiting room, and there, dwarfing one of the two comfy chairs was, not Smister, but beautiful, inspirational Pierre. *And he brought Electra.*

She stood on her hind legs with her forepaws on my shoulders. Upright she was almost as tall as me. She didn't do anything sloppy, like licking my face but she tucked her head under my chin and made little whiffling sounds. I put my arms around her and we stood like that for several minutes. I thought I'd never see her again, but here she was—warm, smelling of London rain and Yum-Chum.

I ran my hands from her ears, down her slim flanks. You can always feel her ribs of course, but I could tell she'd been fed and brushed. When I sat down she pressed up close and laid her head on my knee. I bent over her and pretended to search her ears for mites, but actually I was telling her how glad I was to see her.

Pierre said, 'The message from the group is "one step at a time", and "use this period of adversity as an opportunity".' He was looking round the room for microphones. He wore jeans, a Harvard sweatshirt and had a baseball cap on his head which said Praise the Lord—just the sort of thing Smister would find funny.

He went on, 'We're all praying for you, of course, but your sister wants you to know that she's moved away from her previous address and is staying with me and Cherry. She says she found out what Abbie did and she's so, so sorry.'

'Abbie? *Abbie* gave me to Drives Badly Bradley?'

'We must all forgive and rely on a Higher Power to right our wrongs.' Pierre raised his eyes piously to the ceiling. He was so camp I couldn't imagine how he'd fooled anyone. 'Meanwhile,' he went on, 'I've had a word with your Ms Yost and she's given us her card so should you wish to pursue legal redress, we can communicate through her.'

'Thank you so, so much for coming,' I said, wiping my streaming eyes on the cuff of my sweatshirt. 'I thought I was lost forever. Unforgiven and dogless.'

'Your sister and the whole group insisted.'

'How is she?'

'She's doing better. She's tackling her addictions and, with our help and God's love, trying to keep better company. She sends her love. She wanted to come herself.'

'She mustn't.'

'No shit,' Pierre said, sounding more like himself. 'She may be a masochist but she's not a total jerk-wad.'

'Do you pray for her too?'

'Every day, my child, every day.'

'Aren't you confusing an AA sponsor with a Catholic priest?'

'I could be both. Catholics have all the best uniforms.'

Electra was sniffing me all over, reading me like a book. She stopped at my badly bandaged foot and whined.

'What's that?'

'It's where Drives Badly Bradley slammed his car door. I took the strapping off to shower and I can't get it back on again. Thanks so much for the soap and clean clothes. I'd been sick.'

'Your sister seems to know you pretty damn well. Get that foot up here and I'll sort it out.'

I put my foot on his knee and he untangled the strapping. I sat and watched the huge hands. I wished he had been my mother. He'd brought comfort. He'd told me that Smister wasn't the one who snitched on me. He'd brought Electra. Plus he'd brought just enough mouthwash to perk me up for a moment.

I sat back in a comfortable chair with my arm round Electra's shoulders and just for an instant I felt cared for. The Abomination must've been looking the other way.

Chapter 40

... After Which
It Gets Even Worse

///

The next morning I was on fire and coughing up chesty brown lava. The custody sergeant allowed me an extra roll of bog paper.

DC Anderson fetched me and made me stand in a room with a glass wall. Then he took me back to the custody suite without asking any questions. I was glad of my clean hair and clothes.

Later he woke me up again and took me to the same place, only this time I was on the other side of the glass looking first at Georgie, then at Joss. Kaylee told me that all three of us were identified by an Australian *au pair*, but I didn't see her. Joss and Georgie didn't see me.

The boiling lava hurt my lungs and throat so badly I couldn't eat breakfast or lunch. But the custody sergeant brought me a choc-ice and a bottle of water. Maybe, now that I couldn't talk, I wasn't so annoying.

A doctor came in, listened to my chest and checked my bandages. I could hear her outside the door giving the sergeant a lecture about how all the homeless should be given flu vaccinations. 'Why?' he asked, sounding genuinely puzzled.

I dreamed about being hanged.

I dreamed the Devil loved me and took me to the bedroom. When I lay down for him he cut off my foot. He said it smelled rotten.

I dreamed hornets crawled under my skin and laid their eggs in my heart.

No one came to see me—not even Dl Sprague.

The next time someone fetched me it was a WPC called Linda. She took me to another interview room with a grey plastic-topped table. DC Anderson was in charge.

'You've been downgraded,' Kaylee whispered. 'Are you feeling better? They told me you were quite sick and couldn't eat. Can I bring you anything in from outside?'

'Ice cream,' I croaked. 'Ice lollies, banana custard.'

'Okay, okay,' she said. 'I'll see what I can do.'

Anderson turned to WPC Linda and said, 'Go and pick up some ice cream and a spoon. If they haven't got any in the canteen, go to Tesco's and I'll reimburse you later.'

When she'd gone he said, 'Listen, Lady Bag, you're in a position to help me and I'm in a position to help you. On the other hand you can screw up royally in which case I can make things tough for you. Do you understand?'

Kaylee said, 'Are you offering my client a d-deal?'

Anderson pointed at the recorder on the table. It was not running. 'I'm talking about good will and maybe recommending treatment instead of a custodial sentence. All I want is a sensible chat, during which we agree to call the Devil by the name of Graham Attwood, and that the Lord of Lust and Wrath doesn't stick his nose in too many times. I don't want you to make up shit to please me—that's not what I'm saying—I just want a reasonable account of what you remember and what you don't. Is that too much to ask?'

Kaylee said, 'As f-far as I know, my client has not been charged with an offence meriting a custodial sentence.'

'Assaulting a police officer—namely me. Last time she pushed me out the door, started screaming about ghosts and ran away.'

My cough bubbled over but I said, 'When I see a ghost what do you want me to call it—a sausage sandwich?'

'She wasn't a ghost; you know that.'

'But I thought she was.'

'Why?'

'Because I thought she was Natalie Munrow who everyone said was dead. So she had to be Natalie Munrow's ghost.'

'Do you really believe in ghosts?'

'I believe in Satan and restless spirits,' I said. 'I don't see why visions of Satan or ghosts should be any less valid than visions of the Virgin Mary.'

'The Virgin Mary notwithstanding,' Anderson interrupted, looking tired, 'when you're talking about the human manifestation of Satan, please would you call him Graham Attwood? It'll make a huge difference to the tone of your witness statement. It would make you sound less deranged and me less of a prat.'

'Who's a prat?' WPC Linda asked coming through the door with a tray bearing a heaped bowl of vanilla ice cream with chocolate sauce and four cups of tea. She was a sight for sore eyes, to say nothing of throats.

Soft, sweet frozen gloop slid from spoon to mouth to gullet like honeyed anaesthetic. I smiled at DC Anderson. He really wasn't bad for a cop.

He burned his tongue on the hot tea, switched on the recorder and said, 'You've said on a number of occasions that you think Graham Attwood killed Natalie Munrow. Can you tell us why?'

'Start with the easy ones, why don't you?' I said.

'Ah-ahem,' said Kaylee, so I had to think about it.

In the end I said, 'Because he was there and he must've had his own key. Because the little stone lion's gone from outside the house. Because J… Whatsisname and Whatsisname didn't do it or I'd be dead too. Because they both said she was already dead when they got there and they wouldn't bother to lie to me.'

'What about the little stone lion?'

'It stood on the edge of that phoney horse trough. I remember because Electra thought it was so bogus. But next time we went there it was gone. Joss and Georgie wouldn't have nicked it cos it was heavy and they chose stuff that's easy to carry and quick to sell—CDs and DVDs.'

'Would you explain how you know about the stolen items?'

'When I went back there after the hospital—those were things that were in a mess.'

'And why did you go back after the hospital?'

'I thought it was where I lived. The keys fit the door. I had all my identity in my handbag and everyone including a police lady called me Miss Munrow. I couldn't recognise my own face in the mirror.'

'Photographs taken of my client at the t-time are in the file—plus doctors' reports about the extent of her i-injuries, including a skull fracture.'

'No one knows quite what to make of that,' DC Anderson said. 'The CPS is still considering charges of Breaking and Entering and Theft, for instance.'

'C-concussion and/or hysterical fugue brought on by the influence of legally prescribed painkillers,' Kaylee said. 'Any number of doctors including the one who originally treated her could convince a jury th-that… '

'Okay, okay.'

I smiled at Kaylee. She was hitting her stride.

'But you do know who you are now?' WPC Linda spoke up for the first time.

'I am the Dowager Lady Bag of Denmark Street, also known as Mad Old Bat with Dog.' Reasonableness only gets you so far with the police. After that they start taking advantage. I turned my back on the cops and finished my ice cream.

'Try not to help again,' Anderson said to his colleague. He paused, giving me time to lick the bowl. Then he said, 'So let me get this straight: when you entered 14 Harrison Mews for the first time, after being kicked in the head... '

'And ribs—don't forget the ribs.'

'And ribs, Ms Munrow was already dead and her property had been burglarised.'

'I didn't see a body. I didn't notice her property. Not then. I just wanted a drink.'

'Situation normal,' Linda muttered, and Anderson kicked her under the table.

'The trouble is,' he said, 'it has been suggested that you had blood on you *before* anyone kicked you. It has been suggested that you were only kicked because *you* were committing an assault on John Farmer who thought *you* were already a murderer and was in fear for his life and defending himself.'

I should've expected it, I really should. The Devil turns friends into enemies; he renders the just unjust, and the unjust unjuster.

'Don't start mumbling rubbish,' Anderson said.

I tried to collect myself, but all I could think of to say was, 'Have you *seen* Joss?'

Kaylee said, 'D-DC Anderson are you seriously accusing... ?'

'I have to mention it.'

'I'm s-sorry,' she said, 'b-but I don't think much of this non-confrontational style you promised me.'

'An accusation has been made—in the same way that she's accused Mr Attwood.'

'But I've never hurt anyone.'

'You pushed *me*,' he said reasonably.

'But it didn't hurt, did it? Besides, I needed a wee and you were standing between me and the toilet.'

He took a moment to collect himself. He'd begun to sweat. Then he said, 'What makes you think Mr Attwood had Miss Munrow's key?'

'Stands to reason, doesn't it?' I started to cough.

'Would you like more ice cream?' he asked, sighing.

I nodded, and after WPC Linda left the room I said, 'He went to Natalie's house while she was at the theatre. Why would he do that if he couldn't go in?'

'My problem is this—suppose the woman you saw Attwood with was not Miss Munrow? Suppose it was Chantelle Cain?'

'So what?' I said. 'He still took a taxi to Harrison Mews. Chantelle doesn't live there, does she?'

'But suppose he only went there to leave a secret note for Miss Munrow about the surprise party they were planning for Chantelle's birthday, and then he went straight home to Acton. Suppose he didn't have a key to the house in Harrison Mews and he never went inside.'

My heart double-knocked. The cops had talked to the Devil. He'd told them a story which I really hoped they would check. I said, 'When's her birthday?'

'In about a month, apparently.'

'Then I'd want to see the note *and* Chantelle's passport and birth certificate and send them away for forensic testing to make sure they weren't faked. He could make a nun lie for him.'

'But you never actually saw him there.'

'No, but she had the jasmine-scented bubbly bath oil he loves and his favourite candles, and soap from Fortnum's. That's why I thought it was my bathroom. He trained me too, you see. The pillows smelled of almond and citrus so I thought it was my bedroom. I'm not lying—the Devil's head lay on those pillows.'

'You said… '

'Gram,' I cried. 'In his earthly manifestation Gram Attwood luxuriated in that bath and slept in that bed.'

'Have you checked the product in the b-bathroom?' Kaylee asked, as WPC Linda came in with more tea and ice cream.

'No I fucking haven't,' he said. 'And I'm not going to. I can't see the Crown Prosecutors setting much store by a vagrant's sense of smell.'

Kaylee agreed. 'She's never going to be a prosecution witness anyway, is she?'

'God, I hope not. But she might still have to defend herself. She might find she's the only one left in the frame.'

'So you m-might check if any of the same products that are in his house are in Natalie's house too. You might want to check for his DNA on the sheets… '

'Too late, the brother's been staying there… '

I let the chilly gloop anaesthetise my throat again.

I could tell my story but I couldn't sell it.

Decent Middle-English juries, senior police officers, the CPS, barristers and judges would all reject my story because they rejected me. I live on the outer edge of the known universe, a scrounger who drinks red wine, who doesn't bathe regularly, who's had her head kicked in—leaving her grotesque and ugly. But for exactly the same reasons they'd probably accept me as a mad, bad killer.

The spoon was rattling like maracas against the bowl. My spine was strung tight as piano wire.

'Can we take a break?' Kaylee asked.

Kaylee said, 'You're damaging your liver, you know. You could die a horrible painful death.'

'Beats a horrible painful life.'

'What?'

'If I go to prison for life… '

The custody sergeant came in with a plastic cup of water and a pill—only one pill. I panicked.

'Strictly speaking, your medication isn't due for another hour and a half,' he said. 'Take it or leave it but don't make so much fuss.'

One whole hour and a half, ninety minutes to be endured one by one—how could they torture me like that? Shouldn't the Red Cross have something to say about it?

'You're sick.' Kaylee hovered in the doorway to my cell. 'I could ask for you to be transferred… '

'No!' I'd be sectioned for sure and then I'd never get out—never see Electra again, never be free from their medication. That's not living. Although, why should I care? The Devil is covering his tracks with webs of eight-legged lies. And I am his fly—encased in the sticky ropes that hold me helpless while he sucks at my viscera. The pain and emptiness started in my chest and corkscrewed everywhere.

I thought the Master of Spiders had forgotten one tiny corner of his web where I could be cared for and at peace with Electra. I was wrong. He lured Pierre and Electra in and gave me moments of comfort with them only to rip them away. The Craftsman of Pain gave me the Poisoned Draught. It's called Foul Hope and it kills slowly.

A couple of hours later, back in the interview room, DC Anderson said, 'Tell me more about the little stone lion that you noticed was gone from outside 14 Harrison Mews.'

'It was there, and then it was gone. What's to tell?' I was numb now, three-quarters dead. Everyone seemed to prefer me that way. DI Sprague was back again, squatting like a scorpion in the corner. WPC Linda brought ice cream and custard, and then went away. Kaylee sat beside me chewing on a hangnail. I couldn't be bothered to ask for a chair for my foot. I knew it was throbbing but I couldn't really feel it.

'What made you notice it?'

'I didn't, Electra did. I told you, she thought it was bogus.'

'But when you came out of hospital it was gone?'

I nearly corrected him—the fact is that when I came back from hospital I didn't notice a thing. But I couldn't tell that to Anderson and Sprague because, when I did finally check up on it, Smister was with me.

'Where do you think it is now?'

'How should I know?' I didn't want to say, 'Under the Devil's kitchen sink'. He'd ask how I knew and that too would mean talking about Smister.

'But you suspect it might have been the weapon that killed Natalie?'

I shrugged.

'Good question.' DI Sprague stood up and stretched his long arms over his head. 'How would you know any of this unless you broke into 17 Milton Way, assaulted Chantelle Cain and found a bloodstained stone lion under the kitchen sink?'

I was horrified. I turned to Kaylee with what I hoped was an expression of stupefied ignorance on my face.

Kaylee looked horrified too. 'Where is this accusation c-coming from, Detective Inspector?'

'Information received from the Acton Police.'

'W-why wasn't I informed?'

'Only just received. They were waiting for forensics. *For your information*, Ms Yost, Angela Mary Sutherland's fingerprints were found in the premises.'

'I-is this true?'

'My mother, my brother and me—we lived there all our lives. Now I don't live anywhere. The Devil lives there and I haven't a pot to piss in or a window to jump out of.'

'About "the Devil",' Anderson put in.

'Gram lives there.'

'How do you know?'

'He's in the fricking phonebook,' I cried. 'Just cos he's the Prince of Pain doesn't mean you can't look him up.' I was so grateful to Smister just then: remembering him with the phonebook was almost as good as having him beside me.

'Stay c-calm. You were doing so well.'

'But you haven't lived there for what—four, five, years? Surely Mr Attwood's redecorated, had building work done, since then?'

Oh the crafty bastard! He wanted me to tell him about Gram turning my brother's room into a home gym. Then he'd know I was there.

I shook my head. 'They took away my key. I can't go in. There's a force field protecting the house…'

'Y-you're mumbling again,' Kaylee said. 'I can't understand you.'

I pointed at Sprague. 'He's got Satan riding on his back, whispering in his ear. He knows I can't go home but he taunts me. Make him stop.' With that I folded my arms on the plastic-topped table, lay my head down and closed my eyes. Electra would be pleased, she's always telling me to keep my head down and my mouth shut. There was a blessed silence for a few moments, and then I heard Sprague go back to his corner and sit.

Kaylee touched my shoulder and said, 'Do you want anything?'

'Sleep,' I said, 'ice cream, a comfier pillow, a bottle of red wine and Electra.'

'Ice cream it is,' DC Anderson said cheerfully.

He waited for it to come and allowed me four spoonfuls before saying, 'You were keeping company with a young woman calling herself Josepha Munrow. It was about the time of the fire at that block of flats at South Side Docks. She appeared on TV with you and said she was your daughter. Who is she?'

I kept my hand steady on the spoon that was stirring the ice cream. I said, 'What's she done now?'

'She's not your daughter, is she?'

'Of course not. She just wanted to get on telly. They wanted to interview Electra. She's a heroine, you know.'

'She isn't even a young woman, is she?'

'She's a dog,' I said, pretending to misunderstand. The fearful thing had happened—Jerry-cop had spread his evil in bits and bytes on the Corrupter's Spider Web.

'Josepha,' Anderson said.

'She's a thief and a liar but she has a heart the size of a horse. Where is she? She walked off with my umbrella and didn't come back.'

'That's not all he-she walked off with, was it?'

'What do you mean?'

'He was caught using Natalie Munrow's stolen credit card.'

I said, 'It wasn't stolen. It was mine. I was Natalie. The police told me so. *They* gave me the card. I gave it to Josepha because she's got small fingers. My fingers got swollen in the cold and then the Lord O'Disorder made machines too small for my hands and too big for my brains. My feet are too big too and I can't buy shoes. Bad Brad tried to chop one in half, but it didn't work.'

'S-slow down, you're r-rambling again.'

'That's the point,' I wailed. 'How can I ramble when I've only got half a foot? How can I ramble when I'm in here and you won't let me out?'

Nobody could think of any reply to that so I finished my ice cream. Then I said, 'She didn't steal the card or the phone. I gave them to her but if you find my umbrella, I'd like that back, please.'

A loud sigh from the corner told me that Sprague was reaching his limit.

Anderson said quickly, 'The original question was, who is the person calling him or herself Josepha Munrow?'

'I don't know,' I said because it was the Devil's own truth. 'I heard her called Jo, Josey, Jody, Josephine and Josepha. There were four of us—her, Electra, Too-Tall Tina and me. They took TT away in an ambo after the fire. I think she died. Josepha and I split up soon after. That's what happens when you're homeless. The only one left is Electra and you're keeping us apart, thank you so fucking much.'

Smister, poor little Smister, was out on public display. I'd tried so hard to keep her private. But the Commander of Catastrophe keeps his army of eight-legged probes to attack the last corners of private life. Those long, jointed palps reach in through your mouth to suck information out of you and stick it on their web of lies. It doesn't matter if the information is wrong—like my name, or what Jerry-cop said about Smister—what matters is that it lives forever. It exists like supermarket plastic bags floating, indestructible, in the ocean.

It won't matter how horribly Smister mutilates his body to be a girl, somewhere on the steel spider's web lurks the information that he is a boy. Unless he's very careful and restrains all his natural urges, that bit of byte will persist, waiting to bite him on the arse.

'Take her away,' Sprague shouted to WPC Linda. 'She's a raving lunatic. Take her away and section her. I can't deal with it anymore.'

Chapter 41

Toxic Hope

///

T hey charged me with Assaulting a Police Officer and
sent me to HMP Holloway on remand.

That first night I dreamed that Electra and I were
in a supermarket. We could take anything we wanted. I loaded
goodies into my backpack but it weighed a ton and hard
objects, like tins and boxes, dug into my back. I was exhausted,
but Smister and Pierre were waiting for us in the car park.
Smister opened the boot of a car so that I could put the
backpack in. To my horror I found that the heavy, painful bag
was empty. All our goods had fallen out. I had to retrace my
steps alone until I found myself in a grubby white interview
room in front of a supermarket manager, dressed like a cop,
who was laughing his nasty head off. It was all a cruel joke.
'That's life,' he said, just as I woke up.

At the medical screening I was diagnosed with alcoholism,
depression, paranoia, three cracked ribs, two cracked
metatarsals and a severe chest infection.

Well, no shit! Wouldn't you be depressed, paranoid and in
need of a drink if you'd been through what I'd been through?

There were warders and Prisoner Advice people but I
didn't want to talk to anyone. This was not my life so I didn't
want anyone advising me on how to live with it. Besides, I'd
been there before. I knew how to remove myself from my
own body.

On the fourth day Kaylee Yost came to see me. She said I could have visitors because I was only on remand. But no dogs. She said Pierre and Smister had sent a parcel of clean clothes which she'd left at reception.

I was torn. I wanted Smister to see the inside of a prison for his education; so that he'd take more care. But I didn't want him to see me there. Plus it was too dangerous because the cops still wanted to talk to him.

All I needed from Kaylee was to know how long I'd have to wait. I hadn't been to court yet because everyone thought I was unfit to plead. She said I'd been given twenty-one days to detox and then they'd review my case. She said Holloway ran a good detox unit and I should make the most of the opportunity.

I knew. But they'd turned me into an anti-depressant dependant last time. Well, not Holloway, but the prison system—I couldn't remember where exactly cos they move you around. And they take heroin addicts and turn them into methadone addicts.

Kaylee said I was seeing the negative side and that I should be more aware of the best in people and circumstances. If I did that, she said, I'd feel all the benefits of a positive mental attitude.

'Like hope?' I asked.

'That's the s-spirit,' she said.

She understands nothing. You'd think, being a junior in a law firm and being dumped with all the Legal Aid cases, that she'd have learned something about who benefits from the system and why. Then she'd understand how toxic hope is to the likes of me.

'Would you like to meet with your AA sponsor?' she asked.

I looked at her very carefully but she didn't seem to be kidding.

'I can arrange a visiting order for him,' she went on.

'Can you find out about Too-Tall Tina for me?'

'What's her real name?' She clicked her biro in a competent legal way.

Smister would ask why I cared about TT when it was obvious she didn't care for me. Of course he didn't know I'd made a pact with the Devil—Tina's life for Electra's. Electra was alive so TT must be dead and I must be responsible for her death. So if I end up locked away for all time or sectioned to a secure wing at least I'll know I deserve it. And that might be some comfort.

But I can't forgive myself for being so naïve. There was a fire and Electra stopped breathing. I asked for her life. But I didn't ask for her life *with me*, did I? So the Devil laughed and said, 'Okay, wish granted.'

I was so grateful. I remember it clearly. He lulled me and duped me. Then he said, 'Ha-ha, but I forgot to mention, Electra has to live with Smister and you have to live in the chokey. You'll never see each other again. But don't complain—I did what you asked.' The Shah of Shattered Dreams is considered a wit in his circle of Hell.

My circle of hell was filled with young women; some of them still teenagers, barely out of school. Sheer incompetence had brought them to Holloway—theirs, their parents', their teachers', the care homes'. How does a girl become an addict with a personality disorder by the age of thirteen, and be unable to read and write unless many, many people older than her let her down? Its one thing for someone like me to find solace at the bottom of the heap—I came here almost by choice—but the bottom of the heap is where these kids started. No one gave *them* a choice.

—◦◦◦—

For the first few days I could smell anger and distress the same way I could hear shouts and screams in the night. I'd lie on my bed and imagine Electra and me in the West End, sitting on the steps at Trafalgar Square watching people have fun in the fountains, shrieking their pleasure, and wonder if I'd ever hear screams like that again. I'd think, this is where I live now, in Satan's palace of iron and ice, among his handmaidens. It's my duty to watch him thrust the icicles of want and need under their fingernails and hear them scream for love and comfort.

I took my pills every day and waited for the misty grey gauze to settle in front of my eyes and cut me off from pleasure, pain and life. The pills don't fill the hole in the middle of your chest. It's still there, vaster than ever, but I don't seem to care.

I was waiting for the time when the taste of good red wine left my mouth, when the feel of Electra's soft ears left my fingertips, when the smell of Smister's girly boy hair disappeared from my nose. Then, when I heard the screams in the night, I'd pull the blanket up to my ears and go back to sleep. I'd be cured of hope.

———

A week later Kaylee Yost came back. She said, 'You're looking b-better. You're not l-limping so badly. How're they treating you?'

'How's Electra?' I asked because I wasn't cured of hope yet.

'Your friends are fine, and your dog's b-being well looked after, but she's missing you.'

'You've seen her?'

'Well, yes… '

'How's her arthritis? Is her nose cool? And her ears? Are they remembering to put her coat on in the rain? She likes canned tuna but she mustn't have it cos it runs straight through her.'

'Er… she seemed p-perfectly healthy to me. I'll remind Pierre about the coat and the tuna.'

I should've just thanked her because going to see Electra was more than most lawyers would do for a client like me.

Kaylee said, 'I've brought good news.'

'Good booze?' I said, because my heart was still full of Electra.

'N-no. Chantelle Cain has confessed to Natalie's murder.'

'*No*,' I said, horrified.

'Yes.' Kaylee's brow wrinkled in puzzlement.

'You're joking. That can't be right.'

'I-I thought you'd be relieved. If you had any lingering fears that the police might still try to i-implicate you.'

'But she didn't do it.'

'W-what d'you mean?'

'*He* did.' How could she be so blind?

'Graham Attwood? But why w-would Mr Attwood kill Natalie? He loved her. He was going to marry her. That's why Chantelle killed her. It was a classic case of murderous jealousy.'

'No, no,' I shouted. 'That's what he would *make* her say. But it isn't true.'

'Well, that's what the police believe. They say she's pleading temporary insanity. Graham Attwood knew nothing about it whatsoever.'

'How can they possibly believe that?' I cried. 'If she did it, it was his idea. He drove her to it. He benefited from it.'

'But you were right about the murder weapon,' Kaylee said, sounding discouraged. 'It was the stone lion you noticed outside Natalie's house. The police think Chantelle put it under Mr Attwood's sink to implicate him.'

'You're wrong. It's the other way round. *He* kept it there so that he'd always have something to blackmail *her* with.'

'But what would be the p-point?'

'Maybe he wanted to dump Chantelle but keep her car. Maybe she's got a cute little riverside house and he's tired of living in Acton. I don't know. But the corporeal manifestation of the Devil has material ambitions. He'll end up grabbing everything. You wait and see.'

Suddenly I couldn't care less what everyone else thought or why. They were wrong. They were being controlled by forces they didn't understand. Maybe one day someone would wake up to what advantage Gram took from Natalie's death and Chantelle's confession. But by the time that happened Chantelle would be old, and bitterness would have ripped at her hair and skin. Her fine tanned ankles would be puffy, veiny and white.

'I think you're quite wrong,' Kaylee said. 'But I didn't mean to upset you. I wanted to cheer you up before telling you the bad news. Your friend, er, T-too-Tall Tina Smith… '

'I know,' I said dully, 'she's dead.'

'Not exactly. She was very, very sick in St George's for a while, but she was beginning to recover, and then she set fire to her hospital bed. Now she's pretty badly burned. Even if she get's better she'll end up in a secure hospital somewhere. Arson seems to be h-habitual.'

It *sounded* like a death to me. The Devil has many interesting interpretations of the word and they don't all include a box and a hole in the ground.

'When can I see a judge?' I asked.

'When your twenty-one days are up they'll reassess your medical condition and then I'll see what I c-can do. Do you want my advice?'

'Not really. Also, I didn't assault a police officer. I'm innocent.'

'It's n-not what you've done,' she said. 'It's who you are. Weirdly, I quite admire your independence. You've wangled a lot of advantages from being someone no one wants. The police couldn't get rid of you fast enough; the social services can't handle you so they leave you alone. I think, in your own way, you've benefited from that. I don't know how c-crazy you really are but prison is different. When a prison gets fed up with you they don't let you go. They just move you to another prison—*ad infinitum*. In prison the system always wins. Always.'

Kaylee Yost was not a total div. She was shy but she wasn't stupid. And nor am I—I knew she was right.

So here I am, in chokey, pretending to be sane in order to claim the privileges of the mad. I'm enduring imprisonment so that I can walk away free with Electra. I'm lonely so that I can protect my friends. I'm obedient so that I can indulge my habit of sticking two fingers up to authority. And I'm teetotal because there isn't any booze.

Who knows what will happen next?

I no longer dream about Trafalgar Square; I dream about what I'll say to Chantelle Cain when we meet. Because word on the wing says she'll be remanded to Holloway, and if that happens maybe we'll meet at Association. Will she ever smell of *Rive Gauche* and truffle oil again?

I play games with myself. In them Electra says, 'You will have three and a half minutes with Chantelle—you can ask her only one question. What will it be?' Electra looks dignified and fair, like a good judge.

What would I ask? Was it Chantelle or Natalie who I saw with Gram Satan Attwood that day, long ago, outside the National Portrait Gallery? Or, whose idea was it to kill Natalie? Or, was she the one who left the mews house the morning Natalie died, and if so, who picked her up in the sexy little red car?

'No,' Electra says, 'that's a bunch of questions. You aren't Old Fanny—you can't ask multiple questions and pretend it's only one.'

'Okay then,' I say. 'I'll just ask her this—how did Gram persuade you to take the rap for him?'

Because I know he did. He did it to me.

I remember how his tears scorched my naked shoulder. I thought he was so young and that he should remain free. If he were to be locked up, I thought, he'd never have a chance to blossom and grow. He would be corrupted in prison I thought. And he promised to love me forever if I took all the blame. What a sick, sick joke. Listen to me laugh.

I don't care what the cops or Kaylee think. Gram *is* the Devil, and who knows what game he has in mind next? He got away with murder this time and another poor woman is paying the price.

But however hard he tried he didn't succeed in framing *me*. Maybe my luck is turning. I'll be ready for him next time. Ready in tooth and claw. His deeds shall not go unrecorded. I will be watching. If they ever let me out of here.

About the Author

L IZA CODY is the award-winning author of many novels and short stories. Her Anna Lee series introduced the professional female private detective to British mystery fiction. It was adapted for television and broadcast in the UK and US. Cody's ground-breaking Bucket Nut Trilogy featured professional wrestler, Eva Wylie. Other novels include Rift, Gimme More, Ballad of a Dead Nobody (2011), and Miss Terry (2012). Her novels have been widely translated.

Cody's short stories have been published in many magazines and anthologies. A collection of her first seventeen appeared in the widely praised Lucky Dip and other stories.

Liza Cody was born in London and most of her work is set there. Her career before she began writing was mostly in the visual arts. Currently she lives in Bath. Her informative website can be found at www.LizaCody.com and you can follow LizaCody on twitter.

CPSIA information can be obtained at www.ICGtesting.com
Printed in the USA
LVOW07s0006171114

414026LV00001B/94/P